PLANET STORIES
1939–1955

During the golden age of the pulps—those fabulous magazines featuring larger-than-life heroes battling monstrous aliens on hostile planets or pursuing the luscious goddesses of golden worlds—some 70 issues of **Planet Stories** were published. When the magazine folded, along with most of the other pulps, the space opera all but disappeared. Gone were those marvelous stories that drew us out beyond our narrow skies into the vastness of interstellar space where a billion nameless planets might harbor life forms infinitely numerous and strange.

Now Leigh Brackett—whose thrilling tales of wonder and high adventure filled the pages of **Planet**—has selected seven of the most dazzling stories ever published in that magazine.

The Best of
PLANET STORIES
#1

Strange Adventures on Other Worlds

Edited by

Leigh Brackett

BALLANTINE BOOKS • NEW YORK

BALLANTINE BOOKS
A Division of Random House, Inc.
201 East 50th Street, New York, N.Y. 10022
Simultaneously published by
Ballantine Books, Ltd., Toronto, Canada

For T. T. Scott,
who made Fiction House a home.

Acknowledgments

"Lorelei of the Red Mist," copyright © 1946 by Love Romances Publishing Co., Inc.; reprinted by permission of the authors' agents, Harold Matson Co., Inc., for Ray Bradbury, and Lurton Blasingame for Leigh Brackett.

"The Star Mouse," copyright © 1942 by Love Romances Publishing Co., Inc.; reprinted by permission of the author and his agent, Scott Meredith Literary Agency, Inc.

"Return of a Legend," copyright © 1952 by Love Romances Publishing Co., Inc.; reprinted by permission of the author.

"Quest of Thig," copyright © 1942 by Love Romances Publishing Co., Inc.; reprinted by permission of the author.

"The Rocketeers Have Shaggy Ears," copyright © 1949 by Love Romances Publishing Co., Inc.; reprinted by arrangement with Forrest J Ackerman, 2495 Glendower Ave., Hollywood/CA 90027.

"The Diversifal," copyright © 1951 by Love Romances Publishing Co., Inc.; reprinted by permission of the author and his agent, Scott Meredith Literary Agency, Inc.

"Duel on Syrtis," copyright © 1951 by Love Romances Publishing Co., Inc.; reprinted by permission of the author and his agent, Scott Meredith Literary Agency, Inc.

Contents

Introduction: Beyond
Our Narrow Skies

It is seldom enough that one has the opportunity to stand up publicly and say "Thank you" to an old friend. Therefore it gives me great pleasure to be writing this introduction to the first of a new series: THE BEST OF PLANET STORIES.

For fifteen years, from 1940 to 1955, when the magazine ceased publication, I had the happiest relationship possible for a writer with the editors of *Planet Stories*. They gave me, in the beginning, a proving-ground where I could gain strength and confidence in the exercise of my fledgeling skills, a thing of incalculable value for a young writer. They sent me checks, which enabled me to keep on eating. In later years, they provided a steady market for the kind of stories I liked best to write. In short, I owe them much. To Malcolm Reiss, and to Wilbur Peacock, Chester Whitehorn, Paul L. Payne, Jack O'Sullivan, and Jerome Bixby, my fondest salutations.

It was fashionable for a while, among certain elements of science-fiction fandom, to hate *Planet Stories*. They hated the magazine, apparently, because it was not *Astounding Stories*, a view which I found ridiculous at the time, and still do. (They come now—to be truthful, not those identical fans—and say, "Gee, *Planet* was a great magazine, I wish we had it back!") Of course *Planet* wasn't *Astounding;* it never pretended to be *Astounding*, and that was a mercy for a lot of us who would have starved to death if John W. Campbell, Jr., had been the sole and only market for our wares. Apart from everything else, there wasn't room enough for all of us in that one magazine. And we who wrote for *Planet* tended to be more interested in wonders than we were in differential calculus or the theory and practice of the hydraulic ram, even if we knew all about such things. (I didn't.) *Astounding* went for the cerebrum, *Planet* for the gut, and it always seemed to me that one target was as valid as the other. *Chacun à son goût.*

Planet, unashamedly, published "space opera." Space opera, as every reader doubtless knows, is a pejorative term often applied to a story that has an element of adventure. Over the decades, brilliant and talented new writers appear, receiving great acclaim, and each and every one of them can be expected to write at least one article stating flatly that the day of space opera is over and done, thank goodness, and that henceforward these crude tales of interplanetary nonsense will be replaced by whatever type of story that writer happens to favor—closet dramas, psychological dramas, sex dramas, etc., but by God *important* dramas, containing nothing but Big Thinks.

Ten years later, the writer in question may or may not still be around, but the space opera can be found right where it always was, sturdily driving its dark trade in heroes.

There's a reason for this. The tale of adventure—of great courage and daring, of battle against the forces of darkness and the unknown—has been with the human race since it first learned to talk. It began as part of the primitive survival technique, interwoven with magic and ritual, to explain and propitiate the vast forces of nature with which man could not cope in any other fashion. The tales grew into religions. They became myth and legend. They became the Mabinogion and the Ulster Cycle and the Voluspa. They became Arthur and Robin Hood, and Tarzan of the Apes.

The so-called space opera is the folk-tale, the hero-tale, of our particular niche in history. No more than a few years back, Ziolkovsky was a visionary theoretician. Goddard, a genius before his time, had to pretend that his rockets were for high-altitude research only because he was afraid to use the word "space." The important men, who were carrying their brains in their hip-pockets, continued to sit upon them, sneering, until Sputnik went up and frightened the daylights out of them. But the space opera has been telling us tales of spaceflight, of journeys to other worlds in this solar system, of journeys to the world of other stars, even to other galaxies; the space opera has been telling them of decades, with greater or less skill but with enormous love and enthusiasm. These stories served to stretch our little minds, to draw us out beyond our narrow skies into the vast glooms of interstellar space, where the great suns ride in splendor and the bright nebulae fling their veils of fire parsecs-long across the universe; where the Coal-sack and the Horsehead make patterns of black mystery; where the Cepheid variables blink their evil eyes and a billion nameless planets may harbor life-forms infinitely numerous and strange. Escape fiction? Yes, indeed! But in its own ironic way, as we see now, it was an escape into a reality which even now some people are still trying to fight off as the Devil fights holy water, afraid to look up and Out.

Usually the space opera was firmly based, in its essentials, upon current knowledge and/or advanced speculation in technology, astronomy, physics, chemistry, biology, mathematics, etc. And wild-eyed as some of them may have been, the stories taught us a lot about the universe we live in. They taught us the difference between a planet, a moon, a sun, a solar system, and a galaxy, things which still, incredibly, seem not to be understood by a large number of citizens; taught us something about celestial mechanics, and the origins of life, and the ultimate deaths of stars. They also taught us to beware of scientific absolutes. Science once knew as a fact that communication between Earth and an orbiting spaceship would be quite impossible because of the Heaviside Layer, through which radio waves could not penetrate. Technology took a step ahead, and we're getting excellent results. Einstein has caused a deal of trouble with his apparently irrefutable theory that the speed of light is the limiting speed of the universe, thereby cutting the continuum out from under the faster-than-light drives necessary to take a spaceship from one star to another in a manageable (for story purposes) length of time. Well, there are ways of getting around that, fictionally, and meanwhile some hateful little particles have been caught moving at speeds exceeding that of light . . . so who knows? The most important thing about the space opera was that, besides offering adventure and excitement, it shook us loose from the dead weight of conventional thinking that denied the existence of anything beyond cheese, fence-post, and the income tax.

Now we have seen the actuality. We have seen, via television, those footprints on the Moon, man's first step into the wider universe which he must seek out or perish. We have seen space opera of the noblest sort in the flight of Apollo Thirteen, where brave and gallant men fought for survival against incredible odds, and won. We have seen the faces of alien planets, strange and forbidding. We have learned a little. We shall learn much more.

So where does this leave space opera—especially the space opera of yesteryear? And why should we bring back even the best stories from a magazine like *Planet*, which passed on to that Great Distributor in the Sky almost twenty years ago? Surely much of the science is outdated. We know now that Venus is a hellhole of impossible heat where no man could survive for a moment. We know that Mercury is even worse. We know that Mars—but hold on there, no we don't. We're having second thoughts about Mars, after a much longer and closer look. There was once an abundance of water there, and a thicker atmosphere; and even now human survival on that planet would be possible, with a measure of assistance. One imagines that it might be easy for men to live on equatorial Mars as it is for them to live on the continent of Antarctica—something they manage to do, albeit not comfortably. We have not yet landed on Mars, so we cannot yet be sure what will be found there in the way of life-forms —past or present—though some sort of vegetation seems at least possible. It's probably too much to hope for the Twin Cities of Helium, but discoveries may well be made which will be far more exciting and of profoundly greater importance.

In any case, Mars is still fun. So is Venus—not, perhaps, as the actual and factual worlds so named, but simply as creations of a writer's imagination, full of wonders that may perfectly well exist on *some* world, somewhere.

Stories such as these that we present to you, from the heyday of *Planet Stories*, are not intended to be read as educational texts. If you want accurate up-to-date science, buy a book, and be prepared to buy a new one every week or so as the state of knowledge continues to move ahead in quantum jumps. Furthermore, if you are looking for the delights of cannibalism, incest, *outré* sex, or a general feeling of dismal gloom, you will not find them here. These stories, shameful as it may seem, were written to be entertaining, to be exciting, to impart to the reader some of the pleasure we had in writing them. You may also sense a vigor and vitality that are not too often found these days—perhaps because we were dealing with heroes and thought no shame to ourselves for that.

A persistent myth flourishes about space opera which says that stories of the genre were all about troops of bug-eyed monsters, wooden men with ray-guns, senseless slaughter and a cretinous jingoism that portrayed the dominant Earthman happily tramping all over an assortment of extraterrestrials invariably imagined as vile, low and menacing. I have even read supposedly eminent critics who went so far as to say that science fiction had failed miserably in that it had never considered alien psychologies or the problems of communication with alien intelligences—something that leads me to wonder what, if any, science fiction these gentlemen have read. The stories contained herein ought to help prove the falsity of those several assumptions.

Two of the stories, "Duel on Syrtis," by Poul Anderson, and "Return of a Legend," by Raymond Z. Gallun, are laid on Mars—in each case, an astonishingly believable Mars even in the light of our latest knowledge. In each case the background is meticulously constructed, interesting in itself and a vital element in the plot. Both are psychological stories. "Return of a Legend" concerns itself powerfully with the effect of an alien environment on Earthmen. "Duel on Syrtis" has excellent action coupled with a sensitive portrayal of a Martian and his attempts to cope with what is to him an alien life-form, only partly understood and direly menacing—an Earthman.

"Quest of Thig," by Basil Wells, is a look at Earth through the eyes of a visitor from a distant star, and we see how Earth and its people react upon the alien, affecting him and his mission. Here, too, the emphasis is on psychology rather than on ray-guns, though the ray-guns are present when needed. "The Diversifal," by Ross Rocklynne, is again Earth-based; it's a down-to-earth, grim story of time-travel and betrayal, uncompromisingly honest in its downbeat ending.

"The Star-Mouse," by Frederic Brown, is sheer humor and sheer delight, with a sly stinger in its tail. If Mitkey Mouse qualifies as a BEM, then I wish we had more of him! Look for that marvelous line describing the asteroids, plus Brown's deft handling of some highly unusual and likable aliens and their peculiar world.

Of the two stories laid on Venus, one is bitterly realistic in its background. "The Rocketeers Have Shaggy Ears," by Keith Bennett, is a powerfully understated story of quiet heroism that really generates the old tingle and an impulse to stand up and cheer at the end. Unpleasant Venusians we have here. But they are quite convincing, and do not at all register a sense of Hail-the-conquering-Earthman-comes. The cumulative effect of this day-to-day struggle for survival in a totally unfamiliar and totally hostile environment is gut-tightening. You won't put this yarn down.

The other Venusian tale, "Lorelei of the Red Mist," by myself and Ray Bradbury, shows a different sort of Venus, purely fanciful—a background I used more than once and had a lot of fun with. And by the way, I offer no apology for including in this collection a story with which I was personally concerned. The nice people at Ballantine gave me a choice—one Brackett story per issue, or you don't edit the series. Since I'm not asked to edit a series every day, and since I'm not totally immune to flattery, I managed to acquiesce gracefully.

In this case, of course, the story is as much Ray Bradbury's as it is mine—exactly as much. I've heard all sorts of conjecture about who wrote what in this sole and only collaboration between us—that Bradbury wrote the poetic bits, Brackett the action, etc., etc. The truth is quite simple. In late summer of 1944 I had finished about half of a 20,000-worder for *Planet*. Suddenly lightning struck and (no one more amazed than I) I had a job working on the screenplay of *The Big Sleep*, for Howard Hawks. Obviously I wasn't going to have time to finish the story, and I asked Ray if he would like to tackle it. He had nothing to go on but what I had down on paper. I never worked from an outline in those days (and often regretted it) and I had no idea where the story was going. Ray took the story and finished it, completely on his own. I never read a word of it until he handed me the manuscript, and I never changed a word after that. I'm convinced to this day that he did a better job with the second half than I would have done. Bradbury's section begins with the line, "He saw the flock, herded by more of the golden hounds." Ray did some of the best of his early writing for *Planet*, and this was some of that.

One thing for which I will offer a belated apology is the use of the name "Conan." Conan is, of course, an authentic Celtic name and therefore in public domain. In using it I intended a sort of gesture of respect and affection toward a writer I greatly admired. However, Robert E. Howard had made that name so peculiarly his own, and so strongly identified for all time with his character, that I really had no right to use it, whatever my reason. Suffice it to say that I'm sorry, even though Conan-called-Starke bears absolutely no resemblance to Conan the Cimmerian.

Getting back to the mention of Big Thinks—like Dr. Moreau's beast-men, writers of adventure stories aren't allowed to have them. Sometimes we manage to sneak one in even so, and all that saves us is that no one realizes it's there. Who looks for a statement of any *Real Importance* in a space opera? I won't tell you whether any such are lurking among these stories—but if you should happen to think you see one here and there, you just might be right.

Anyway, here you are with a handful of good yarns. We hope, with this and subsequent volumes, to bring to you the best of a magazine much too long neglected, both for the enjoyment of young readers who have heard about *Planet* but have never seen it except on the huckster's tables at prohibitive prices, and for the older ones who may take their own nostalgic pleasure in welcoming back an old friend. We hope also to reach a third and even larger group—people who have never read much, or any, science fiction but who are looking simply for entertainment.

The planets are yours. Read and have fun.

—LEIGH BRACKETT
Kinsman, Ohio
26 July, 1974

Lorelei of the Red Mist

Leigh Brackett and
Ray Bradbury

He died—and then awakened in a new
body. He found himself on a world of bizarre
loveliness, a powerful, rich man. He took
pleasure in his turn of good luck . . . until he
discovered that his new body was hated by
all on this strange planet, that his soul was
owned by Rann, devil-goddess of Falga, who
was using him for her own gain.

The Company dicks were good. They were
plenty good. Hugh Starke began to think maybe this
time he wasn't going to get away with it.

His small stringy body hunched over the control
bank, nursing the last ounce of power out of the
Kallman. The hot night sky of Venus fled past the
ports in tattered veils of indigo. Starke wasn't sure
where he was any more. Venus was a frontier planet,
and still mostly a big X, except to the Venusians—who
weren't sending out any maps. He did know that he
was getting dangerously close to the Mountains of
White Cloud. The backbone of the planet, towering
far into the stratosphere, magnetic trap, with God knew
what beyond. Maybe even God wasn't sure.

But it looked like over the mountains or out. Death
under the guns of the Terro-Venus Mines, Incorpo-

rated, Special Police, or back to the Luna cell blocks for life as an habitual felon.

Starke decided he would go over.

Whatever happened, he'd pulled off the biggest lone-wolf caper in history. The T-V Mines payroll ship, for close to a million credits. He cuddled the metal strongbox between his feet and grinned. It would be a long time before anybody equaled that.

His mass indicators began to jitter. Vaguely, a dim purple shadow in the sky ahead, the Mountains of White Cloud, stood like a wall against him. Starke checked the positions of the pursuing ships. There was no way through them. He said flatly, "All right, damn you," and sent the Kallman angling up into the thick blue sky.

He had no very clear memories after that. Crazy magnetic vagaries, always a hazard on Venus, made his instruments useless. He flew by the seat of his pants and he got over, and the T-V men didn't. He was free, with a million credits in his kick.

Far below in the virgin darkness he saw a sullen crimson smear on the night, as though someone had rubbed it with a bloody thumb. The Kallman dipped toward it. The control bank flickered with blue flame, the jet timers blew, and then there was just the screaming of air against the falling hull.

Hugh Starke sat still and waited . . .

He knew, before he opened his eyes, that he was dying. He didn't feel any pain, he didn't feel anything, but he knew just the same. Part of him was cut loose. He was still there, but not attached anymore.

He raised his eyelids. There was a ceiling. It was a long way off. It was black stone veined with smoky reds and ambers. He had never seen it before.

His head was tilted toward the right. He let his gaze move down that way. There were dim tapestries, more of the black stone, and three tall archways giving onto a balcony. Beyond the balcony was a sky veiled and clouded with red mist. Under the mist, spreading away from a murky line of cliffs, was an ocean. It wasn't water and it didn't have any waves on it, but there was nothing else to call it. It burned, deep down inside itself, breathing up the red fog. Little angry bursts of flame coiled up under the flat surface, sending circles of sparks flaring out like ripples from a dropped stone.

He closed his eyes and frowned and moved his head restively. There was the texture of fur against his skin. Through the cracks of his eyelids he saw that he lay on a high bed piled with silks and soft tanned pelts. His body was covered. He was rather glad he couldn't see it. It didn't matter because he wouldn't be using it any more anyway, and it hadn't been such a hell of a body to begin with. But he was used to it, and he didn't want to see it now, the way he knew it would have to look.

He looked along over the foot of the bed, and he saw the woman.

She sat watching him from a massive carved chair softened with a single huge white pelt like a drift of snow. She smiled, and let him look. A pulse began to beat under his jaw, very feebly.

She was tall and sleek and insolently curved. She wore a sort of tabard of pale grey spider-silk, held to her body by a jeweled girdle, but it was just a nice piece of ornamentation. Her face was narrow, finely cut, secret, faintly amused. Her lips, her eyes, and her flowing silken hair were all the same pale cool shade of aquamarine.

Her skin was white, with no hint of rose. Her shoulders, her forearms, the long flat curve of her thighs, the pale-green tips of her breasts, were dusted with tiny particles that glistened like powdered diamond. She sparkled softly like a fairy thing against the snowy fur, a creature of foam and moonlight and clear shallow water. Her eyes never left his, and they were not human, but he knew that they would have done things to him if he had had any feeling below the neck.

He started to speak. He had no strength to move his tongue. The woman leaned forward, and as though her movement were a signal four men rose from the tapestried shadows by the wall. They were like her. Their eyes were pale and strange like hers.

She said, in liquid High Venusian, "You're dying, in this body. But *you* will not die. You will sleep now, and wake in a strange body, in a strange place. Don't be afraid. My mind will be with yours, I'll guide you, don't be afraid. I can't explain now, there isn't time, but don't be afraid."

He drew back his thin lips baring his teeth in what might have been a smile. If it was, it was wolfish and bitter, like his face.

The woman's eyes began to pour coolness into his skull. They were like two little rivers running through the channels of his own eyes, spreading in silver-green quiet across the tortured surface of his brain. His brain relaxed. It lay floating on the water, and then the twin streams became one broad, flowing stream, and his mind, or ego, the thing that was intimately himself, vanished along it.

It took him a long, long time to regain consciousness. He felt as though he'd been shaken until pieces of him were scattered all over inside. Also, he had an instinctive premonition that the minute he woke up he would be sorry he had. He took it easy, putting himself together.

He remembered his name, Hugh Starke. He remembered the mining asteroid where he was born. He remembered the Luna cell blocks where he had once come near dying. There wasn't much to choose between them. He remembered his face decorating half the bulletin boards between Mercury and The Belt. He remembered hearing about himself over the telecasts, stuff to frighten babies with, and he thought of himself committing his first crime—a stunted scrawny kid of eighteen swinging a spanner on a grown man who was trying to steal his food.

The rest of it came fast, then. The T-V Mines job, the getaway that didn't get, the Mountains of White Cloud. The crash . . .

The woman.

That did it. His brain leaped shatteringly. Light, feeling, a naked sense of reality swept over him. He lay perfectly still with his eyes shut, and his mind clawed at the picture of the shining woman with sea-green hair and the sound of her voice saying, *You will not die, you will wake in a strange body, don't be afraid* . . .

He was afraid. His skin pricked and ran cold with it. His stomach knotted with it. His skin, his stomach, and yet somehow they didn't feel just right, like a new coat that hasn't shaped to you . . .

He opened his eyes, a cautious crack.

He saw a body sprawled on its side in dirty straw. The body belonged to him, because he could feel the straw pricking it, and the itch of little things that crawled and ate and crawled again.

It was a powerful body, rangy and flat-muscled, much bigger than his old one. It had obviously not been starved the first twenty-some years of its life. It was stark naked. Weather and violence had written history on it, wealed white marks on leathery bronze, but nothing seemed to be missing. There was black hair on its chest and thighs and forearms, and its hands were lean and sinewy for killing.

It was a human body. That was something. There were so many other things it might have been that his racial snobbery wouldn't call human. Like the nameless shimmering creature who smiled with strange pale lips.

Starke shut his eyes again.

He lay, the intangible self that was Hugh Starke, bellied down in the darkness of the alien shell, quiet, indrawn, waiting. Panic crept up on its soft black paws. It walked around the crouching ego and sniffed and patted and nuzzled, whining, and then struck with its raking claws. After a while it went away, empty.

The lips that were now Starke's lips twitched in a thin, cruel smile. He had done six months once in the Luna solitary crypts. If a man could do that, and come out sane and on his two feet, he could stand anything. Even this.

It came to him then, rather deflatingly, that the woman and her four companions had probably softened the shock by hypnotic suggestion. His subconscious understood and accepted the change. It was only his conscious mind that was superficially scared to death.

Hugh Starke cursed the woman with great thoroughness, in seven languages and some odd dialects. He became healthily enraged that any dame should play around with him like that. Then he thought, What the hell, I'm alive. And it looks like I got the best of the trade-in!

He opened his eyes again, secretly, on his new world.

He lay at one end of a square stone hall, good sized, with two straight lines of pillars cut from some dark Venusian wood. There were long crude benches and tables. Fires had been burning on round brick hearths spaced between the pillars. They were embers now. The smoke climbed up, tarnishing the gold and bronze of shields hung on the walls and pediments, dulling the blades of longswords, the spears, the tapestries and hides and trophies.

It was very quiet in the hall. Somewhere outside of it there was fighting going on. Heavy, vicious fighting. The noise of it didn't touch the silence, except to make it deeper.

There were two men besides Starke in the hall.

They were close to him, on a low dais. One of them sat in a carved high seat, not moving, his big scarred hands flat on the table in front of him. The other crouched on the floor by his feet. His head was bent forward so that his mop of lint-white hair hid his face and the harp between his thighs. He was a little man, a swamp-edger from his albino coloring. Starke looked back at the man in the chair.

The man spoke harshly. "Why doesn't she send word?"

The harp gave out a sudden bitter chord. That was all.

Starke hardly noticed. His whole attention was drawn to the speaker. His heart began to pound. His muscles coiled and lay ready. There was a bitter taste in his mouth. He recognized it. It was hate.

He had never seen the man before, but his hands twitched with the urge to kill.

He was big, nearly seven feet, and muscled like a draft horse. But his body, naked above a gold-bossed leather kilt, was lithe and quick as a greyhound in spite of its weight. His face was square, strong-boned, weathered, and still young. It was a face that had laughed a lot once, and liked wine and pretty girls. It had forgotten those things now, except maybe the wine. It was drawn and cruel with pain, a look as of something in a cage. Starke had seen that look before, in the Luna blocks. There was a thick white scar across the man's forehead. Under it his blue eyes were sunken and dark behind half-closed lids. The man was blind.

Outside, in the distance, men screamed and died.

Starke had been increasingly aware of a soreness and stricture around his neck. He raised a hand, careful not to rustle the straw. His fingers found a long tangled beard, felt under it, and touched a band of metal.

Starke's new body wore a collar, like a vicious dog.

There was a chain attached to the collar. Starke couldn't find any fastening. The business had been welded on for keeps. His body didn't seem to have liked it much. The neck was galled and chafed.

The blood began to crawl up hot into Starke's head. He'd worn chains before. He didn't like them. Especially around the neck.

A door opened suddenly at the far end of the hall. Fog and red daylight spilled in across the black stone floor. A man came in. He was big, half naked, blond, and bloody. His long blade trailed harshly on the flags. His chest was laid open to the bone and he held the wound together with his free hand.

"Word from Beudag," he said. "They've driven us back into the city, but so far we're holding the Gate."

No one spoke. The little man nodded his white head. The man with the slashed chest turned and went out again, closing the door.

A peculiar change came over Starke at the mention of the name Beudag. He had never heard it before, but it hung in his mind like a spear point, barbed with strange emotion. He couldn't identify the feeling, but it brushed the blind man aside. The hot simple hatred cooled. Starke relaxed in a sort of icy quiet, deceptively calm as a sleeping cobra. He didn't question this. He waited, for Beudag.

The blind man struck his hands down suddenly on the table and stood up. "Romna," he said, "give me my sword."

The little man looked at him. He had milk-blue eyes and a face like a friendly bulldog. He said, "Don't be a fool, Faolan."

Faolan said softly, "Damn you. Give me my sword."

Men were dying outside the hall, and not dying silently. Faolan's skin was greasy with sweat. He made a sudden, darting grab toward Romna.

Romna dodged him. There were tears in his pale eyes. He said brutally, "You'd only be in the way. Sit down."

"I can find the point," Faolan said, "to fall on it."

Romna's voice went up to a harsh scream. "Shut up. Shut up and sit down."

Faolan caught the edge of the table and bent over it. He shivered and closed his eyes, and the tears ran out hot under the lids. The bard turned away, and his harp cried out like a woman.

Faolan drew a long sighing breath. He straightened slowly, came round the carved high seat, and walked steadily toward Starke.

"You're very quiet, Conan," he said. "What's the matter? You ought to be happy, Conan. You ought to laugh and rattle your chain. You're going to get what you wanted. Are you sad because you haven't a mind any more, to understand that with?"

He stopped and felt with one sandaled foot across the straw until he touched Starke's thigh. Starke lay motionless.

"Conan," said the blind man gently, pressing Starke's belly with his foot. "Conan the dog, the betrayer, the butcher, the knife in the back. Remember what you did at Falga, Conan? No, you don't remember now. I've been a little rough with you, and you don't remember any more. But I remember, Conan. As long as I live in darkness, I'll remember."

Romna stroked the harp strings and they wept,

savage tears for strong men dead of treachery. Low music, distant but not soft. Faolan began to tremble, a shallow animal twitching of the muscles. The flesh of his face was drawn, iron shaping under the hammer. Quite suddenly he went down on his knees. His hands struck Starke's shoulders, slid inward to the throat, and locked there.

Outside, the sound of fighting had died away.

Starke moved, very quickly. As though he had seen it and knew it was there, his hand swept out and gathered in the slack of the heavy chain and swung it.

It started out to be a killing blow. Starke wanted with all his heart to beat Faolan's brains out. But at the last second he pulled it, slapping the big man with exquisite judgment across the back of the head. Faolan grunted and fell sideways, and by that time Romna had come up. He had dropped his harp and drawn a knife. His eyes were startled.

Starke sprang up. He backed off, swinging the slack of the chain warningly. His new body moved magnificently. Outside everything was fine, but inside his psycho-neural setup had exploded into civil war. He was furious with himself for not having killed Faolan. He was furious with himself for losing control enough to want to kill a man without reason. He hated Faolan. He did not hate Faolan because he didn't know him well enough. Starke's trained, calculating unemotional brain was at grips with a tidal wave to baseless emotion.

He hadn't realized it was baseless until his mental monitor, conditioned through years of bitter control, had stopped him from killing. Now he remembered the woman's voice saying, *My mind will be with yours, I'll guide you . . .*

Catspaw, huh? Just a hired hand, paid off with a new body in return for two lives. Yeah, two. This Beudag, whoever he was. Starke knew now what that cold alien emotion had been leading up to.

"Hold it," said Starke hoarsely. "Hold everything. *Catspaw! You green-eyed she-devil! You picked the wrong guy this time.*"

Just for a fleeting instant he saw her again, leaning forward with her hair like running water across the soft foam-sparkle of her shoulders. Her sea-pale eyes were full of mocking laughter, and a direct, provocative admiration. Starke heard her quite plainly:

"You may not have any choice, Hugh Starke. They know Conan, even if you don't. Besides, it's of no great importance. The end will be the same for them—it's just a matter of time. You can save your new body or not, as you wish." She smiled. "I'd like it if you did. It's a good body. I knew it, before Conan's mind broke and left it empty."

A sudden thought came to Starke. "My box, the million credits."

"Come and get them." She was gone. Starke's mind was clear, with no alien will tramping around in it. Faolan crouched on the floor, holding his head. He said:

"Who spoke?"

Romna the bard stood staring. His lips moved, but no sound came out.

Starke said, "I spoke. Me, Hugh Starke. I'm not Conan, and I never heard of Falga, and I'll brain the first guy that comes near me."

Faolan stayed motionless, his face blank, his breath sobbing in his throat. Romna began to curse, very softly, not as though he were thinking about it. Starke watched them.

Down the hall the doors burst open. The heavy reddish mist coiled in with the daylight across the flags, and with them a press of bodies hot from battle, bringing a smell of blood.

Starke felt the heart contract in the hairy breast of the body named Conan, watching the single figure that led the pack.

Romna called out, "Beudag!"

She was tall. She was built and muscled like a lioness, and she walked with a flat-hipped arrogance, and her hair was like coiled flame. Her eyes were blue, hot and bright, as Faolan's might have been once. She looked like Faolan. She was dressed like him, in a leather kilt and sandals, her magnificent body bare above the waist. She carried a longsword slung across her back, the hilt standing above the left shoulder. She had been using it. Her skin was smeared with blood and grime. There was a long cut on her thigh and another across her flat belly, and bitter weariness lay on her like a burden in spite of her denial of it.

"We've stopped them, Faolan," she said. "They can't breach the Gate, and we can hold Crom Dhu as long as we have food. And the sea feeds us." She laughed, but there was a hollow sound to it. "Gods, I'm tired!"

She halted then, below the dais. Her flame-blue gaze swept across Faolan, across Romna, and rose to meet Hugh Starke's, and stayed there.

The pulse began to beat under Starke's jaw again, and this time his body was strong, and the pulse was like a drum throbbing.

Romna said, "His mind has come back."

There was a long, hard silence. No one in the hall moved. Then the men back of Beudag, big brawny kilted warriors, began to close in on the dais, talking in low snarling undertones that rose toward a mob howl. Faolan rose up and faced them, and bellowed them to quiet.

"He's mine to take! Let him alone."

Beudag sprang up onto the dais, one beautiful flowing movement. "It isn't possible," she said. "His mind broke under torture. He's been a drooling idiot with barely the sense to feed himself. And now, suddenly, you say he's normal again?"

Starke said, "You know I'm normal. You can see it in my eyes."

"Yes."

He didn't like the way she said that. "Listen, my name is Hugh Starke. I'm an Earthman. This isn't Conan's brain come back. This is a new deal. I got shoved into his body. What it did before I got it I don't know, and I'm not responsible."

Faolan said, "He doesn't remember Falga. He doesn't remember the longships at the bottom of the sea." Faolan laughed.

Romna said quietly, "He didn't kill you, though.

He could have, easily. Would Conan have spared you?"

Beudag said, "Yes, if he had a better plan. Conan's mind was like a snake. It crawled in the dark, and you never knew where it was going to strike."

Starke began to tell them how it happened, the chain swinging idly in his hand. While he was talking he saw a face reflected in a polished shield hung on a pillar. Mostly it was just a tangled black mass of hair, mounted on a frame of long, harsh, jutting bone. The mouth was sensuous, with a dark sort of laughter on it. The eyes were yellow. The cruel, brilliant yellow of a killer hawk.

Starke realized with a shock that the face belonged to him.

"A woman with pale green hair," said Beudag softly. "Rann," said Faolan, and Romna's harp made a sound like a high-priest's curse.

"Her people have that power," Romna said. "They can think a man's soul into a spider, and step on it."

"They have many powers. Maybe Rann followed Conan's mind, wherever it went, and told it what to say, and brought it back again."

"Listen," said Starke angrily. "I didn't ask . . ."

Suddenly, without warning, Romna drew Beudag's sword and threw it at Starke.

Starke dodged it. He looked at Romna with ugly yellow eyes. "That's fine. Chain me up so I can't fight and kill me from a distance." He did not pick up the sword. He'd never used one. The chain felt better, not being too different from a heavy belt or a length of cable, or the other chains he'd swung on occasion.

Romna said, "Is that Conan?"

Faolan snarled, "What happened?"

"Romna threw my sword at Conan. He dodged it, and left it on the ground." Beudag's eyes were narrowed. "Conan could catch a flying sword by the hilt, and he was the best fighter on the Red Sea, barring you, Faolan."

"He's trying to trick us. Rann guides him."

"The hell with Rann!" Starke clashed his chain. "She wants me to kill the both of you, I still don't know why. All right. I could have killed Faolan, easy. But I'm not a killer. I never put down anyone except to save my own neck. So I didn't kill him in spite of Rann. And I don't want any part of you, or Rann either. All I want is to get the hell out of here!"

Beudag said, "His accent isn't Conan's. And the look in his eyes is different, too." Her voice had an odd note in it. Romna glanced at her. He fingered a few rippling chords on his harp, and said:

"There's one way you could tell for sure."

A sullen flush began to burn on Beudag's cheekbones. Romna slid unobtrusively out of reach. His eyes danced with malicious laughter.

Beudag smiled, the smile of an angry cat, all teeth and no humor. Suddenly she walked toward Starke, her head erect, her hands swinging loose and empty at her sides. Starke tensed warily, but the blood leaped pleasantly in his borrowed veins.

Beudag kissed him.

Starke dropped the chain. He had something better to do with his hands.

After a while he raised his head for breath, and she stepped back, and whispered wonderingly,

"It isn't Conan."

The hall had been cleared. Starke had washed and shaved himself. His new face wasn't bad. Not bad at all. In fact, it was pretty damn good. And it wasn't known around the System. It was a face that could own a million credits and no questions asked. It was a face that could have a lot of fun on a million credits.

All he had to figure out now was a way to save the neck the face was mounted on, and get his million credits back from that beautiful she-devil named Rann.

He was still chained, but the straw had been cleaned up and he wore a leather kilt and a pair of sandals. Faolan sat in his high seat nursing a flagon of wine. Beudag sprawled wearily on a fur rug beside him. Romna sat cross-legged, his eyes veiled sleepily, stroking soft wandering music out of his harp. He looked fey. Starke knew his swamp-edgers. He wasn't surprised.

"This man is telling the truth," Romna said. "But there's another mind touching his. Rann's, I think. Don't trust him."

Faolan growled, "I couldn't trust a god in Conan's body"

Starke said, "What's the setup? All the fighting out there, and this Rann dame trying to plant a killer on the inside. And what happened at Falga? I never heard of this whole damn ocean, let alone a place called Falga."

The bard swept his hand across the strings. "I'll tell you, Hugh Starke. And maybe you won't want to stay in that body any longer."

Starke grinned. He glanced at Beudag. She was watching him with a queer intensity from under lowered lids. Starke's grin changed. He began to sweat. Get rid of this body, hell! It was really a body. His own stringy little carcass had never felt like this.

The bard said, "In the beginning, in the Red Sea, was a race of people having still their fins and scales. They were amphibious, but after a while part of this race wanted to remain entirely on land. There was a quarrel, and a battle, and some of the people left the sea forever. They settled along the shore. They lost their fins and most of their scales. They had great mental powers and they loved ruling. They subjugated the human peoples and kept them almost in slavery. They hated their brothers who still lived in the sea, and their brothers hated them.

"After a time a third people came to the Red Sea. They were rovers from the North. They raided and reaved and wore no man's collar. They made a settlement on Crom Dhu, the Black Rock, and built longships, and took toll of the coastal towns.

"But the slave people didn't want to fight against the rovers. They wanted to fight with them and destroy the sea-folk. The rovers were human, and blood calls to blood. And the rovers liked to rule, too, and this is a rich country. Also, the time had come in their tribal development when they were ready to change from nomadic warriors to builders in their own country.

"So the rovers, and the sea-folk, and the slave-people who were caught between the two of them, began their struggle for the land."

The bard's fingers thrummed against the strings so that they beat like angry hearts. Starke saw that Beudag was still watching him, weighing every change of expression on his face. Romna went on:

"There was a woman named Rann, who had green hair and great beauty, and ruled the sea-folk. There was a man called Faolan of the Ships, and his sister Beudag, which means Dagger-in-the-Sheath, and they two ruled the outland rovers. And there was the man called Conan."

The harp crashed out like a sword-blade striking.

"Conan was a great fighter and a great lover. He was next under Faolan of the Ships, and Beudag loved him, and they were plighted. Then Conan was taken prisoner by the sea-folk during a skirmish, and Rann saw him—and Conan saw Rann."

Hugh Starke had a fleeting memory of Rann's face smiling, and her low voice saying, *It's a good body. I knew it, before* . . .

Beudag's eyes were two stones of blue vitriol under her narrow lids.

"Conan stayed a long time at Falga with Rann of the Red Sea. Then he came back to Crom Dhu, and said that he had escaped, and had discovered a way to take the longships into the harbor of Falga, at the back of Rann's fleet; and from there it would be easy to take the city, and Rann with it. And Conan and Beudag were married."

Starke's yellow hawk eyes slid over Beudag, sprawled like a long lioness in power and beauty. A muscle began to twitch under his cheekbone. Beudag flushed, a slow deep color. Her gaze did not waver.

"So the longships went out from Crom Dhu, across the Red Sea. And Conan led them into a trap at Falga, and more than half of them were sunk. Conan thought his ship was free, that he had Rann and all she'd promised him, but Faolan saw what had happened and went after him. They fought, and Conan laid his sword across Faolan's brow and blinded him; but Conan lost the fight. Beudag brought them home.

"Conan was chained naked in the market place. The people were careful not to kill him. From time to time other things were done to him. After a while his mind broke, and Faolan had him chained here in the hall, where he could hear him babble and play with his chain. It made darkness easier to bear.

"But since Falga, things have gone badly from Crom Dhu. Too many men were lost, too many ships. Now Rann's people have us bottled up here. They can't break in, we can't break out. And so we stay, until . . ." The harp cried out a bitter question, and was still.

After a minute or two Starke said slowly, "Yeah, I get it. Stalemate for both of you. And Rann figured if I could kill off the leaders, your people might give up." He began to curse. "What a lousy, dirty, sneaking trick! And who told her she could use me . . ." He paused. After all, he'd be dead now. After all, a new body, and a cool million credits. Ah, the hell with Rann. He hadn't asked her to do it. And he was nobody's hired killer. Where did she get off, sneaking around his mind, trying to make him do things he didn't even know about? Especially to someone like Beudag.

Still, Rann herself was nobody's crud.

And just where was Hugh Starke supposed to cut in on this deal? Cut was right. Probably with a longsword, right through the belly. Swell spot he was in, and a good three strikes on him already.

He was beginning to wish he'd never seen the T-V Mines payroll ship, because then he might never have seen the Mountains of White Cloud.

He said, because everybody seemed to be waiting for him to say something, "Usually when there's a deadlock like this, somebody calls in a third party. Isn't there somebody you can yell for?"

Faolan shook his rough red head. "The slave people might rise, but they haven't arms and they're not used to fighting. They'd only get massacred, and it wouldn't help us any."

"What about those other—uh—people that live in the sea? And just what is that sea, anyhow? Some radiation from it wrecked my ship and got me into this bloody mess."

Beudag said lazily, "I don't know what it is. The seas our forefathers sailed on were water, but this is different. It will float a ship, if you know how to build the hull—very thin, of a white metal we mine from the foothills. But when you swim in it, it's like being in a cloud of bubbles. It tingles, and the farther down you go in it the stranger it gets, dark and full of fire. I stay down for hours sometimes, hunting the beasts that live there."

Starke said, "For hours? You have diving suits, then. What are they?"

She shook her head, laughing. "Why weigh yourself down that way? There's no trouble to breathe in this ocean."

"For cripesake," said Starke. "Well I'll be damned. Must be a heavy gas, then, radioactive, surface tension under atmospheric pressure, enough to float a light hull, and high oxygen content without any dangerous mixture. Well, well. Okay, why doesn't somebody go down and see if the sea-people will help? They don't like Rann's branch of the family, you said."

"They don't like us, either," said Faolan. "We stay out of the southern part of the sea. They wreck our ships, sometimes." His bitter mouth twisted in a smile. "Did you want to go to them for help?"

Starke didn't quite like the way Faolan sounded. "It was just a suggestion," he said.

Beudag rose, stretching, wincing as the stiffened wounds pulled her flesh. "Come on, Faolan. Let's sleep."

He rose and laid his hand on her shoulder. Romna's harpstrings breathed a subtle little mockery of sound. The bard's eyes were veiled and sleepy. Beudag did not look at Starke, called Conan.

Starke said, "What about me?"

"You stay chained," said Faolan. "There's plenty

of time to think. As long as we have food—and the sea feeds us."

He followed Beudag, through a curtained entrance to the left. Romna got up, slowly, slinging the harp over one white shoulder. He stood looking steadily into Starke's eyes in the dying light of the fires.

"I don't know," he murmured.

Starke waited, not speaking. His face was without expression.

"Conan we knew. Starke we don't know. Perhaps it would have been better if Conan had come back." He ran his thumb absently over the hilt of the knife in his girdle. "I don't know. Perhaps it would have been better for all of us if I'd cut your throat before Beudag came in."

Starke's mouth twitched. It was not exactly a smile.

"You see," said the bard seriously, "to you, from Outside, none of this is important, except as it touches you. But we live in this little world. We die in it. To us, it's important."

The knife was in his hand now. It leaped up glittering into the dregs of the firelight, and fell, and leaped again.

"You fight for yourself, Hugh Starke. Rann also fights through you. I don't know."

Starke's gaze did not waver.

Romna shrugged and put away the knife. "It is written of the gods," he said, sighing. "I hope they haven't done a bad job of the writing."

He went out. Starke began to shiver slightly. It was competely quiet in the hall. He examined his collar, the rivets, every separate link of the chain, the staple to which it was fixed. Then he sat down on the fur rug provided for him in place of the straw. He put his face in his hands and cursed, steadily, for several minutes, and then struck his fists down hard on the floor. After that he lay down and was quiet. He thought Rann would speak to him. She did not.

The silent black hours that walked across his heart were worse than any he had spent in the Luna crypts.

She came soft-shod, bearing a candle. Beudag, the Dagger-in-the-Sheath. Starke was not asleep. He rose and stood waiting. She set the candle on the table and came, not quite to him, and stopped. She wore a length of thin white cloth twisted loosely at the waist and dropping to her ankles. Her body rose out of it straight and lovely, touched mystically with shadows in the little wavering light.

"Who are you?" she whispered. "What are you?"

"A man. Not Conan. Maybe not Hugh Starke any more. Just a man."

"I loved the man called Conan, until . . ." She caught her breath, and moved closer. She put her hand on Starke's arm. The touch went through him like white fire. The warm clean healthy fragrance of her tasted sweet in his throat. Her eyes searched his.

"If Rann has such great powers, couldn't it be that Conan was forced to do what he did? Couldn't it be that Rann took his mind and moulded it her way, perhaps without his knowing it?"

"It could be."

"Conan was hot-tempered and quarrelsome, but he . . ."

Starke said slowly, "I don't think you could have loved him if he hadn't been straight."

Her hand lay still on his forearm. She stood looking at him, and then her hand began to tremble, and in a moment she was crying, making no noise about it. Starke drew her gently to him. His eyes blazed yellowly in the candlelight.

"Woman's tears," she said impatiently, after a bit. She tried to draw away. "I've been fighting too long, and losing, and I'm tired."

He let her step back, not far. "Do all the women of Crom Dhu fight like men?"

"If they want to. There have always been shield-maidens. And since Falga, I would have had to fight anyway, to keep from thinking." She touched the collar on Starke's neck. "And from seeing."

He thought of Conan in the market square, and Conan shaking his chain and gibbering in Faolan's hall, and Beudag watching it. Starke's fingers tightened.

He slid his palms upward along the smooth muscles of her arms, across the straight, broad planes of her shoulders, onto her neck, the proud strength of it pulsing under his hands. Her hair fell loose. He could feel the redness of it burning him.

She whispered, "You don't love me."

"No."

"You're an honest man, Hugh Starke."

"You want me to kiss you."

"Yes."

"You're an honest woman, Beudag."

Her lips were hungry, passionate, touched with the bitterness of tears. After a while Starke blew out the candle . . .

"I could love you, Beudag."

"Not the way I mean."

"The way you mean. I've never said that to any woman before. But you're not like any woman before. And—I'm a different man."

"Strange—so strange. Conan, and yet not Conan."

"I could love you, Beudag—if I lived."

Harpstrings gave a thrumming sigh in the darkness, the faintest whisper of sound. Beudag started, sighed, and rose from the fur rug. In a minute she had found flint and steel and got the candle lighted. Romna the bard stood in the curtained doorway, watching them.

Presently he said, "You're going to let him go."

Beudag said, "Yes."

Romna nodded. He did not seem surprised. He walked across the dais, laying his harp on the table, and went into another room. He came back almost at once with a hacksaw.

"Bend your neck," he said to Starke.

The metal of the collar was soft. When it was cut through Starke got his fingers under it and bent the ends outward, without trouble. His old body could never have done that. His old body could never have done a lot of things. He figured Rann hadn't cheated him. Not much.

He got up, looking at Beudag. Beudag's head was dropped forward, her face veiled behind shining hair.

"There's only one possible way out of Crom Dhu,"

she said. There was no emotion in her voice. "There's a passage leading down through the rock to a secret harbor, just large enough to moor a skiff or two. Perhaps, with the night and the fog, you can slip through Rann's blockade. Or you can go aboard one of her ships, for Falga." She picked up the candle. "I'll take you down."

"Wait," Starke said. "What about you?"

She glanced at him, surprised. "I'll stay, of course."

He looked into her eyes. "It's going to be hard to know each other that way."

"You can't stay here, Hugh Starke. The people would tear you to pieces the moment you went into the street. They may even storm the hall, to take you. Look here." She set the candle down and led him to a narrow window, drawing back the hide that covered it.

Starke saw narrow twisting streets dropping steeply toward the sullen sea. The longships were broken and sunk in the harbor. Out beyond, riding lights flickering in the red fog, were other ships. Rann's ships.

"Over there," said Beudag, "is the mainland. Crom Dhu is connected to it by a tongue of rock. The seafolk hold the land beyond it, but we can hold the rock bridge as long as we live. We have enough water, enough food from the sea. But there's no soil nor game on Crom Dhu. We'll be naked after a while, without leather or flax, and we'll have scurvy without grain and fruit. We're beaten, unless the gods send us a miracle. And we're beaten because of what was done at Falga. You can see how the people feel."

Starke looked at the dark streets and the silent houses leaning on each other's shoulders, and the mocking lights out in the fog. "Yeah," he said. "I can see."

"Besides, there's Faolan. I don't know whether he believes your story. I don't know whether it would matter."

Starke nodded. "But you won't come with me?"

She turned away sharply and picked up the candle again. "Are you coming, Romna?"

The bard nodded. He slung his harp over his

shoulder. Beudag held back the curtain of a small doorway far to the side. Starke went through it and Romna followed, and Beudag went ahead with the candle. No one spoke.

They went along a narrow passage, past store rooms and armories. They paused once while Starke chose a knife, and Romna whispered: "Wait!" He listened intently. Starke and Beudag strained their ears along with him. There was no sound. Romna shrugged. "I thought I heard sandals scraping stone," he said. They went on.

The passage lay behind a wooden door. It led downward steeply through the rock, a single narrow way without side galleries or branches. In some places there were winding steps. It ended, finally, in a flat ledge low to the surface of the cove, which was a small cavern closed in with the black rock. Beudag set the candle down.

There were two little skiffs built of some light metal moored to rings in the ledge. Two long sweeps leaned against the cave wall. They were of a different metal, oddly vaned. Beudag laid one across the thwarts of the nearest boat. Then she turned to Starke. Romna hung back in the shadows by the tunnel mouth.

Beudag said qiuetly, "Goodbye, man without a name."

"It has to be goodbye?"

"I'm leader now, in Faolan's place. Besides, these are my people." Her fingers tightened on his wrists. "If you could . . ." Her eyes held a brief blaze of hope. Then she dropped her head and said, "I keep forgetting you're not one of us. Goodbye."

"Goodbye, Beudag."

Starke put his arms around her. He found her mouth, almost cruelly. Her arms were tight about him, her eyes half closed and dreaming. Starke's hands slipped upward, toward her throat, and locked on it.

She bent back, her body like a steel bow. Her eyes got fire in them, looking into Starke's but only for a moment. His fingers pressed expertly on the nerve centers. Beudag's head fell forward limply, and then

Romna was on Starke's back and his knife was pricking Starke's throat.

Starke caught his wrist and turned the blade away. Blood ran onto his chest, but the cut was not into the artery. He threw himself backward onto the stone. Romna couldn't get clear in time. The breath went out of him in a rushing gasp. He didn't let go of the knife. Starke rolled over. The little man didn't have a chance with him. He was tough and quick, but Starke's sheer size smothered him. Starke could remember when Romna would not have seemed small to him. He hit the bard's jaw with his fist. Romna's head cracked hard against the stone. He let go of the knife. He seemed to be through fighting. Starke got up. He was sweating, breathing heavily, not because of his exertion. He mouth was glistening and eager, like a dog's. His muscles twitched, his belly was hot and knotted with excitement. His yellow eyes had a strange look.

He went back to Beudag.

She lay on the black rock, on her back. Candlelight ran pale gold across her brown skin, skirting the sharp strong hollows between her breasts and under the arching rim of her rib-case. Starke knelt, across her body, his weight pressed down against her harsh breathing. He stared at her. Sweat stood out on his face. He took her throat between his hands again.

He watched the blood grow dark in her cheeks. He watched the veins coil on her forehead. He watched the redness blacken in her lips. She fought a little, very vaguely, like someone moving in a dream. Starke breathed hoarsely, animal-like through an open mouth.

Then, gradually his body became rigid. His hands froze, not releasing pressure, but not adding any. His yellow eyes widened. It was as though he were trying to see Beudag's face and it was hidden in dense clouds.

Back of him, back in the tunnel, was the soft, faint whisper of sandals on uneven rock. Sandals, walking slowly. Starke did not hear. Beudag's face glimmered deep in a heavy mist below him, a blasphemy of a face, distorted, blackened.

Starke's hands began to open.

They opened slowly. Muscles stood like coiled ropes in his arms and shoulders, as though he moved them against heavy weights. His lips peeled back from his teeth. He bent his neck, and sweat dropped from his face and glittered on Beudag's breast.

Starke was now barely touching Beudag's neck. She began to breathe again, painfully.

Starke began to laugh. It was not nice laughter. "Rann," he whispered. "Rann, you she-devil." He half fell away from Beudag and stood up, holding himself against the wall. He was shaking violently. "I wouldn't use your hate for killing, so you tried to use my passion." He cursed her in a flat sibilant whisper. He had never in his profane life really cursed anyone before.

He heard an echo of laughter dancing in his brain.

Starke turned. Faolan of the Ships stood in the tunnel mouth. His head was bent, listening, his blind dark eyes fixed on Starke as though he saw him.

Faolan said softly "I hear you, Starke. I hear the others breathing, but they don't speak."

"They're all right. I didn't mean to do . . ."

Faolan smiled. He stepped out on the narrow ledge. He knew where he was going, and his smile was not pleasant.

"I heard your steps in the passage beyond my room. I knew Beudag was leading you, and where, and why. I would have been here sooner, but it's a slow way in the dark."

The candle lay in his path. He felt the heat of it close to his leg, and stopped and felt for it, and ground it out. It was dark, then. Very dark, except for a faint smudgy glow from the scrap of ocean that lay along the cave floor.

"It doesn't matter," Faolan said, "as long as I came in time."

Starke shifted his weight warily. "Faolan . . ."

"I wanted you alone. On this night of all nights

I wanted you alone. Beudag fights in my place now, Conan. My manhood needs proving."

Starke strained his eyes in the gloom, measuring the ledge, measuring the place where the skiff was moored. He didn't want to fight Faolan. In Faolan's place he would have felt the same. Starke understood perfectly. He didn't hate Faolan, he didn't want to kill him, and he was afraid of Rann's power over him when his emotions got control. You couldn't keep a determined man from killing you and still be uninvolved emotionally. Starke would be damned if he'd kill anyone to suit Rann.

He moved, silently, trying to slip past Faolan on the outside and get into the skiff. Faolan gave no sign of hearing him. Starke did not breathe. His sandals came down lighter than snowflakes. Faolan did not swerve. He would pass Starke with a foot to spare. They came abreast.

Faolan's hand shot out and caught in Starke's long black hair. The blind man laughed softly and closed in.

Starke swung one from the floor. Do it the quickest way and get clear. But Faolan was fast. He came in so swiftly that Starke's fist jarred harmlessly along his ribs. He was bigger than Starke, and heavier, and the darkness didn't bother him.

Starke bared his teeth. Do it quick, brother, and clear out! Or that green-eyed she-cat . . . Faolan's brute bulk weighed him down. Faolan's arm crushed his neck. Faolan's fist was knocking his guts loose. Starke got moving.

He'd fought in a lot of places. He'd learned from stokers and tramps, Martian Low-Canalers, red-eyed Nahali in the running gutters of Lhi. He didn't use his knife. He used his knees and feet and elbows and his hands, fist and flat. It was a good fight. Faolan was a good fighter, but Starke knew more tricks.

One more, Starke thought. One more and he's out. He drew back for it, and his heel struck Romna, lying on the rock. He staggered, and Faolan caught him with a clean swinging blow. Starke fell backward against the cave wall. His head cracked the rock. Light

flooded crimson across his brain and then paled and
grew cooler, a wash of clear silver-green like water.
He sank under it . . .

He was tired, desperately tired. His head ached.
He wanted to rest, but he could feel that he was sitting
up, doing something that had to be done. He opened
his eyes.

He sat in the stern of a skiff. The long sweep was
laid into its crutch, held like a tiller bar against his
body. The blade of the sweep trailed astern in the red
sea, and where the metal touched there was a spurt
of silver fire and a swirling of brilliant motes. The skiff
moved rapidly through the sullen fog, through a mist
of blood in the hot Venusian night.

Beudag crouched in the bow, facing Starke. She
was bound securely with strips of the white cloth she
had worn. Bruises showed dark on her throat. She was
watching Starke with the intent, unwinking, perfectly
expressionless gaze of a tigress.

Starke looked away, down at himself. There was
blood on his kilt, a brown smear of it across his chest.
It was not his blood. He drew the knife slowly out
of its sheath. The blade was dull and crusted, still a
little wet.

Starke looked at Beudag. His lips were stiff, swollen.
He moistened them and said hoarsely, "What happened?"

She shook her head, slowly, not speaking. Her eyes
did not waver.

A black, cold rage took hold of Starke and shook
him. Rann! He rose and went forward, letting the
sweep go where it would. He began to untie Beudag's
wrists.

A shape swam toward them out of the red mist.
A longship with two heavy sweeps bursting fire astern
and a slender figurehead shaped like a woman. A
woman with hair and eyes of aquamarine. It came
alongside the skiff.

A rope ladder snaked down. Men lined the low rail.
Slender men with skin that glistened white like
powdered snow, and hair the color of distant shallows.

One of them said, "Come aboard, Hugh Starke."

Starke went back to the sweep. It bit into the sea, sending the skiff in a swift arc away from Rann's ship.

Grapnels flew, hooking the skiff at thwart and gunwale. Bows appeared in the hands of the men, wicked curving things with barbed metal shafts on the string. The man said again, politely, "Come aboard."

Hugh Starke finished untying Beudag. He didn't speak. There seemed to be nothing to say. He stood back while she climbed the ladder and then followed. The skiff was cast loose. The longship veered away, gathering speed.

Starke said, "Where are we going?"

The man smiled. "To Falga."

Starke nodded. He went below with Beudag into a cabin with soft couches covered with spider-silk and panels of dark wood beautifully painted, dim fantastic scenes from the past of Rann's people. They sat opposite each other. They still did not speak.

They raised Falga in the opal dawn—a citadel of basalt cliffs rising sheer from the burning sea, with a long arm holding a harbor full of ships. There were green fields inland, and beyond, cloaked in the eternal mists of Venus, the Mountains of White Clouds lifted spaceward. Starke wished that he had never seen the Mountains of White Cloud. Then, looking at his hands, lean and strong on his long thighs, he wasn't so sure. He thought of Rann waiting for him. Anger, excitement, a confused violence of emotion set him pacing nervously.

Beudag sat quietly, withdrawn, waiting.

The longship threaded the crowded moorings and slid into place alongside a stone quay. Men rushed to make fast. They were human men, as Starke judged humans, like Beudag and himself. They had the shimmering silver hair and fair skin of the plateau peoples, the fine-cut faces and straight bodies. They wore leather collars with metal tags and they went naked like beasts, and they were gaunt and bowed with labor. Here and there a man with pale blue-green hair and resplendent harness stood godlike above the swarming masses.

Starke and Beudag went ashore. They might have been prisoners or honored guests, surrounded by their escort from the ship. Streets ran back from the harbor, twisting and climbing crazily up the cliffs. Houses climbed on each other's backs. It had begun to rain, the heavy steaming downpour of Venus, and the moist heat brought out the choking stench of people, too many people.

They climbed, ankle deep in water sweeping down the streets that were half stairway. Thin naked children peered out of the houses, out of narrow alleys. Twice they passed through market squares where women with the blank faces of defeat drew back from stalls of coarse food to let the party through.

There was something wrong. After a while Starke realized it was the silence. In all that horde of humanity no one laughed, or sang, or shouted. Even the children never spoke above a whisper. Starke began to feel a little sick. Their eyes had a look in them . . .

He glanced at Beudag, and away again.

The waterfront streets ended in a sheer basalt face honeycombed with galleries. Starke's party entered them, still climbing. They passed level after level of huge caverns, open to the sea. There was the same crowding, the same stench, the same silence. Eyes glinted in the half-light, bare feet moved furtively on stone. Somewhere a baby cried thinly, and was hushed at once.

They came out on the cliff top, into the clean high air. There was a city here. Broad streets, lined with trees, low rambling villas of the black rock set in walled gardens, drowned in brilliant vines and giant ferns and flowers. Naked men and women worked in the gardens, or hauled carts of rubbish through the alleys, or hurried on errands, slipping furtively across the main streets where they intersected the mews.

The party turned away from the sea, heading toward an ebon palace that sat like a crown above the city. The steaming rain beat on Starke's bare body, and up here you could get the smell of the rain, even through the heavy perfume of the flowers. You could smell Venus in the rain—musky and primitive and savagely alive, a fecund giantess with passion flowers in her outstretched hands. Starke set his feet down like a panther and his eyes burned a smoky amber.

They entered the palace of Rann. . . .

She received them in the same apartment where Starke had come to after the crash. Through a broad archway he could see the high bed where his old body had lain before the life went out of it. The red sea steamed under the rain outside, the rusty fog coiling languidly through the open arches of the gallery. Rann watched them lazily from a raised couch set massively into the wall. Her long sparkling legs sprawled arrogantly across the black spider-silk draperies. This time her tabard was a pale yellow. Her eyes were still the color of shoal-water, still amused, still secret, still dangerous.

Starke said, "So you made me do it after all."

"And you're angry." She laughed, her teeth showing white and pointed as bone needles. Her gaze held Starke's. There was nothing casual about it. Starke's hawk eyes turned molten yellow, like hot gold, and did not waver.

Beudag stood like a bronze spear, her forearms crossed beneath her bare sharp breasts. Two of Rann's palace guards stood behind her.

Starke began to walk toward Rann.

She watched him come. She let him get close enough to reach out and touch her, and then she said slyly, "It's a good body, isn't it?"

Starke looked at her for a moment. Then he laughed. He threw back his head and roared, and struck the great corded muscles of his belly with his fist. Presently he looked straight into Rann's eyes and said:

"I know you."

She nodded. "We know each other. Sit down, Hugh Starke." She swung her long legs over to make room, half erect now, looking at Beudag. Starke sat down. He did not look at Beudag.

Rann said, "Will your people surrender now?"

Beudag did not move, not even her eyelids. "If Faolan is dead—yes."

"And if he's not?"

Beudag stiffened. Starke did too.

"Then," said Beudag quietly, "They'll wait."

"Until he is?"

"Or until they must surrender."

Rann nodded. To the guards she said, "See that this woman is well fed and well treated."

Beudag and her escort had turned to go when Starke said, "Wait." The guards looked at Rann, who nodded, and glanced quizzically at Starke. Starke said:

"Is Faolan dead?"

Rann hesitated. Then she smiled. "No. You have the most damnably tough mind, Starke. You struck deep, but not deep enough. He may still die, but . . . No, he's not dead." She turned to Beudag and said with easy mockery, "You needn't hold anger against Starke. I'm the one who should be angry." Her eyes came back to Starke. They didn't look angry.

Starke said, "There's something else. Conan—the Conan that used to be, before Falga."

"Beudag's Conan."

"Yeah. Why did he betray his people?"

Rann studied him. Her strange pale lips curved, her sharp white teeth glistening wickedly with barbed humor. The she turned to Beudag. Beudag was still standing like a carved image, but her smooth muscles were ridged with tension, and her eyes were not the eyes of an image.

"Conan or Starke," said Rann, "she's still Beudag, isn't she? All right, I'll tell you. Conan betrayed his people because I put it into his mind to do it. He fought me. He made a good fight of it. But he wasn't quite as tough as you are, Starke."

There was a silence. For the first time since entering the room, Hugh Starke looked at Beudag. After a moment she sighed and lifted her chin and smiled, a deep, faint smile. The guards walked out beside her, but she was more erect and lighter of step than either of them.

"Well," said Rann, when they were gone, "and what about you, Hugh-Starke-Called-Conan."

"Have I any choice?"

"I always keep my bargains."

"Then give me my dough and let me clear the hell out of here."

"Sure that's what you want?"

"That's what I want."

"You could stay a while, you know."

"With you?"

Rann lifted her frosty-white shoulders. "I'm not promising half my kingdom, or even part of it. But you might be amused."

"I got no sense of humor."

"Don't you even want to see what happens to Crom Dhu?"

"And Beudag."

"And Beudag." He stopped, then fixed Rann with uncompromising yellow eyes. "No. Not Beudag. What are you going to do to her?"

"Nothing."

"Don't give me that."

"I say again, nothing. Whatever is done, her own people will do."

"What do you mean?"

"I mean that little Dagger-in-the-Sheath will be rested, cared for, and fattened, for a few days. Then I shall take her aboard my own ship and join the fleet before Crom Dhu. Beudag will be made quite comfortable at the masthead, where her people can see her plainly. She will stay there until the Rock surrenders. It depends on her own people how long she stays. She'll be given water. Not much, but enough."

Starke stared at her. He stared at her a long time. Then he spat deliberately on the floor and said in a perfectly flat voice: "How soon can I get out of here?"

Rann laughed, a small casual chuckle. "Humans," she said, "are so damned queer. I don't think I'll ever understand them." She reached out and struck a gong that stood in a carved frame beside the couch. The soft deep shimmering note had a sad quality of nostalgia. Rann lay back against the silken cushions and sighed.

"Goodbye, Hugh Starke."
A pause. Then, regretfully:
"Goodbye—Conan!"

They had made good time along the rim of the Red
Sea. One of Rann's galleys had taken them to the edge
of the Southern Ocean and left them on a narrow
shingle beach under the cliffs. From there they had
climbed to the rimrock and gone on foot—Hugh-Starke-
Called-Conan and four of Rann's arrogant shining
men. They were supposed to be guide and escort. They
were courteous, and they kept pace uncomplainingly
though Starke marched as though the devil were
pricking his heels. But they were armed, and Starke
was not.

Sometimes, very faintly, Starke was aware of Rann's
mind touching his with the velvet delicacy of a cat's
paw. Sometimes he started out of his sleep with her
image sharp in his mind, her lips touched with the
mocking, secret smile. He didn't like that. He didn't
like it at all.

But he liked even less the picture that stayed with
him waking or sleeping. The picture he wouldn't look
at. The picture of a tall women with hair like loose
fire on her neck, walking on light proud feet between
her guards.

She'll be given water, Rann said. Not much, but
enough.

Starke gripped the solid squareness of the box that
held his mililon credits and set the miles reeling backward from under his sandals.

On the fifth night one of Rann's men spoke quietly
across the campfire. "Tomorrow," he said, "we'll reach
the pass."

Starke got up and went away by himself, to the edge
of the rimrock that fell sheer to the burning sea. He
sat down. The red fog wrapped him like a mist of
blood. He thought of the blood on Beudag's breast
the first time he saw her. He thought of the blood on
his knife, crusted and dried. He thought of the blood
poured rank and smoking into the gutters of Crom
Dhu. The fog has to be red, he thought. Of all the

goddam colors in the universe, it has to be red. Red like Beudag's hair.

He held out his hands and looked at them, because he could still feel the silken warmth of that hair against his skin. There was nothing there now but the old white scars of another man's battles.

He set his fists against his temples and wished for his old body back again—the little stunted abortion that had clawed and scratched its way to survival through sheer force of mind. A most damnably tough mind, Rann had said. Yeah. It had had to be tough. But a mind was a mind. It didn't have emotions. It just figured out something coldly and then went ahead and never questioned, and it controlled the body utterly, because the body was only the worthless machinery that carried the mind around. Worthless. Yeah. The few women he'd ever looked at had told him that—and he hadn't even minded much. The old body hadn't given him any trouble.

He was having trouble now.

Starke got up and walked.

Tomorrow we reach the pass.

Tomorrow we go away from the Red Sea. There are nine planets and the whole damn Belt. There are women on all of them. All shapes, colors, and sizes, human, semi-human, and God knows what. With a million credits a guy could buy half of them, and with Conan's body he coud buy the rest. What's a woman, anyway? Only a . . .

Water. She'll be given water. Not much, but enough.

Conan reached out and took hold of a spire of rock, and his muscles stood out like knotted ropes. "Oh God,' he whispered, "what's the matter with me?"

"Love."

It wasn't God who answered. It was Rann. He saw her plainly in his mind, heard her voice like a silver bell.

"Conan was a man, Hugh Starke. He was whole, body and heart and brain. He knew how to love, and with him it wasn't women, but one woman—and her name was Beudag. I broke him, but it wasn't easy. I can't break you."

Starke stood for a long, long time. He did not move, except that he trembled. Then he took from his belt the box containing his million credits and threw it out as far as he could over the cliff edge. The red mist swallowed it up. He did not hear it strike the surface of the sea. Perhaps in that sea there was no splashing. He did not wait to find out.

He turned back along the rimrock, toward a place where he remembered a cleft, or chimney, leading down. And the four shining men who wore Rann's harness came silently out of the heavy luminous night and ringed him in. Their sword-points caught sharp red glimmers from the sky.

Starke had nothing on him but a kilt and sandals, and a cloak of tight-woven spider-silk that shed the rain.

"Rann sent you?" he said.

The men nodded.

"To kill me?"

Again they nodded. The blood drained out of Starke's face, leaving it grey and stony under the bronze. His hand went to his throat, over the gold fastening of his cloak.

The four men closed in like dancers.

Starke loosed his cloak and swung it like a whip across their faces. It confused them for a second, for a heartbeat—no more, but long enough. Starke left two of them to tangle their blades in the heavy fabric and leaped aside. A sharp edge slipped and turned along his ribs, and then he had reached in low and caught a man around the ankles, and used the thrashing body for a flail.

The body was strangely light, as though the bones in it were no more than rigid membrane, like a fish.

If he had stayed to fight, they would have finished him in seconds. They were fighting men, and quick. But Starke didn't stay. He gained his moment's grace and used it. They were hard on his heels, their points all but pricking his back as he ran, but he made it. Along the rimrock, out along a narrow tongue that jutted over the sea, and then outward, far outward, into red fog and dim fire that rolled around his plummeting body.

Oh God, he thought, if I guessed wrong and there *is* a beach . . .

The breath tore out of his lungs. His ears cracked, went dead. He held his arms out beyond his head, the thumbs locked together, his neck braced forward against the terrific upward push. He struck the surface of the sea.

There was no splash.

Dim coiling fire that drifted with infinite laziness around him, caressing his body with slow, tingling sparks. A feeling of lightness, as though his flesh had become one with the drifting fire. A sense of suffocation that had no basis in fact and gave way gradually to a strange exhilaration. There was no shock of impact, no crushing pressure. Merely a cushioning softness, like dropping into a bed of compressed air. Starke felt himself turning end over end, pinwheel fashion, and then that stopped, so that he sank quietly and without haste to the bottom.

Or rather, into the crystalline upper reaches of what seemed to be a forest.

He could see it spreading away along the downward-sloping floor of the ocean, into the vague red shadows of distance. Slender fantastic trunks upholding a maze of delicate shining branches, without leaves or fruit. They were like trees exquisitely molded from ice, transparent, holding the lambent shifting fire of the strange sea. Starke didn't think they were, or ever had been, alive. More like coral, he thought, or some vagary of mineral deposit. Beautiful, though. Like something you'd see in a dream. Beautiful, silent, and somehow deadly.

He couldn't explain that feeling of deadliness. Nothing moved in the red drifts between the trunks. It was nothing about the trees themselves. It was just something he sensed.

He began to move among the upper branches, following the downward drop of the slope.

He found that he could swim quite easily. Or perhaps it was more like flying. The dense gas buoyed him up, almost balancing the weight of his body, so that it was easy to swoop along, catching a crystal branch and using it as a lever to throw himself forward to the next one.

He went deeper and deeper into the heart of the forbidden Southern Ocean. Nothing stirred. The fairy forest stretched limitless ahead. And Starke was afraid.

Rann came into his mind abruptly. Her face, clearly outlined, was full of mockery.

"I'm going to watch you die, Hugh-Starke-Called-Conan. But before you die, I'll show you something. Look."

Her face dimmed, and in its place was Crom Dhu rising bleak into the red fog, the longships broken and sunk in the harbor, and Rann's fleet around it in a shining circle.

One ship in particular. The flagship. The vision in Starke's mind rushed toward it, narrowed down to the masthead platform. To the woman who stood there, naked, erect, her body lashed tight with thin cruel cords.

A woman with red hair blowing in the slow wind, and blue eyes that looked straight ahead like a falcon's, at Crom Dhu.

Beudag.

Rann's laughter ran across the picture and blurred it like a ripple of ice-cold water.

"You'd have done better," she said, "to take the clean steel when I offered it to you."

She was gone, and Starke's mind was as empty and cold as the mind of a corpse. He found that he was standing still, clinging to a branch, his face upturned as though by some blind instinct, his sight blurred.

He had never cried before in all his life, nor prayed.

There was no such thing as time, down there in the smoky shadows of the sea bottom. It might have been minutes or hours later than Hugh Starke discovered he was being hunted.

There were three of them, slipping easily among the shining branches. They were pale golden, almost phosphorescent, about the size of large hounds. Their eyes were huge, jewel-like in their slim sharp faces. They possessed four members that might have been legs and arms, retracted now against their arrowing bodies. Golden membranes spread wing-like from head to flank, and they moved like wings, balancing expertly the thrust of the flat, powerful tails.

They could have closed in on him easily, but they didn't seem to be in any hurry. Starke had sense enough not to wear himself out trying to get away. He kept on going, watching them. He discovered that the crystal branches could be broken, and he selected himself one with a sharp forked tip, shoving it swordwise under his belt. He didn't suppose it would do much good, but it made him feel better.

He wondered why the things didn't jump him and get it over with. They looked hungry enough, the way they were showing him their teeth. But they kept about the same distance away, in a sort of crescent formation, and every so often the ones on the outside would make a tentative dart at him, then fall back as he swerved away. It wasn't like being hunted so much as . . .

Starke's eyes narrowed. He began suddenly to feel much more afraid than he had before, and he wouldn't have believed that possible.

The things weren't hunting him at all. They were herding him.

There was nothing he could do about it. He tried stopping, and they swooped in and snapped at him, working expertly together so that while he was trying to stab one of them with his clumsy weapon, the others were worrying his heels like sheepdogs at a recalcitrant wether.

Starke, like the wether, bowed to the inevitable and went where he was driven. The golden hounds showed their teeth in animal laughter and sniffed hungrily at the thread of blood he left behind him in the slow red coils of fire.

After a while he heard the music.

It seemed to be some sort of a harp, with a strange quality of vibration in the notes. It wasn't like anything he'd ever heard before. Perhaps the gas of which the

sea was composed was an extraordinarily good con-
ductor of sound, with a property of diffusion that made
the music seem to come from everywhere at once—
softly at first, like something touched upon in a dream,
and then, as he drew closer to the source, swelling into a racing, rippling flood of melody that wrapped itself around his nerves with a demoniac shiver of
ecstasy.

The golden hounds began to fret with excitement,
spreading their shining wings, driving him impatiently
faster through the crystal branches.

Starke could feel the vibration growing in him—the
very fibers of his muscles shuddering in sympathy with
the unearthly harp. He guessed there was a lot of the
music he couldn't hear. Too high, too low for his ears
to register. But he could feel it.

He began to go faster, not because of the hounds,
but because he wanted to. The deep quivering in his
flesh excited him. He began to breathe harder, partly
because of increased exertion, and some chemical
quality of the mixture he breathed made him slightly
drunk.

The thrumming harp-song stroked and stung him,
waking a deeper, darker music, and suddenly he saw
Beudag clearly—half-veiled and mystic in the candlelight at Faolan's dun; smooth curving bronze, her
hair loose fire about her throat. A great stab of agony
went through him. He called her name, once, and the
harp-sound swept it up and away, and then suddenly
there was no music any more, and no forest, and
nothing but cold embers in Starke's heart.

He could see everything quite clearly in the time
it took him to float from the top of the last tree to
the floor of the plain. He had no idea how long a time
that was. It didn't matter. It was one of those moments
when time doesn't have any meaning.

The rim of the forest fell away in a long curve that
melted glistening into the spark-shot sea. From it the
plain stretched out, a level glassy floor of black obsidian, the spew of some long-dead volcano. Or was
it dead? It seemed to Starke that the light here was

redder, more vital, as though he were close to the source from which it sprang.

As he looked farther over the plain, the light seemed to coalesce into a shimmering curtain that wavered like the heat veils that dance along the Mercurian Twilight Belt at high noon. For one brief instant he glimpsed a picture on the curtain—a city, black, shining, fantastically turreted, the gigantic reflection of a Titan's dream. Then it was gone, and the immediate menace of the foreground took all of Starke's attention.

He saw the flock, herded by more of the golden hounds. And he saw the shepherd, with the harp held silent between his hands.

The flock moved slightly, phosphorescently.

One hundred, two hundred silent, limply floating warriors drifting down the red dimness. In pairs, singly, or in pallid clusters they came. The golden hounds winged silently, leisurely around them, channeling them in tides that sluiced toward the fantastic ebon city.

The shepherd stood, a crop of obsidian, turning his shark-pale face. His sharp, aquamarine eyes found Starke. His silvery hand leapt beckoning over hardthreads, striking them a blow. Reverberations ran out, seized Starke, shook him. He dropped his crystal dagger.

Hot screens of fire exploded in his eyes, bubbles whirled and danced in his eardrums. He lost all muscular control. His dark head fell forward against the thick blackness of hair on his chest; his golden eyes dissolved into weak, inane yellow, and his mouth loosened. He wanted to fight, but it was useless. This shepherd was one of the sea-people he had come to see, and one way or another he would see him.

Dark blood filled his aching eyes. He felt himself led, nudged, forced first this way, then that. A golden hound slipped by, gave him a pressure which rolled him over into a current of sea-blood. It ran down past where the shepherd stood with only a harp for a weapon.

Starke wondered dimly whether these other warriors in the flock, drifting, were dead or alive like himself. He had another surprise coming.

They were all Rann's men. Men of Falga. Silver men with burning green hair. Rann's men. One of them, a huge warrior colored like powdered salt, wandered aimlessly by on another tide, his green eyes dull. He looked dead.

What business had the sea-people with the dead warriors of Falga? Why the hounds and the shepherd's harp? Questions eddied like lifted silt in Starke's tired, hanging head. Eddied and settled flat.

Starke joined the pilgrimage.

The hounds were deft flickerings of wings ushered him into the midst of the flock. Bodies brushed against him. *Cold* bodies. He wanted to cry out. The cords of his neck constricted. In his mind the cry went forward:

"Are you alive, men of Falga?"

No answer; but the drift of scarred, pale bodies. The eyes in them knew nothing. They had forgotten Falga. They had forgotten Rann for whom they had lifted blade. Their tongues lolling in mouths asked nothing but sleep. They were getting it.

A hundred, two hundred strong they made a strange human river slipping toward the gigantic city wall. Starke-called-Conan and his bitter enemies going together. From the corners of his eyes, Starke saw the shepherd move. The shepherd was like Rann and her people who had years ago abandoned the sea to live on land. The shepherd seemed colder, more fish-like, though. There were small translucent webs between the thin fingers and spanning the long-toed feet. Thin, scar-like gills in the shadow of his tapered chin, lifted and sealed in the current, eating, taking sustenance from the blood-colored sea.

The harp spoke and the golden hounds obeyed. The harp spoke and the bodies twisted uneasily, as in a troubled sleep. A triple chord of it came straight at Starke. His fingers clenched.

"—and the dead shall walk again—"

Another ironic ripple of music.

"—and Rann's men will rise again, this time against her—"

Starke had time to feel a brief, bewildered shivering,

before the current hurled him forward. Clamoring drunkenly, witlessly, all about him, the dead, muscleless warriors of Falga tried to crush past him, all of them at once . . .

Long ago some vast sea Titan had dreamed of avenues struck from black stone. Each stone the size of three men tall. There had been a dream of walls going up and up until they dissolved into scarlet mist. There had been another dream of sea-gardens in which fish hung like erotic flowers, on tendrils of sensitive film-tissue. Whole beds of fish clung to garden base, like colonies of flowers aglow with sunlight. And on occasion a black amoebic presence filtered by, playing the gardener, weeding out an amber flower here, an amythystine bloom there.

And the sea Titan had dreamed of endless balustrades and battlements, of windowless turrets where creatures swayed like radium-skinned phantoms, carrying their green plumes of hair in their lifted palms, and looked down with curious, insolent eyes from on high. Women with shimmering bodies like some incredible coral harvested and kept high over these black stone streets, each in its archway.

Starke was alone. Falga's warriors had gone off along a dim subterranean vent, vanished. Now the faint beckoning of harp and the golden hounds behind him turned him down a passage that opened out into a large circular stone room, one end of which opened out into a hall. Around the ebon ceiling, slender schools of fish swam. It was their bright effulgence that gave light to the room. They had been there, breeding, eating, dying, a thousand years, giving light to the place, and they would be there, breeding and dying, a thousand more.

The harp faded until it was only a murmur.

Starke found his feet. Strength returned to him. He was able to see the man in the center of the room well. Too well.

The man hung in the fire tide. Chains of wrought bronze held his thin fleshless ankles so he couldn't escape. His body desired it. It floated up.

It had been dead a long time. It was gaseous with

decomposition and it wanted to rise to the surface of
the Red Sea. The chains prevented this. Its arms
weaved like white scarves before a sunken white face.
Black hair trembled on end.

He was one of Faolan's men. One of the Rovers.
One of those who had gone down at Falga because of
Conan.

His name was Geil.

Starke remembered.

The part of him that was Conan remembered the
name.

The dead lips moved.

"Conan. What luck is this! Conan. I make you
welcome."

The words were cruel, the lips around them loose
and dead. It seemed to Starke an anger and embittered
wrath lay deep in those hollow eyes. The lips twitched
again.

"I went down at Falga for you and Rann, Conan.
Remember?"

Part of Starke remembered and twisted in agony.

"We're all here, Conan. All of us. Clev and Mannt
and Bron and Aesur. Remember Aesur, who could
shape metal over his spine, prying it with his fingers?
Aesur is here, big as a sea-monster, waiting in a niche,
cold and loose as string. The sea-shepherds collected
us. Collected us for a purpose of irony. Look!"

The boneless fingers hung out, as in a wind, pointing.

Starke turned slowly, and his heart pounded an
uneven, shattering drum beat. His jaw clinched and
his eyes blurred. That part of him that was Conan cried
out. Conan was so much of him and he so much of
Conan it was impossible for a cleavage. They'd grown
together like pearl material around sand-specule, layer
on layer. Starke cried out.

In the hall which this circular room overlooked,
stood a thousand men.

In lines of fifty across, shoulder to shoulder, the
men of Crom Dhu stared unseeingly up at Starke. Here
and there a face became shockingly familiar. Old
memory cried their names.

"Bron! Clev! Mannt! Aesur!"

The collected decomposition of their bodily fluids raised them, drifted them above the flaggings. Each of them was chained, like Geil.

Geil whispered. "We have made a union with the men of Falga!"

Starke pulled back.

"Falga!"

"In death, all men are equals." He took his time with it. He was in no hurry. Dead bodies under-sea are never in a hurry. They sort of bump and drift and bide their time. "The dead serve those who give them a semblance of life. Tomorrow we march against Crom Dhu."

"You're crazy! Crom Dhu is *your* home! It's the place of Beudag and Faolan—"

"And—" interrupted the hanging corpse, quietly, "Conan? Eh?" He laughed. A crystal dribble of bubbles ran up from the slack mouth. "Especially Conan. Conan who sank us at Falga . . ."

Starke moved swiftly. Nobody stopped him. He had the corpse's short blade in an instant. Geil's chest made a cold, silent sheath for it. The blade went like a fork through butter.

Coldly, without noticing this, Geil's voice spoke out:

"Stab me, cut me. You can't kill me any deader. Make sections of me. Play butcher. A flank, a hand, a heart! And while you're at it, I'll tell you the plan."

Snarling, Starke seized the blade out again. With blind violence he gave sharp blow after blow at the body, cursing bitterly, and the body took each blow, rocking in the red tide a little, and said with a matter-of-fact-tone:

"We'll march out of the sea to Crom Dhu's gates. Romna and the others, looking down, recognizing us, will have the gates thrown wide to welcome us." The head tilted lazily, the lips peeled wide and folded down languidly over the words. "Think of the elation, Conan! The moment when Bron and Mannt and Aesur and

I and yourself, yes, even yourself, Conan, return to Crom Dhu!"

Starke saw it, vividly. Saw it like a tapestry woven for him. He stood back, gasping for breath, his nostrils flaring, seeing what his balde had done to Geil's body, and seeing the great stone gates of Crom Dhu crashing open. The deliberation. The happiness, the elation to Faolan and Romna to see old friends returned. Old Rovers, long thought dead. Alive again, come to help! It made a picture!

With great deliberation, Starke struck flat across before him.

Geil's head, severed from its lazy body, began, with infinite tiredness, to float toward the ceiling. As it traveled upward, now facing, now bobbling the back of its skull toward Starke, it finished its nightmare speaking:

"And then, once inside the gates, what then, Conan? Can you guess? Can you guess what we'll do, Conan?"

Starke stared at nothingness, the sword tembling in his fist. From far away he heard Geil's voice:

"—we will kill Faolan in his hall. He will die with surprised lips. Romna's harp will lie in his disemboweled stomach. His heart with its last pulsings will sound the strings. And as for Beudag—"

Starke tried to push the thoughts away, raging and helpless. Geil's body was no longer anything to look at. He had done all he could to it. Starke's face was bleached white and scraped down to the insane bone of it, "You'd kill your own people!"

Geil's separated head lingered at the ceiling, light-fish illuminating its ghastly features. "Our people? But we have no people! We're another race now. The dead. We do the biddings of the sea-shepherds."

Starke looked out into the hall, then he looked at circular wall.

"Okay," he said, without tone in his voice. "Come out. Wherever you're hiding and using this voice-throwing act. Come on out and talk straight."

In answer, an entire section of ebon stones fell back on silent hingework. Starke saw a long slender black marble table. Six people sat behind it in carven mid-night thrones.

They were all men. Naked except for film-like garments about their loins. They looked at Starke with no particular hatred or curiosity. One of them cradled a harp. It was the shepherd who'd drawn Starke through the gate. Amusedly, his webbed fingers lay on the strings, now and then bringing out a clear sound from one of the two hundred strands.

The shepherd stopped Starke's rush forward with a cry of that harp!

The blade in his hand was red hot. He dropped it.

The shepherd put a head on the story. "And then? And then we will march Rann's dead warriors all the way to Falga. There, Rann's people, seeing the warriors, will be overjoyed, hysterical to find their friends and relatives returned. They, too, will fling wide Falga's defenses. And death will walk in, disguised as resurrection."

Starke nodded, slowly, wiping his hand across his cheek. "Back on Earth we call that psychology. *Good* psychology. But will it fool Rann?"

"Rann will be with her ships at Crom Dhu. While she's gone, the innocent population will let in their lost warriors gladly." The shepherd had amused green eyes. He looked like a youth of some seventeen years. Deceptively young. If Starke guessed right, the youth was nearer to two centuries old. That's how you lived and looked when you were under the Red Sea. Something about the emanations of it kept part of you young.

Starke lidded his yellow hawk's eyes thoughtfully. "You've got all aces. You'll win. But what's Crom Dhu to you? Why not just Rann? She's one of you; you hate her more than you do the Rovers. Her ancestors came up on land; you never got over hating them for that—"

The shepherd shrugged. "Toward Crom Dhu we have little actual hatred. Except that they are by nature land-men, even if they do rove by boat, and pillagers. One day they might try their luck on the sunken devices of this city."

Starke put a hand out. "We're fighting Rann, too. Don't forget, we're on your side!"

"Whereas we are on no one's," retorted the green-haired youth, "Except our own. Welcome to the army which will attack Crom Dhu."

"Me! By the gods, over my dead body!"

"That," said the youth, amusedly, "is what we intend. We've worked many years, you see, to perfect the plan. We're not much good out on land. We needed bodies that could do the work for us. So, every time Faolan lost a ship or Rann lost a ship, we were there, with our golden hounds, waiting. Collecting. Saving. Waiting until we had enough of each side's warriors. They'll do the fighting for us. Oh, not for long, of course. The Source energy will give them a semblance of life, a momentary electrical ability to walk and combat, but once out of water they'll last only half an hour. But that should be time enough once the gates of Crom Dhu and Falga are open."

Starke said, "Rann will find some way around you. Get her first. Attack Crom Dhu the following day."

The youth deliberated. "You're stalling. But there's sense in it. Rann is most important. We'll get Falga first, then. You'll have a bit of time in which to raise false hopes."

Starke began to get sick again. The room swam.

Very quietly, very easily, Rann came into his mind again. He felt her glide in like the merest touch of a sea fern weaving in a tide pool.

He closed his mind down, but not before she snatched at a shred of thought. Her aquamarine eyes reflected desire and inquiry.

"Hugh Starke, you're with the sea people?"

Her voice was soft. He shook his head.

"Tell me, Hugh Starke. How are you plotting against Falga?

He said nothing. He thought nothing. He shut his eyes.

Her fingernails glittered, raking at his mind. "Tell me!"

His thoughts rolled tightly into a metal sphere which nothing could dent.

Rann laughed unpleasantly and leaned forward until she filled every dark horizon of his skull with her shimmering body. "All right. I *gave* you Conan's body. Now I'll take it away."

She struck him a combined blow of her eyes, her writhing lips, her bone-sharp teeth. "Go back to your old body, go back to your old body, Hugh Starke," she hissed. "Go back! Leave Conan to his idiocy. Go back to your old body!"

Fear had him. He fell down upon his face, quivering and jerking. You could fight a man a sword. But how could you fight this thing in your brain? He began to suck sobbing breaths through his lips. He was screaming. He could not hear himself. Her voice rushed in from the dim outer red universe, destroying him.

"Hugh Starke! Go back to your old body!"

His old body was—dead!

And she was sending him back into it.

Part of him shot endwise through red fog.

He lay on a mountain plateau overlooking the harbor of Falga.

Red fog coiled and snaked around him. Flame birds dived eerily down at his staring, blind eyes.

His old body held him.

Putrefaction stuffed his nostrils. The flesh sagged and slipped greasily on his loosened structure. He felt small again and ugly. Flame birds nibbled, picking, choosing between his ribs. Pain gorged him. Cold, blackness, nothingness filled him. Back in his old body. Forever.

He didn't want that.

The plateau, the red fog vanished. The flame birds, too.

He lay once more on the floor of the sea shepherds, struggling.

"That was just a start," Rann told him. "Next time, I'll leave you up there on the plateau in that body. *Now,* will you tell the plans of the sea people? And go on living in Conan? He's yours, if you tell." She smirked. "You don't want to be dead."

Starke tried to reason it out. Any way he turned

was the wrong way. He grunted out a breath. "If I tell, you'll still kill Beudag."

"Her life in exchange for what you know, Hugh Starke."

Her answer was too swift. It had the sound of treachery. Starke did not believe. He would die. That would solve it. Then, at least, Rann would die when the sea people carried out their strategy. That much revenge, at least, damn it.

Then he got the idea.

He coughed out a laugh, raised his weak head to look at the startled sea shepherd. His little dialogue with Rann had taken about ten seconds, actually, but it had seemed a century. The sea shepherd stepped forward.

Starke tried to get to his feet. "Got—got a proposition for you. You with the harp. Rann's inside me. *Now.* Unless you guarantee Crom Dhu and Beudag's safety, I'll tell her some things she might want to be in on!"

The sea shepherd drew a knife.

Starke shook his head, coldly. "Put it away. Even if you get me I'll give the whole damned strategy to Rann."

The shepherd dropped his hand. He was no fool.

Rann tore at Starke's brain. "Tell me! Tell me their plan!"

He felt like a guy in a revolving door. Starke got the sea men in focus. He saw that they were afraid now, doubtful and nervous. "I'll be dead in a minute," said Starke. "Promise me the safety of Crom Dhu and I'll die without telling Rann a thing."

The sea shepherd hesitated, then raised his palm upward. "I promise," he said. "Crom Dhu will go untouched."

Starke sighed. He let his head fall forward until it hit the floor. Then he rolled over, put his hands over his eyes. "It's a deal. Go give Rann hell for me, will you, boys? Give her hell!

As he drifted into mind darkness, Rann waited for him. Feebly, he told her, "Okay, duchess. You'd kill me even if I'd told you the idea. I'm ready. Try your god-awfullest to shove me back into that stinking body of mine. I'll fight you all the way there!"

Rann screamed. It was a pretty frustrated scream. Then the pains began. She did a lot of work on his mind in the next minute.

That part of him that was Conan held on like a clam holding to its precious contents.

The odor of putrid flesh returned. The blood mist returned. The flame birds fell down at him in spirals of sparks and blistering smoke, to winnow his naked ribs.

Starke spoke one last word before the blackness took him.

"Beudag."

He never expected to awaken again.

He awoke just the same.

There was red sea all around him. He lay on a kind of stone bed, and the young sea shepherd sat beside him, looking down at him, smiling delicately.

Starke did not dare move for a while. He was afraid his head might fall off and whirl away like a big fish, using its ears as propellers. "Lord," he muttered, barely turning his head.

The sea creature stirred. "You won. You fought Rann, and won."

Starke groaned. "I feel like something passed through a wild-cat's intestines. She's gone. Rann's gone." He laughed. "That makes me sad. Somebody cheer me up. Rann's gone." He felt of his big, flat-muscled body. "She was bluffing. Trying to decide to drive me batty. She knew she couldn't really tuck me back into that carcass, but she didn't want me to know. It was like a baby's nightmare before it's born. Or maybe you haven't got a memory like me." He rolled over, stretching. "She won't ever get in my head again. I've locked the gate and swallowed the key." His eyes dilated. "What's *your* name?"

"Linnl," said the man with the harp. "You didn't tell Rann our strategy?"

"What do *you* think?"

Linnl smiled sincerely. "I think I like you, man

of Crom Dhu. I think I like your hatred for Rann.
I think I like the way you handled the entire matter,
wanted to kill Rann and save Crom Dhu, and being
so willing to die to accomplish either."

"That's a lot of thinking. Yeah, and what about
that promise you made?"

"It will be kept."

Starke gave him a hand. "Linnl, you're okay. If
I ever get back to Earth, so help me, I'll never bait
a hook again and drop it in the sea." It was lost to
Linnl. Starke forgot it, and went on, laughing. There
was an edge of hysteria to it. Relief. You got booted
around for days, people milled in and out of your mind
like it was a bargain basement counter, pawing over
the treads and convolutions, yelling and fighting; the
woman you loved was starved on a ship masthead,
and as a climax a lady with green eyes tried to make
you a filling for an accident-mangled body. And now
you had an ally.

And you couldn't believe it.

He laughed in little starts and stops, his eyes shut.

"Will you let me take care of Rann when the time
comes?"

His fingers groped hungrily upward, closed on an
imaginary figure of her, pressed, tightened, choked.

Linnl said, "She's yours. I'd like the pleasure, but
you have as much if not more of a revenge to take.
Come along. We start now. You've been asleep for
one entire period."

Starke let himself down gingerly. He didn't want
to break a leg off. He felt if someone touched him he
might disintegrate.

He managed to let the tide handle him, do all the
work. He swam carefully after Linnl down three
passageways where an occasional silver inhabitant of
the city slid by.

Drifting below them in a vast square hall, each
gravitating but imprisoned by leg-shackles, the warriors
of Falga looked up with pale cold eyes at Starke and
Linnl. Occasional discharges of light-fish from in-
terstices in the walls passed luminous, fleeting glows
over the warriors. The light-fish flirted briefly in a long

shining rope that tied knots around the dead faces and as quickly untied them. Then the light-fish pulsed away and the red color of the sea took over.

Bathed in wine, thought Starke, without humor. He leaned forward.

"Men of Falga!"

Linnl plucked a series of harp-threads.

"Aye." A deep suggestion of sound issued from a thousand dead lips.

"We go to sack Rann's citadel!"

"Rann!" came the muffled thunder of voices.

At the sound of another tune, the golden hounds appeared. They touched the chains. The men of Falga, released, danced through the red sea substance.

Siphoned into a valve mouth, they were drawn out into a great volcanic courtyard. Starke went close after. He stared down into a black ravine, at the bottom of which was a blazing caldera.

This was the Source Life of the Red Sea. Here it had begun a millennium ago. Here the savage cyclones of sparks and fire energy belched up, shaking titanic black garden walls, causing currents and whirlpools that threatened to suck you forward and shoot you violently up to the surface, in cannulas of force, thrust, in capillaries of ignited mist, in chutes of color that threatened to cremate but only exhilarated you, gave you a seething rebirth!

He braced his legs and fought the suction. An unbelievable sinew of fire sprang up from out the ravine, crackling and roaring.

The men of Falga did not fight the attraction.

They moved forward in their silence and hung over the incandescence.

The vitality of the Source grew upward in them. It seemed to touch their sandaled toes first, and then by a process of shining osmosis, climb up the limbs, into the loins, into the vitals, delineating their strong bone structure as mercury delineates the glass thermometer with a rise of temperature. The bones flickered like carved polished ivory through the momentarily film-like flesh. The ribs of a thousand men expanded like silvered spider legs, clenched, then expanded again. Their spines straightened, their shoulders flattened back. Their eyes, the last to take the fire, now were ignited and glowed like candles in refurbished sepulchers. The chins snapped up, the entire outer skins of their bodies broke into silver brilliance.

Swimming through the storm of energy like nightmare figments, entering cold, they reached the far side of the ravine resembling smelted metal from blast furnaces. When they brushed into one another, purple sparks sizzled, jumped from head to head, from hand to hand.

Linnl touched Starke's arm. "You're next."

"No thank you."

"Afraid?" laughed the harp-shepherd. "You're tired. It will give you new life. You're next."

Starke hesitated only a moment. Then he let the tide drift him rapidly out. He was afraid. Damned afraid. A belch of fire caught him as he arrived in the core of the ravine. He was wrapped in layers of ecstasy. Beudag pressed against him. It was her consuming hair that netted him and branded him. It was her warmth that crept up his body into his chest and into his head. Somebody yelled somewhere in animal delight and unbearable passion. Somebody danced and threw out his hands and crushed that solar warmth deeper into his huge body. Somebody felt all tiredness, oldness flumed away, a whole new feeling of warmth and strength inserted.

That somebody was Starke.

Waiting on the other side of the ravine were a thousand men of Falga. What sounded like a thousand harps began playing now, and as Starke reached the other side, the harps began marching, and the warriors marched with them. They were still dead, but you would never know it. There were no minds inside those bodies. The bodies were being activated from outside. But you would never know it.

They left the city behind. In embering ranks, the soldier-fighters were led by golden hounds and distant harps to a place where a huge intra-coastal tide swept by.

They got on the tide for a free ride. Linnl beside him, using his harp, Starke felt himself sucked down through a deep where strange monsters sprawled. They looked at Starke with hungry eyes. But the harp wall swept them back.

Starke glanced about at the men. They don't know what they're doing, he thought. Going home to kill their parents and their children, to set the flame to Falga, and they don't know it. Their alive-but-dead faces tilted up, always upward, as though visions of Rann's citadel were there.

Rann. Starke let the wrath simmer in him. He let it cool. Then it was cold. Rann hadn't bothered him now for hours. Was there a chance she'd read his thought in the midst of that fighting nightmare? Did she know this plan for Falga? Was that an explanation for her silence now?

He sent his mind ahead, subtly. *Rann. Rann.* The only answer was the move of silver bodies through the fiery deeps.

Just before dawn they broke surface of the sea.

Falga drowsed in the red-smeared fog silence. Its slave streets were empty and dew-covered. High up, the first light was bathing Rann's gardens and setting her citadel aglow.

Linnl lay in the shallows beside Starke. They both were smiling half-cruel smiles. They had waited long for this.

Linnl nodded. "This is the day of the carnival. Fruit, wine and love will be offered the returned soldiers of Rann. In the streets there'll be dancing."

Far over to the right lay a rise of mountain. At its blunt peak—Starke stared at it intently—rested a body of a little, scrawny Earthman, with flame-birds clustered on it. He'd climb that mountain later. When it was over and there was time.

"What are you searching for?" asked Linnl.

Starke's voice was distant. "Someone I used to know."

Filing out on the stone quays, their rusling sandals eroded by time, the men stood clean and bright. Starke paced, a caged animal, at their center, so his dark body would pass unnoticed.

They were seen.

The cliff guard looked down over the dirty slave dwellings, from their arrow galleries, and set up a cry. Hands waved, pointed frosty white in the dawn. More guards loped down the ramps and galleries, meeting, joining others and coming on.

Linnl, in the sea by the quay, suggested a theme on the harp. The other harps took it up. The shuddering music lifted from the water and with a gentle firmness, set the dead feet marching down the quays, upward through the narrow, stifling alleys of the slaves, to meet the guard.

Slave people peered out at them tiredly from their choked quarters. The passing of warriors was old to them, of no significance.

These warriors carried no weapons. Starke didn't like that part of it. A length of chain even, he wanted. But this emptiness of the hands. His teeth ached from too long a time of clenching his jaws tight. The muscles of his arms were feverish and nervous.

At the edge of the slave community, at the cliff base, the guard confronted them. Running down off the galleries, swords naked, they ran to intercept what they took to be an enemy.

The guards stopped in blank confusion.

A little laugh escaped Starke's lips. It was a dream. With fog over, under and in between its parts. It wasn't real to the guard, who couldn't believe it. It wasn't real to these dead men either, who were walking around. He felt alone. He was the only live one. He didn't like walking with dead men.

The captain of the guard came down warily, his green eyes suspicious. The suspicion faded. His face fell apart. He had lain on his fur pelts for months thinking of his son who had died to defend Falga.

Now his son stood before him. Alive.

The captain forgot he was captain. He forgot everything. His sandals scraped over stones. You could hear the air go out of his lungs and come back in in a numbed prayer.

"My son! In Rann's name. They said you were slain by Faolan's men one hundred darknesses ago. My son!"

A harp tinkled somewhere.

The son stepped forward, smiling.

They embraced. The son said nothing. He couldn't speak.

This was the signal for the others. The whole guard, shocked and surprised, put away their swords and sought out old friends, brothers, fathers, uncles, sons!

They moved up the galleries, the guard and the returned warriors, Starke in their midst. Threading up the cliff, through passage after passage, all talking at once. Or so it seemed. The guards did the talking. None of the dead warriors replied. They only *seemed* to. Starke heard the music strong and clear everywhere.

They reached the green gardens atop the cliff. By this time the entire city was awake. Women came running, bare-breasted and sobbing, and throwing themselves forward into the ranks of their lovers. Flowers showered over them.

"So this is war," muttered Starke, uneasily.

They stopped in the center of the great gardens. The crowd milled happily, not yet aware of the strange silence from their men. They were too happy to notice.

"Now," cried Starke to himself. "Now's the time. Now!"

As if in answer, a wild skirling of harps out of the sky.

The crowd stopped laughing only when the returned warriors of Falga swept forward, their hands lifted and groping before them . . .

The crying in the streets was like a far siren wailing. Metal made a harsh clangor that was sheathed in silence at the same moment metal found flesh to lie in. A vicious pantomime was concluded in the green moist gardens.

Starke watched from Rann's empty citadel. Fog plumes strolled by the archways and a thick rain fell.

It came like a blood squall and washed the garden below until you could not tell rain from blood.

The returned warriors had gotten their swords by now. First they killed those nearest them in the celebration. Then they took the weapons from the victims. It was very simple and very unpleasant.

The slaves had joined battle now. Swarming up from the slave town, plucking up fallen daggers and short swords, they circled the gardens, happening upon the arrogant shining warriors of Rann who had so far escaped the quiet, deadly killing of the alive-but-dead men.

Dead father killed startled, alive son. Dead brother garroted unbelieving brother. Carnival indeed in Falga.

An old man waited alone. Starke saw him. The old man had a weapon, but refused to use it. A young warrior of Falga, harped on by Linnl's harp, walked quietly up to the old man. The old man cried out. His mouth formed words. "Son! What *is* this?" He flung down his blade and made to plead with his boy.

The son stabbed him with silent efficiency, and without a glance at the body, walked onward to find another.

Starke turned away, sick and cold.

A thousand such scenes were being finished.

He set fire to the black spider-silk tapestries. They whispered and talked with flame. The stone echoed his feet as he searched room after room. Rann had gone, probably last night. That meant that Crom Dhu was on the verge of falling. Was Faolan dead? Had the people of Crom Dhu, seeing Beudag's suffering, given in? Falga's harbor was completely devoid of ships, except for small fishing skiffs.

The fog waited him when he returned to the garden. Rain found his face.

The citadel of Rann was fire-encrusted and smoke-shrouded as he looked up at it.

A silence lay in the garden. The fight was over.

The men of Falga, still shining with Source-Life, hung their blades from uncomprehending fingers, the light beginning to leave their green eyes. Their skin looked dirty and dull.

Starke wasted no time getting down the galleries, through the slave quarter, and to the quays again.

Linnl awaited him, gently petting the obedient harp.

"It's over. The slaves will own what's left. They'll be our allies, since we've freed them."

Starke didn't hear. He was squinting off over the Red Sea.

Linnl understood. He plucked two tones from the harp, which pronounced the two words uppermost in Starke's thought.

"Crom Dhu."

"If we're not too late." Starke leaned forward. "If Faolan lives. If Beudag still stands at the masthead."

Like a blind man he walked straight ahead, until he fell into the sea.

It was not quite a million miles to Crom Dhu. It only seemed that far.

A sweep of tide picked them up just off shore from Falga and siphoned them rapidly, through deeps along coastal latitudes, through crystal forests. He cursed every mile of the way.

He cursed the time it took to pause at the Titan's city to gather fresh men. To gather Clev and Mannt and Aesur and Bron. Impatiently, Starke watched the whole drama of the Source-Fire and the bodies again. This time it was the bodies of Crom Dhu men, hung like beasts on slow-turned spits, their limbs and vitals soaking through and through, their skins taking bronze color, their eyes holding flint-sparks. And then the harps wove a garment around each, and the garment moved the men instead of the men the garment.

In the tidal basilic now, Starke twisted. Coursing behind him were the new bodies of Clev and Aesur! The current elevated them, poked them through obsidian needle-eyes like spider-silk threads.

There was good irony in this. Crom Dhu's men, fallen at Falga under Conan's treachery, returned now under Conan to exonerate that treachery.

Suddenly they were in Crom Dhu's outer basin. Shadows swept over them. The long dark falling shadows of Falga's longboats lying in that harbor. Shadows like black culling-nets let down. The school of men cleaved the shadow nets. The tide ceased here, eddied and distilled them.

Starke glared up at the immense silver bottom of a Falgian ship. He felt his face stiffen and his throat tighten. Then, flexing knees, he rammed upward; night air broke dark red around his head.

The harbor held flare torches on the rims of long ships. On the neck of land that led from Crom Dhu to the mainland the continuing battle sounded. Faint cries and clashing made their way through the fog veils. They sounded like echoes of past dreams.

Linnl let Starke have the leash. Starke felt something pressed into his fist. A coil of slender green woven reeds, a rope with hooked weights on the end of it. He knew how to use it without asking. But he wished for a knife now, even though he realized carrying a knife in the sea was all but impossible if you wanted to move fast.

He saw the sleek naked figurehead of Rann's best ship a hundred yards away, a floating silhouette, its torches hanging fire like Beudag's hair.

He swam toward it, breathing quietly. When at last the silvered figurehead with the mocking green eyes and the flag of shoal-shallow hair hung over him, he felt the cool white ship metal kiss his fingers.

The smell of torch-smoke lingered. A rise of faint shouts from the land told of another rush upon the Gate. Behind him—a ripple. Then—a thousand ripples.

The resurrected men of Crom Dhu rose in dents and stirrings of sparkling wine. They stared at Crom Dhu and maybe they knew what it was and maybe they didn't. For one moment, Starke felt apprehension. Suppose Linnl was playing a game. Suppose, once these men had won the battle, they went on into Crom Dhu to rupture Romna's harp and make Faolan the blinder? He shook the thought away. That would have to be handled in time. On either side of him Clev and Mannt appeared. They looked at Crom Dhu, their

lips shut. Maybe they saw Faolan's eyrie and heard
a harp that was more than these harps that sang them
to blade and plunder—Romna's instrument telling bard-
tales of the rovers and the coastal wars and the old,
living days. Their eyes looked and looked at Crom
Dhu, but saw nothing.

The sea shepherds appeared now, the followers of
Linnl, each with his harp; and the harp music began,
high. So high you couldn't hear it. It wove a tension
on the air.

Silently, with a grim certainty, the dead-but-not-dead
gathered in a bronze circle about Rann's ship. The
very silence of their encirclement made your skin crawl
and sweat break cold on your cheeks.

A dozen ropes went raveling, looping over the ship
side. They caught, held, grapnelled, hooked.

Starke had thrown his, felt it bite and hold. Now
he scrambled swiftly, cursing, up its length, kicking
and slipping at the silver hull.

He reached the top.

Beudag was there.

Half over the low rail he hesitated, just looking at
her.

Torchlight limned her, shadowed her. She was still
erect; her head was tired and her eyes closed, her face
thinned and less brown, but she was still alive. She
was coming out of a deep stupor now, at the whistle
of ropes and the grate of metal hooks on the deck.

She saw Starke and her lips parted. She did not look
away from him. His breath came out of him,
choking.

It almost cost him his life, his standing there, looking at her.

A guard, with flesh like new snow, shafted his bow
from the turret and let it loose. A chain lay on deck.
Thankfully, Starke took it.

Clev came over the rail beside Starke. His chest
took the arrow. The shaft burst half through and
stopped, held. Clev kept going after the man who had
shot it. He caught up with him.

Beudag cried out. "Behind you, Conan!"

Conan! In her excitement, she gave the old name.

Conan he *was*. Whirling, he confronted a wiry little fellow, chained him brutally across the face, seized the man's falling sword, used it on him. Then he walked in, got the man's jaw, unbalanced him over into the sea.

The ship was awake now. Most of the men had been down below, resting from the battles. Now they came pouring up, in a silver spate. Their yelling was in strange contrast to the calm silence of Crom Dhu's men. Starke found himself busy.

Conan had been a healthy animal, with great recuperative powers. Now his muscles responded to every trick asked of them. Starke leaped cleanly across the deck, watching for Rann, but she was nowhere to be seen. He engaged two blades, dispatched one of them. More ropes raveled high and snaked him. Every ship in the harbor was exploding with violence. More men swarmed over the rail behind Starke, silently.

Above the shouting, Beudag's voice came, at sight of the fighting men. "Clev! Mannt! Aesur!"

Starke was a god; anything he wanted he could have. A man's head? He could have it. It meant acting the guillotine with knife and wrist and lunged body. Like— *this!* His eyes were smoking amber and there were deep lines of grim pleasure tugging at his lips. An enemy cannot fight without hands. One man, facing Starke, suddenly displayed violent stumps before his face, not believing them.

Are you watching, Faolan? cried Starke inside himself, delivering blows. Look here, Faolan! God, no, you're blind. *Listen* then! Hear the ring of steel on steel. Does the smell of hot blood and hot bodies reach you? Oh, if you could see this tonight, Faolan. Falga would be forgotten. This is Conan, out of idiocy, with a guy named Starke wearing him and telling him where to go!

It was not safe on deck. Starke hadn't particularly noticed before, but the warriors of Crom Dhu didn't care whom they attacked now. They were beginning to do surgery to one another. They excised one another's shoulders, severed limbs in blind instantaneous obedience. This was no place for Beudag and himself.

He cut her free of the masthead, drew her quickly to the rail.

Beudag was laughing. She could do nothing but laugh. Her eyes were shocked. She saw dead men alive again, lashing out with weapons; she had been starved and made to stand night and day, and now she could only laugh.

Starke shook her.

She did not stop laughing.

"Beudag! You're all right. You're free."

She stared at nothing. "I'll—I'll be all right in a minute."

He had to ward off a blow from one of his own men. He parried the thrust, then got in and pushed the man off the deck, over into the sea. That was the only thing to do. You couldn't kill them.

Beudag stared down at the tumbling body.

"Where's Rann?" Starke's yellow eyes narrowed, searching.

"She *was* here." Beudag trembled.

Rann looked out of her eyes. Out of the tired numbness of Beudag, an echo of Rann. Rann was nearby, and this was her doing.

Instinctively, Starke raised his eyes.

Rann appeared at the masthead, like a flurry of snow. Her green-tipped breasts were rising and falling with emotion. Pure hatred lay in her eyes. Starke licked his lips and readied his sword.

Rann snapped a glance at Beudag. Stooping, as in a dream, Beudag picked up a dagger and held it to her own breast.

Starke froze.

Rann nodded, with satisfaction. "Well, Starke? How will it be? Will you come at me and have Beudag die? Or will you let me go free?"

Starke's palms felt sweaty and greasy. "There's no place for you to go. Falga's taken. I can't guarantee your freedom. If you want to go over the side, into the sea, that's your chance. You might make shore and your own men."

"Swimming? With the *sea-beasts* waiting?" She accented the *beasts* heavily. She was one of the sea-*people*. They, Linnl and his men, were sea-*beasts*. "No, Hugh Starke. I'll take a skiff. Put Beudag at the rail where I can watch her all the way. Guarantee my passage to shore and my own men there, and Beudag lives."

Starke waved his sword. "Get going."

He didn't want to let her go. He had other plans, good plans for her. He shouted the deal down at Linnl. Linnl nodded back, with much reluctance.

Rann, in a small silver skiff, headed toward land. She handled the boat and looked back at Beudag all the while. She passed through the sea-beasts and touched the shore. She lifted her hand and brought it smashing down.

Whirling, Starke swung his fist against Beudag's jaw. Her hand was already striking the blade into her breast. Her head flopped back. His fist carried through. She fell. The blade clattered. He kicked it overboard. Then he lifted Beudag. She was warm and good to hold. The blade had only pricked her breast. A small rivulet of blood ran.

On the shore, Rann vanished upward on the rocks, hurrying to find her men.

In the harbor the harp music paused. The ships were taken. Their crews lay filling the decks. Crom Dhu's men stopped fighting as quickly as they'd started. Some of the bright shining had dulled from the bronze of their arms and bare torsos. The ships began to sink.

Linnl swam below, looking up at Starke. Starke looked back at him and nodded at the beach. "Swell. Now, let's go get that she-devil," he said.

Faolan waited on his great stone balcony, overlooking Crom Dhu. Behind him the fires blazed high and their eating sound of flame on wood filled the pillared gloom with sound and furious light.

Faolan leaned against the rim, his chest swathed in bandage and healing ointment, his blind eyes flickering, looking down again and again with a fixed intensity, his head tilted to listen.

Romna stood beside him, filled and refilled the cup that Faolan emptied into his thirsty mouth, and told him what happened. Told of the men pouring out of the sea, and Rann appearing on the rocky shore. Sometimes Faolan leaned to one side, weakly, toward Romna's words. Sometimes he twisted to hear the thing itself, the thing that happened down beyond the Gate of besieged Crom Dhu.

Romna's harp lay untouched. He didn't play it. He didn't need to. From below, a great echoing of harps, more liquid than his, like a waterfall drenched the city, making the fog sob down red tears.

"Are those harps?" cried Faolan.

"Yes, harps!"

"What was that?" Faolan listened, breathing harshly, clutching for support.

"A skirmish," said Romna.

"Who won?"

"*We* won."

"And *that?*" Faolan's blind eyes tried to see until they watered.

"The enemy falling back from the Gate!"

"And that sound, and that sound?" Faolan went on and on, feverishly, turning this way and that, the lines of his face agonized and attentive to each eddy and current and change of tide. The rhythm of swords through fog and body was a complicated music whose themes he must recognize. "Another fell! I heard him cry. And another of Rann's men!"

"Yes," said Romna.

"But why do our warriors fight so quietly? I've heard nothing from their lips. So quiet."

Romna scowled. "Quiet. Yes—quiet."

"And where did they come from? All our men are in the city?"

"Aye." Romna shifted. He hesitated, squinting. He rubbed his bulldog jaw. "Except those that died at—Falga."

Faolan stood there a moment. Then he rapped his empty cup.

"More wine, bard. More wine."

He turned to the battle again.

"Oh, gods, if I could see it, if I could only see it!"

Below, a ringing crash. A silence. A shouting, a pouring of noise.

"The Gate!" Faolan was stricken with fear. "We've lost! My sword!"

"Stay, Faolan!" Romna laughed. Then he sighed. It was a sigh that did not believe. "In the name of ten thousand mighty gods. Would that I were blind now, or could see better."

Faolan's hand caught, held him. "What *is* it? Tell!"

"Clev! And Tlan! And Conan! And Bron! And Mannt! Standing in the gate, like wine visions! Swords in their hands!"

Faolan's hand relaxed, then tightened. "Speak their names again, and speak them slowly. And tell the truth." His skin shivered like that of a nervous animal. "You said—Clev? Mannt? Bron?"

"And Tlan! And Conan! Back from Falga. They've opened the Gate and the battle's won. It's over, Faolan. Crom Dhu will sleep tonight."

Faolan let him go. A sob broke from his lips. "I will get drunk. Drunker than ever in my life. Gloriously drunk. Gods, but if I could have seen it. Been in it. Tell me again of it, Romna . . ."

Faolan sat in the great hall, on his carved high-seat, waiting.

The pad of sandals on stone outside, the jangle of chains.

A door flung wide, red fog sluiced in, and in the sluice, people walking. Faolan started up. "Clev? Mannt? Aesur?"

Starke came forward into the firelight. He pressed his right hand to the open mouth of wound on his thigh. "No, Faolan. Myself and two others."

"Beudag?"

"Yes." And Beudag came wearily to him.

Faolan stared. "Who's the other? It walks light. It's a woman."

Starke nodded. "Rann."

Faolan rose carefully from his seat. He thought the name over. He took a short sword from a place beside the high seat. He stepped down. He walked toward Starke. "You brought Rann alive to me?"

Starke pulled the chain that bound Rann. She ran forward in little steps, her white face down, her eyes slitted with animal fury.

"Faolan's blind," said Starke. "I let you live for one damned good reason, Rann. Okay, go ahead."

Faolan stopped walking, curious. He waited.

Rann did nothing.

Starke took her hand and wrenched it behind her back. "I said 'go ahead.' Maybe you didn't hear me."

"I will," she gasped, in pain.

Starke released her. "Tell me what happens, Faolan."

Rann gazed steadily at Faolan's tall figure there in the light.

Faolan suddenly threw his hands to his eyes and choked.

Beudag cried out, seized his arm.

"I can see!" Faolan staggered, as if jolted. "I can see!" First he shouted it, then he whispered it. *"I can see."*

Starke's eyes blurred. He whispered to Rann, tightly. "Make him see it, Rann, or you die now. Make him see it!" To Faolan: "What do you see?"

Faolan was bewildered; he swayed. He put out his hands to shape the vision. "I—I see Crom Dhu. It's a good sight. I see the ships of Rann. Sinking!" He laughed a broken laugh. "I—see the fight beyond the gate!"

Silence swam in the room, over their heads.

Faolan's voice went alone, and hypnotized, into that silence.

He put out his big fists, shook them, opened them. "I see Mannt, and Aesur and Clev! Fighting as they always fought. I see Conan as he was. I see Beudag wielding steel again, on the shore! I see the enemy killed! I see men pouring out of the sea with brown skins and dark hair. Men I knew a long darkness ago. Men that roved the sea with me. *I see Rann captured!"* He began to sob with it, his lungs filling and releasing it, sucking on it, blowing it out. Tears ran down from his vacant, blazing eyes. "I see Crom Dhu as it was and is and shall be! *I see, I see, I see!*"

Starke felt the chill on the back of his neck.

"I see Rann captured and held, and her men dead around her on the land before the Gate. I see the Gate thrown open—" Faolan halted. He looked at Starke. "Where are Clev and Mannt? Where is Bron and Aesur?"

Starke let the fires burn on the hearths a long moment. Then he replied.

"They went back into the sea, Faolan."

Faolan's fingers fell emptily. "Yes," he said, heavily. "They had to go back, didn't they? They couldn't stay, could they? Not even for one night of food on the table, and wine in the mouth, and women in the deep warm furs before the hearth. Not even for one toast." He turned. "A drink, Romna. A drink for everyone."

Romna gave him a full cup. He dropped it, fell down to his knees, clawed at his breast. "My heart!"

"Rann, you sea-devil!"

Starke held her instantly by the throat. He put pressure on the small raging pulses on either side of her snow-white neck. "Let him go, Rann!" More pressure. *"Let him go!"* Faolan grunted. Starke held her until her white face was dirty and strange with death.

It seemed like an hour later when he released her. She fell softly and did not move. She wouldn't move again.

Starke turned slowly to look at Faolan.

"You saw, didn't you, Faolan?" he said.

Faolan nodded blindly, weakly. He roused himself from the floor, groping. "I saw. For a moment, I saw everything. And Gods! but it made good seeing! Here, Hugh-Starke-Called-Conan, gave this other side of me something to lean on."

Beudag and Starke climbed the mountain above Falga the next day. Starke went ahead a little way, and with his coming the flame birds scattered, glittering away.

He dug the shallow grave and did what had to be done with the body he found there, and then when the grave was covered with thick grey stones he went back for Beudag. They stood together over it. He had never expected to stand over a part of himself, but here he was, and Beudag's hand gripped his.

He looked suddenly a million years old standing there. He thought of Earth and the Belt and Jupiter, of the joy streets in the Jekkara Low Canals of Mars. He thought of space and the ships going through it, and himself inside them. He thought of the million credits he had taken in that last job. He laughed ironically.

"Tomorrow, I'll have the sea creatures hunt for a little metal box full of credits." He nodded solemnly at the grave. "He wanted that. Or at least he thought he did. He killed himself getting it. So if the sea-people find it, I'll send it up here to the mountain and bury it down under the rocks in his fingers. I guess that's the best place."

Beudag drew him away. They walked down the mountain toward Falga's harbor where a ship waited them. Walking, Starke lifted his face. Beudag was with him, and the sails of the ship were rising to take the wind, and the Red Sea waited for them to travel it. What lay on its far side was something for Beudag and Faolan-of-the-Ships and Romna and Hugh-Starke-Called-Conan to discover. He felt damned good about it. He walked on steadily, holding Beudag near.

And on the mountain, as the ship sailed, the flame birds soared down fitfully and frustratedly to beat at the stone mound, ceased, and mourning shrilly, flew away.

The Star-Mouse

Frederic Brown

Robinson Crusoe . . . Gulliver . . . Paul Bunyan; the story of their adventures is nothing compared to the Saga of Mitkey.

Mitkey, the mouse, wasn't Mitkey then.

He was just another mouse, who lived behind the floorboards and plaster of the house of the great Herr Professor Oberburger, formerly of Vienna and Heidelberg; then a refugee from the excessive admiration of the more powerful of his fellow-countrymen. The excessive admiration had concerned, not Herr Oberburger himself, but a certain gas which had been a by-product of an unsuccessful rocket fuel—which might have been a highly-successful something else.

If, of course, the Professor had given them the correct formula. Which he—Well, anyway, the Professor had made good his escape and now lived in a house in Connecticut. And so did Mitkey.

A small gray mouse, and a small gray man. Nothing unusual about either of them. Particularly there was nothing unusual about Mitkey; he had a family and he liked cheese and if there were Rotarians among mice, he would have been a Rotarian.

The Herr Professor, of course, had his mild eccentricities. A confirmed bachelor, he had no one to talk to except himself, but he considered himself an excellent conversationalist and held constant verbal communion with himself while he worked. That fact, it turned out later, was important, because Mitkey had excellent ears and heard those night-long soliloquies. He didn't understand them, of course. If he thought about them at all, he merely thought of the Professor as a large and noisy super-mouse who squeaked overmuch.

"Und now," he would say to himself, "ve vill see vether this eggshaust tube vas broperly machined. It should fidt vithin vun vun-hundredth thousandth uf an indtch. Ahhh, it iss berfect. Und now—"

Night after night, day after day, month after month. The gleaming thing grew, and the gleam in Herr Oberburger's eyes grew apace.

It was about three and a half feet long, with weirdly shaped vanes, and it rested on a temporary framework on a table in the center of the room that served the Herr Professor for all purposes. The house in which he and Mitkey lived was a four-room structure, but the Professor hadn't yet found it out, seemingly. Originally, he had planned to use the big room as a laboratory only, but he found it more convenient to sleep on a cot in one corner of it, when he slept at all, and to do the little cooking he did over the same gas burner over which he melted down golden grains of TNT into a dangerous soup which he salted and peppered with strange condiments, but did not eat.

"Und now I shall bour it into tubes, und see vether vun tube adjacendt to another eggsplodes der secondt tube vhen der virst tube iss—"

That was the night Mitkey almost decided to move himself and his family to a more stable abode, one that did not rock and sway and try to turn handsprings on its foundations. But Mitkey didn't move after all, because there were compensations. New mouse-holes all over, and—joy of joy!—a big crack in the back of the refrigerator where the Professor kept, among other things, food.

Of course the tubes had been not larger than capillary size, or the house would not have remained around the mouse-holes. And of course Mitkey could not guess what was coming nor understand the Herr

Professor's brand of English (nor any other brand of English, for that matter) or he would not have let even a crack in the refrigerator tempt him.

The Professor was jubilant that morning.

"Der fuel, idt vorks! Der secondt tube, idt did not eggsplode. Und der virst, in *segdtions,* as I had eggspectedt! Und it is more bowerful; there vill be blenty of room for der combartment—"

Ah, yes, the compartment. That was where Mitkey came in, although even the Professor didn't know it yet. In fact the Professor didn't even know that Mitkey existed.

"Und now," he was saying to his favorite listener, "idt is budt a madter of combining der fuel tubes so they vork in obbosite bairs. Und then—"

That was the moment when the Herr Professor's eyes first fell on Mitkey. Rather, they fell upon a pair of gray whiskers and a black, shiny little nose protruding from a hole in the baseboards.

"Vell!" he said, "vot haff ve here! Mitkey Mouse himself! Mitkey, how vould you like to go for a ride, negst veek? Ve shall see."

That is how it came about that the next time the Professor sent into town for supplies, his order included a mousetrap—not one of the vicious kind that kills, but one of the wire-cage kind. And it had not been set, with cheese, for more than ten minutes before Mitkey's sharp little nose had smelled out that cheese and he had followed his nose into captivity.

Not, however, an unpleasant captivity. Mitkey was an honored guest. The cage reposed now on the table at which the Professor did most of his work, and cheese in indigestion-giving abundance was pushed through the bars, and the Professor didn't talk to himself any more.

"You see, Mitkey, I vas going to sendt to der laboratory in Hardtford for a vhite mouse, budt vhy should I, mit you here? I am sure you are more soundt und healthy und able to vithstand a long chourney than those laboratory mices. No? Ah, you viggle your viskers und that means yes, no? Und being used to

living in dargk holes, you should suffer less than they
from glaustrophobia, no?"

And Mitkey grew fat and happy and forgot all about
trying to get out of the cage. I fear that he even forgot
about the family he had abandoned, but he knew, if
he knew anything, that he need not worry about them
in the slightest. At least not until and unless the
Professor discovered and repaired the hole in the
refrigerator. And the Professor's mind was most em-
phatically not on refrigerators.

"Und so, Mitkey, ve shall place this vane so—it iss
only of assistance in der landing, in an atmosphere.
It und these vill bring you down safely und slowly
enough that der shock-absorbers in der movable combartment vill keep you from bumping your head too
hard, I think." Of course, Mitkey missed the ominous
note to that "I think" qualification because he missed
all the rest of it. He did not, as has been explained,
speak English. Not then.

But Herr Oberburger talked to him just the same.
He showed him pictures. "Did you effer see der Mouse
you vas named after, Mitkey? Vhat? No? Loogk, this
is der original Mitkey Mouse, by Valt Dissney. Budt
I think you are cuter, Mitkey."

Probably the Professor was a bit crazy to talk that
way to a little gray mouse. In fact, he must have been
crazy to make a rocket that worked. For the odd thing
was that the Herr Professor was not really an inventor.
There was, as he carefully explained to Mitkey, not
one single thing about that rocket that was *new*. The
Herr Professor was a technician; he could take other
people's ideas and make them work. His only real
invention—the rocket fuel that wasn't one—had been
turned over to the United States Government and had
proved to be something already known and discarded
because it was too expensive for practical use.

As he explained very carefully to Mitkey, "It iss
burely a matter of absolute accuracy and mathematical
correctness, Mitkey. Idt iss all here—ve merely com-
bine—and ve achieff vhat, Mitkey?

"Eggscape velocity, Mitkey! Chust barely, it adds
up to eggscape velocity. Maybe. There are yet unknown

facgtors, Mitkey, in der ubper atmosphere, der troposphere, der stratosphere. Ve think ve know eggsactly how mudch air there iss to calculate resistance against, but are ve absolutely sure? No, Mitkey, ve are not. Ve haff not been there. Und der marchin iss so narrow that so mudch as an air current might affect idt."

But Mitkty cared not a whit. In the shadow of the tapering aluminum-alloy cylinder he waxed fat and happy.

"Der tag, Mitkey, der tag! Und I shall not lie to you, Mitkey. I shall not giff you valse assurances. You go on a dancherous chourney, mein little friendt.

"A vifty-vifty chance ve giff you, Mitkey. Not der moon or bust, but der moon *und* bust, or else maybe safely back to earth. You see, my boor little Mitkey, der moon iss not made of green cheese und if it were, you vould not live to eat it because there iss not enough atmosphere to bring you down safely und vith your viskers still on.

"Und vhy then, you may vell ask, do I send you? Because der rocket may *not* attain eggscape velocity. Und in that case, it iss still an eggsperiment, budt a different vun. Der rocket, if it goes not to der moon, falls back on der earth, no? Und in that case certain instruments shall giff us further information than ve haff yet about things up there in space. Und you shall giff us information, by vether or not you are yet alife, vether der shock absorbers und vanes are sufficient in an earth-equivalent atmosphere. You see?

"Then ladter, vhen ve send rockets to Venus maybe vhere an atmosphere eggsists, ve shall haff data to calculate the needed size of vanes und shock-absorbers, no? Und in either case, und vether or not you return, Mitkey, you shall be vamous! You shall be der virst liffing greature to go oudt beyond der stratosphere of der earth, out into space.

"Mitkey, you shall be der Star-Mouse! I enfy you, Mitkey, und I only vish I vere your size, so I could go, too."

Der tag, and the door to the compartment. "Gootbye, little Mitkey Mouse." Darkness. Silence. Noise!

"Der rocket—if it goes not to der moon—falls back

on der earth, no?" That was what the Herr Professor thought. But the best-laid plans of mice and men gang aft agley. Even star-mice.

All because of Prxl.

II

The Herr Professor found himself very lonely. After having had Mitkey to talk to, soliloquies were somehow empty and inadequate.

There may be some who say that the company of a small gray mouse is a poor substitute for a wife; but others may disagree. And, anyway, the Professor had never had a wife, and he *had* had a mouse to talk to; so he missed one and, if he missed the other, he didn't know it.

During the long night after the launching of the rocket, he had been very busy with his telescope, a sweet little eight-inch reflector, checking its course as it gathered momentum. The exhaust explosions made a tiny fluctuating point of light that was possible to follow, if one knew where to look.

But the following day there seemed to be nothing to do, and he was too excited to sleep, although he tried. So he compromised by doing a spot of housekeeping, cleaning the pots and pans. It was while he was so engaged that he heard a series of frantic little squeaks and discovered that another small gray mouse, with shorter whiskers and a shorter tail than Mitkey, had walked into the wire-cage mousetrap.

"Vell, vell," said the Professor, "vot haff ve here? Minnie? Iss it Minnie come to look for her Mitkey?"

The Professor was not a biologist, but he happened to be right. It *was* Minnie. Rather, it was Mitkey's mate, so the name was appropriate. What strange vagary of mind had induced her to walk into an unbaited trap, the Professor neither knew nor cared, but he was delighted. He promptly remedied the lack of bait by pushing a sizable piece of cheese through the bars.

Thus it was that Minnie came to fill the place of

her far-traveling spouse as repository for the Professor's confidences. Whether she worried about her family or not there is no way of knowing, but she need not have done so. They were now large enough to fend for themselves, particularly in a house that offered abundant cover and easy access to the refrigerator.

"Ah, und now it iss dargk enough, Minnie, that ve can loogk for that husband of yours. His viery trail across the sky. True, Minnie, it iss a very small viery trail und der astronomers vill not notice it, because they do not know vhere to loogk. But ve do.

"He iss going to be a very vamous mouse, Minnie, this Mitkey of ours, vhen ve tell der vorld about him und about mein rocket. You see, Minnie, ve haff not tod them yet. Ve shall vait und giff der gomplete story all at vunce. By dawn of tomorrow ve'll—

"Ah, there he iss, Minnie! Vaint, but there. I'd hold you up to der scope und let you loogk, but it vould not be vocused right for your eyes, und I do not know how to—

"Almost vun hundred thousand miles, Minnie, und still agcelerating, but not for much longer. Our Mitkey iss on schedule; in fagt he iss going vaster than ve had vigured, no? It iss sure now that he vill eggscape the gravitation of der earth, und fall upon der moon!"

Of course, it was purely coincidental that Minnie squeaked.

"Ah, yess, Minnie, little Minnie. I know, I know. Ve shall neffer see our Mitkey again, und I almost vish our eggsperiment hadt vailed. Budt there are gompensations, Minnie. He shall be der most vamous of all mices. Der Star-Mouse! Virst liffing greature effer to go beyond der gravitational bull of earth!"

The night was long. Occasionally high clouds obscured vision.

"Minnie, I shall make your more gomfortable than in that so-small vire cage. You vould like to seem to be vree, vould you not, vithout bars, like der animals at modern zoos, with moats insteadt?"

And so, to fill in an hour when a cloud obscured the sky, the Herr Professor made Minnie her new home. It was the end of a wooden crate, about half an inch thick and a foot square, laid flat on the table, and with no visible barrier around it.

But he covered the top with metal foil at the edges, and he placed the board on another larger board which also had a strip of metal foil surrounding the island of Minnie's home. And he attached wires from the two areas of metal foil to opposite terminals of a small transformer which he placed near by.

"Und now, Minnie, I shall blace you on your island, vhich shall be liberally supplied mitt cheese und vater, und you shall vind it iss an eggceent blace to liff. But you vill get a mild shock or two vhen you try to step off der edge of der island. It vill not hurt much, but you vill not like it, und after a few tries you vill learn not to try again, no? Und—"

And night again.

Minnie was happy on her island, her lesson well learned. She would no longer so much as step on the inner strip of metal foil. It was a mouse-paradise of an island, though. There was a cliff of cheese bigger than Minnie herself. It kept her busy. Mouse and cheese; soon one would be a transmutation of the other.

But Professor Oberburger wasn't thinking about that. The Professor was worried. When he had calculated and recalculated and aimed his eight-inch reflector through the hole in the roof and turned out the lights—

Yes, there *are* advantages to being a bachelor after all. If one wants a hole in the roof, one simply knocks a hole in the roof and there is nobody to tell one that one is crazy. If winter comes, or if it rains, one can always call a carpenter or use a tarpaulin.

But the faint trail of light wasn't there. The Professor frowned and re-calculated and re-re-calculated and shifted his telescope three-tenths of a minute and still the rocket wasn't there.

"Minnie, something iss wrong. Either der tubes haff stopped viring, or—"

Or the rocket was no longer traversing a straight line relative to its point of departure. By straight, of course, is meant parabolically curved relative to everything other than velocity.

So the Herr Professor did the only thing remaining for him to do, and began to search, with the telescope, in widening circles. It was two hours before he found it, five degrees off course already and verring more and more into a—Well, there was only one thing you could call it. A tailspin.

The darned thing was going in circles, circles which appeared to constitute an orbit about something that couldn't possibly be there. Then narrowing into a concentric spiral.

Then—out. Gone. Darkness. No rocket flares.

The Professor's face was pale as he turned to Minnie.

"It iss *imbossible*, Minnie. Mein own eyes, but it could not be. Even if vun side stopped viring, it could not haff gone into such sudden circles." His pencil verified a suspicion. "Und, Minnie, it decelerated vaster than bossible. Even mitt *no* tubes viring, its momentum vould haff been more—"

The rest of the night—telescope and calculus—yielded no clue. That is, no believable clue. Some force not inherent in the rocket itself, and not accountable by gravitation—even of a hypothetical body—had acted.

"Mein poor Mitkey."

The gray, inscrutable dawn. "Mein Minnie, it vill haff to be a secret. Ve dare not bublish vhat ve saw, for it vould not be believed. I am not sure I believe it myself, Minnie. Berhaps because I vas offertired vrom not sleeping, I chust imachined that I saw—"

Later. "But, Minnie, ve shall hope. Vun hundred vifty thousand miles out, it vas. It vill fall back upon der earth. But I gannot tell vhere! I thought that if it did, I vould be able to galculate its course, und—But after those goncentric cirgles—Minnie, not even *Einstein* could galculate vhere it vill land. Not effen *me*. All ve can do iss hope that ve shall hear of vhere it falls."

Cloudy day. Black night jealous of its mysteries.

"Minnie, our poor Mitkey. There iss *nothing* could have gauzed—"

But something had.

Prxl.

Prxl is an asteroid. It isn't called that by earthly astronomers, because—for excellent reasons—they have not discovered it. So we will call it by the nearest possible transliteration of the name its inhabitants use. Yes, it's inhabited.

Come to think of it, Professor Oberburger's attempt to send a rocket to the moon had some strange results. Or rather, Prxl did.

You wouldn't think that an asteroid could reform a drunk, would you? But one Charles Winslow, a besotted citizen of Bridgeport, Connecticut, never took another drink after the time when—right on Grove Street—a mouse asked him the road to Hartford. The mouse was wearing bright red pants and vivid yellow gloves—

But that was fifteen months after the Professor lost his rocket. We'd better start over again.

Prxl is an asteroid. One of those despised celestial bodies which terrestrial astronomers call vermin of the sky, because the darned things leave trails across the plates that clutter up the more important observations of novae and nebulae. Fifty thousand fleas on the dark dog of night.

Tiny things, most of them. Astronomers have been discovering recently that some of them come close to Earth. Amazingly close. There was excitement in 1932 when Amor came within ten million miles; astronomically, a mere mashie shot. Then Apollo cut that almost in half, and in 1936 Adonis came within less than one and a half million miles.

In 1937, Hermes, less than half a million; but the astronomers got really excited when they calculated its orbit and found that the little mile-long asteroid *can* come within a mere 220,000 miles, closer than Earth's own moon.

Some day they may be still more excited, if and when they spot the ⅜-mile asteroid Prxl, that obstacle of space, making a transit across the moon and discover that it frequently comes within a mere hundred thousand miles of our rapidly whirling world.

Only in event of a transit will they ever discover it, though, for Prxl does not reflect light. It hasn't, anyway, for several million years since its inhabitants coated it with a black, light-absorbing pigment derived from its interior. Monumental task, painting a world, for creatures half an inch tall. But worth it, at the time. When they'd shifted its orbit, they were safe from their enemies. There were giants in those days—eight-inch-tall marauding pirates from Diemos. Got to Earth a couple of times too, before they faded out of the picture. Pleasant little giants who killed because they enjoyed it. Records in now-buried cities on Diemos might explain what happened to the dinosaurs. And why the promising Cro-Magnons disappeared at the height of their promise only a cosmic few minutes after the dinosaurs went west.

But Prxl survived. Tiny world no longer reflecting the sun's rays, lost to the cosmic killers when its orbit was shifted.

Prxl. Still civilized, with a civilization millions of years old. Its coat of blackness preserved and renewed regularly, more through tradition than fear of enemies in these later degenerate days. Mighty but stagnant civilization, standing still on a world that whizzes like a bullet.

And Mitkey Mouse.

III

Klarloth, head scientist of a race of scientists, tapped his assistant Bemj on what would have been Bemj's shoulder if he had had one. "Look," he said, "what approaches Prxl. Obviously artificial propulsion."

Bemj looked into the wall-plate and then directed a thought-wave at the mechanism that jumped the magnification of a thousand-fold through an alternation of the electronic field.

The image leaped, blurred, then steadied. "Fabricated," said Bemj. "Extremely crude, I must say. Primitive explosive-powered rocket. Wait, I'll check where it came from."

He took the readings from the dials about the

viewplate, and hurled them as thoughts against the psychocoil of the computer, then waited while that most complicated of machines digested all the factors and prepared the answer. Then, eagerly, he slid his mind into rapport with its projector. Klarloth likewise listened in to the silent broadcast.

Exact point on Earth and exact time of departure. Untranslatable expression of curve of trajectory, and point on that curve where deflected by gravitional pull of Prxl. The destination—or rather the original intended destination—of the rocket was obvious, Earth's moon. Time and place of arrival on Prxl if present course of rocket was unchanged.

"Earth," said Klarloth meditatively. "They were a long way from rocket travel the last time we checked them. Some sort of a crusade, or battle of beliefs, going on, wasn't there?"

Bemj nodded. "Catapults. Bows and arrows. They've taken a long stride since, even if this is only an early experimental thing of a rocket. Shall we destroy it before it gets here?"

Klarloth shook his head thoughtfully. "Let's look it over. May save us a trip to Earth; we can judge their present state of development pretty well from the rocket itself."

"But then we'll have to—"

"Of course. Call the Station. Tell them to train their attracto-repulsors on it and to swing it into a temporary orbit until they prepare a landing-cradle. And not to forget to damp out the explosive before they bring it down."

"Temporary force-field around point of landing—in case?"

"Naturally."

So despite the almost complete absence of atmosphere in which the vanes could have functioned, the rocket came down safely and so softly that Mitkey, in the dark compartment, knew only that the awful noise had stopped.

Mitkey felt better. He ate some more of the cheese with which the compartment was liberally provided. Then he resumed trying to gnaw a hole in the inch-thick wood with which the compartment was lined. That wooden lining was a kind thought of the Herr Professor from Mitkey's mental well-being. He knew that trying to gnaw his way out would give Mitkey something to do en route which would keep him from getting the screaming meamies. The idea had worked; being busy, Mitkey hadn't suffered mentally from his dark confinement. And now that things were quiet, he chewed away more industriously and more happily than ever, sublimely unaware that when he got through the wood, he'd find only metal which he couldn't chew. But better people than Mitkey have found things they couldn't chew.

Meanwhile, Klarloth and Bemj and several thousand other Prxlians stood gazing up at the huge rocket which, even lying on its side, towered high over their heads. Some of the younger ones, forgetting the invisible field of force, walked too close and came back, ruefully rubbing bumped heads.

Klarloth himself was at the psychograph.

"There *is* life inside the rocket," he told Bemj. "But the impressions are confused. One creature, but I cannot follow its thought processes. At the moment it seems to be doing something with its teeth."

"It could not be an Earthling, one of the dominant race. One of them is much larger than this huge rocket. Gigantic creatures. Perhaps, unable to construct a rocket large enough to hold one of themselves, they sent an experimental creature, such as our wooraths."

"I believe you've guessed right, Bemj. Well, when we have explored its mind thoroughly, we may still learn enough to save us a check-up trip to Earth. I am going to open the door."

"But air—creatures of Earth would need a heavy, almost a dense atmosphere. It could not live."

"We retain the force-field, of course. It will keep the air in. Obviously there is a source of supply of air within the rocket or the creature would not have survived the trip."

Klarloth operated controls, and the force-field itself put forth invisible pseudo-pods and turned the outer screw-door, then reached within and unlatched the inner door to the compartment itself.

All Prxl watched breathlessly as a monstrous gray head pushed out of the huge aperture yawning overhead. Thick whiskers, each as long as the body of a Prxlian—

Mitkey jumped down, and took a forward step that bumped his black nose hard—into something that wasn't there. He squeaked, and jumped backwards against the rocket.

There was disgust in Bemj's face as he looked up at the monster. "Obviously much less intelligent than a woorath. Might just as well turn on the ray."

"Not at all," interrupted Klarloth. "You forget certain very obvious facts. The creature is unintelligent, of course, but the subconscious of every animal holds in itself every memory, every impression, every sense-image, to which it has ever been subjected. If this creature has ever heard the speech of the Earthlings, or seen any of their works—besides this rocket—every word and every picture is indelibly graven. You see now what I mean?"

"Naturally. How stupid of me, Klarloth. Well, one things is obvious from the rocket itself: we have nothing to fear from the science of Earth for at least a few millennia. So there is no hurry, which is fortunate. For to send back the creature's memory to the time of its birth, and to follow each sensory impression in the psychograph will require—well, a time at least equivalent to the age of the creature, whatever that is, plus the time necessary for us to interpret and assimilate each."

"But that will not be necessary, Bemj."

"No? Oh, you mean the X-19 waves?"

"Exactly. Focused upon this creature's brain-center, they can, without disturbing his memories, be so delicately adjusted as to increase his intelligence—now probably about .0001 in the scale—to the point where he is a reasoning creature. Almost automatically, during the process, he will assimilate his own memories, and understand them just as he would if he had been intelligent at the time he received those impressions.

"See, Bemj? He will automatically sort out irrevelant data, and will be able to answer our questions."

"But would you make him as intelligent as—?"

"As we? No, the X-19 waves would not work so far. I would say to about .2 on the scale. That, judging from the rocket coupled with what we remember of Earthlings from our last trip there, is about their present place on the intelligence scale."

"Ummm, yes. At that level, he would comprehend his experiences on Earth just sufficiently that he would not be dangerous to us, too. Equal to an intelligent Earthling. Just about right for our purpose. Then, shall we teach him our language?"

"Wait," said Klarloth. He studied the psychograph closely for a while. "No, I do not think so. He will have a language of his own. I see in his subconscious memories of many long conversations. Strangely, they all seem to be monologues by one person. But he will have a language—a simple one. It would take him a long time, even under treatment, to grasp the concepts of our own method of communication. But we can learn his, while he is under the X-19 machine, in a few minutes."

"Does he understand, now, any of that language?"

Klarloth studied the psychograph again. "No, I do not believe he— Wait, there is one word that seems to mean something to him. The word 'Mitkey.' It seems to be his name, and I believe that, from hearing it many times, he vaguely associates it with himself."

"And quarters for him—with air-locks and such?"

"Of course. Order them built."

IV

To say it was a strange experience for Mitkey is understatement. Knowledge is a strange thing, even when it is acquired gradually. To have it thrust upon one—

And there were little things that had to be straightened out. Like the matter of vocal chords. His weren't adapted to the language he now found he knew. Bemj fixed that; you would hardly call it an operation because Mitkey—even with his new awareness—didn't know what was going on, and he was wide awake at the time. And they didn't explain to Mitkey about J-dimension with which one can get at the inwardness of things without penetrating the outside.

They figured things like that weren't in Mitkey's line, and anyway they were more interested in learning from him than teaching him. Bemj and Klarloth, and a dozen others deemed worthy of the privilege. If one of them wasn't talking to him, another was.

Their questioning helped his own growing understanding. He would not, usually, know that he knew the answer to a question until it was asked. Then he'd piece together, without knowing just how he did it (any more than you or I know *how* we know things), and give them the answer.

Bemj: "Iss this language vhich you sbeak a universal vun?"

And Mitkey, even though he'd never thought about it before, had the answer ready: "No, it iss nodt. It iss Englitch, but I remember der Herr Brofessor sbeaking of other tongues. I belieff he sboke another himself originally, budt in America he always sboke Englitch to become more vamiliar mitt it. It iss a beaudiful sbeech, is it nodt?"

"Hmmmm," said Bemj.

Klarloth: "Und your race, the mices. Are they treated vell?"

"Nodt by most people," Mitkey told him. And explained.

"I vould like to do something for them," he added. "Loogk, could I nodt take back mitt me this brocess vhich you used upon me? Abbly it to other mices, und greate a race of super-mices?"

"Vhy not?" asked Bemj.

He saw Klarloth looking at him strangely, and threw his mind into rapport with the chief scientist's, with Mitkey left out of the silent communion.

"Yes, of course," Bemj told Klarloth, "it will lead to trouble on Earth, grave trouble. Two equal classes of beings so dissimilar as mice and men cannot live together in amity. But why should that concern us, other than favorably? The resultant mess will slow down progress on Earth—give us a few more millennia of peace before Earthlings discover we are here, and trouble starts. You know these Earthlings."

"But you would give them the X-19 waves? They might—"

"No, of course not. But we can explain to Mitkey here how to make a very crude and limited machine for them. A primitive one which would suffice for nothing more than the specific task of converting mouse mentality from .0001 to .2, Mitkey's own level and that of the bifurcated Earthlings."

"It is possible," communicated Klarloth. "It is certain that for aeons to come they will be incapable of understanding its basic principle."

"But could they not use even a crude machine to raise their own level of intelligence?"

"You forget, Bemj, the basic limitation of the X-19 rays; that no one can possibly design a projector capable of raising any mentality to a point on the scale higher than his own. Not even we."

All this, of course, over Mitkey's head, in silent Prxlian.

More interviews, and more.

Klarloth again: "Mitkey, ve varn you of vun thing. Avoid carelessness vith electricity. Der new molecular rearranchement of your brain center—it iss unstable, und—"

Bemj: "Mitkey, are you sure your Herr Brofessor iss der most advanced of all who eggsperiment vith der rockets?"

"In cheneral, yess, Bemj. There are others who on vun specific boint, such as eggsplosives, mathematics, astrovisics, may know more, but not much more. Und for combining these knowledges, he iss ahead."

"It iss vell," said Bemj.

Small gray mouse towering like a dinosaur over tinier half-inch Prxlians. Meek, herbivorous creature though he was, Mitkey could have killed any one of them with a single bite. But, of course, it never occurred to him to do so, nor to them to fear that he might.

They turned him inside out mentally. They did a pretty good job of study on him physically, too, but that was through the J-dimension, and Mitkey didn't even know about it.

They found out what made him tick, and they found out everything he knew and some things he didn't even know he knew. And they grew quite fond of him.

"Mitkey," said Klarloth one day, "all der civilized races on Earth vear glothing, do they nodt? Vell, if you are to raise der level of mices to men, vould it not be vitting that you vear glothes, too?"

"An eggcellent idea, Herr Klarloth. Und I know chust vhat kind I vould like. Der Herr Brofessor vunce showed me a bicture of a mouse bainted by der artist Dissney, und der mouse vore glothing. Der mouse vas not a real-life vun, budt an imachinary mouse in a barable, und der Brofessor named me after der Dissney mouse."

"Vot kind of glothing vas it, Mitkey?"

"Bright red bants mitt two big yellow buttons in frondt und two in back, und yellow shoes for der back feet und a pair of yellow gloves for der vront. A hole in der seat of der bants to aggomodate der tail."

"Ogay, Mitkey. Such shall be ready for you in fife minutes."

That was on the eve of Mitkey's departure. Originally, Bemj had suggested awaiting the moment when Prxl's eccentric orbit would again take it within a hundred and fifty thousand miles of Earth. But, as Klarloth pointed out, that would be fifty-five Earth-years ahead, and Mitkey wouldn't last that long. Not unless they— And Bemj agreed that they had better not risk sending a secret like that back to Earth.

So they compromised by refueling Mitkey's rocket with something that would cancel out the million and a quarter odd miles he would have to travel. That secret they didn't have to worry about, because the fuel would be gone by the time the rocket landed.

Day of departure.

"Ve haff done our best, Mitkey, to set und time
der rocket so it vill land on or near der spot from vhich
you left Earth. But you gannot eggspect agguracy in
a voyach so long as this. But you vill land near. The
rest iss up to you. Ve haff equvipped the rocket ship
for effery contingency."

"Thank you, Herr Klarloth, Herr Bemj. Gootbye."

"Gootbye, Mitkey. Ve hate to loose you."

"Gootbye, Mitkey."

"Gootbye, gootbye . . ."

V

For a million and a quarter miles, the aim was really
excellent. The rocket landed in Long Island Sound,
ten miles out from Bridgeport, about sixty miles from
the house of Professor Oberburger near Hartford.

They had prepared for a water landing, of course.
The rocket went down to the bottom, but before it
was more than a few dozen feet under the surface,
Mitkey opened the door—especially reequipped to open
from the inside—and stepped out.

Over his regular clothes he wore a neat little diving
suit that would have protected him at any reasonable
depth, and which, being lighter than water, brought
him to the surface quickly where he was able to open
his helmet.

He had enough synthetic food to last him for a week,
but it wasn't necessary, as things turned out. The night-
boat from Boston carried him in to Bridgeport on its
anchor chain, and once in sight of land he was able
to divest himself of the diving suit and let it sink to
the bottom after he'd punctured the tiny compartments
that made it float, as he'd promised Klarloth he would
do.

Almost instinctively, Mitkey knew that he'd do well
to avoid human beings until he'd reached Professor
Oberburger and told his story. His worst danger proved

to be the rats at the wharf where he swam ashore. They were ten times Mitkey's size and had teeth that could have taken him apart in two bites.

But mind has always triumphed over matter. Mitkey pointed an imperious yellow glove and said, "Scram," and the rats scrammed. They'd never seen anything like Mitkey before, and they were impressed.

So for that matter, was the drunk of whom Mitkey inquired the way to Hartford. We mentioned that episode before. That was the only time Mitkey tried direct communication with strange human beings. He took, of course, every precaution. He addressed his remarks from a strategic position only inches away from a hole into which he could have popped. But it was the drunk who did the popping, without even waiting to answer Mitkey's question.

But he got there, finally. He made his way afoot to the north side of town and hid out behind a gas station until he heard a motorist who had pulled in for gasoline inquire the way to Hartford. And Mitkey was a stowaway when the car started up.

The rest wasn't hard. The calculations of the Prxlians showed that the starting point of the rocket was five Earth miles north-west of what showed on their telescopomaps as a city, and which from the Professor's conversation Mitkey knew would be Hartford.

He got there.

VI

"Hello, Brofessor."

The Herr Professor Oberburger looked up, startled. There was no one in sight. "Vot?" he asked, of the air. "Who iss?"

"It iss I, Brofessor. Mitkey, der mouse whom you sent to der moon. But I vas not there. Insteadt, I—"

"Vot?? It iss imbossible. Somebody blays der choke. Budt—budt nobody *knows* about that rocket. Vhen it vailed, I didn't told nobody. Nobody budt me knows—"

"And me, Brofessor."

The Herr Professor sighed heavily. "Offervork. I am going vhat they call battly in der bel—"

"No, Brofessor. This iss really me, Mitkey. I can talk now. Chust like you."

"You say you can— I do not belief it. Vhy can I not see you, then? Vhere are you? Vhy don't you—"

"I am hiding, Brofessor, in der vall chust behind der big hole. I vanted to be sure efferything vas ogay before I showed myself. Then you vould not get eggcited und throw something at me maybe."

"Vot? Vhy, Mitkey, if it iss really you und I am nodt asleep or going— Vhy Mitkey, you know better than to think I might do something like that!"

"Ogay, Brofessor."

Mitkey stepped out of the hole in the wall, and the Professor looked at him and rubbed his eyes and looked again and rubbed his eyes and—

"I *am* grazy," he said finally. "Red bants he vears yet, und yellow— It gannot be. I *am* grazy."

"No, Brofessor. Listen, I'll tell you all aboudt it."

And Mitkey told him.

Gray dawn, and a small gray mouse still talking earnestly.

"But, Mitkey—"

"Yess, Brofessor. I see your boint, that you think an intelligent race of mices und an intelligent race of men couldt nodt get along side by sides. But it vould not be side by sides; as I said, there are only a ferry few beople in the smallest continent of Australia. Und it vould cost little to bring them back und turn offer that continent to us mices. Ve vould call it Moustralia instead Australia, und ve vould instead of Sydney call der capital Dissney, in honor of—"

"But, Mitkey—"

"But, Brofessor, look vot ve offer for that continent. *All* mices vould go there. Ve civilize a few und the few help us catch others und bring them in to put them under der ray machine, und the others help catch more und build more machines und it grows like a snowball rolling down hill. Und ve sign a non-aggression pact mitt humans und stay on Moustralia und raise our own food und—"

"But, Mitkey—"

"Und look vot ve offer you in eggschange, Herr Brofessor! Ve vill eggsterminate your vorst enemy—der *rats*. Ve do not like them either. Und vun battalion of vun thousand mices, armed mitt gas masks und small gas bombs could go right in effery hole after der rats und could eggsterminate effery rat in a city in vun day or two. In der whole vorld ve could eggsterminate effery last rat in a year, und at the same time catch und civilize effery mouse und ship him to Moustralia, und—"

"But, Mitkey—"

"Vot, Brofessor?"

"It vould vork, but it vould not vork. You could eggsterminate der rats, yess. But how long vould it be before conflicts of interest vould lead to der mices trying to eggsterminate der people or der people trying to eggsterminate der—"

"They vould not dare, Brofessor! Ve could make veapons that vould—"

"You see, Mitkey?"

"But it vould not habben. If men vill honor our rights, ve vill honor—"

The Herr Professor sighed.

"I—I vill act as your intermediary, Mitkey, und offer your broposition, und— Vell, it iss true that getting rid of rats vould be a greadt boon to der human race. Budt—"

"Thank you, Brofessor."

"By der vay, Mitkey. I haff Minnie. Your vife, I guess it iss, unless there vas other mices around. She iss in der other room; I put her there chust before you arriffed, so she vould be in der dark und could sleep. You vant to see her?"

"Vife?" said Mitkey. It had been so long that he had really forgotten the family he had perforce abandoned. The memory returned slowly.

"Vell," he said "—ummm, yess. Ve vill get her und I shall construct quvick a small X-19 prochector und—

Yess, it vill help you in your negotiations mitt der governments if there are sefferal of us already so they can see I am not chust a freak like they might otherwise suspegt."

VII

It wasn't deliberate. It couldn't have been, because the Professor didn't know about Klarloth's warning to Mitkey about carelessness with electricity—"Der new molecular rearranchement of your brain center—it iss unstable, und—"

And the Professor was still back in the lighted room when Mitkey ran into the room where Minnie was in her barless cage. She was asleep, and the sight of her— Memory of his earlier days came back like a flash and suddenly Mitkey knew how lonesome he had been.

"Minnie!" he called, forgetting that she could not understand.

And he stepped up on the board where she lay. "Squeak!" The mild electrical current between the two strips of tinfoil got him.

There was silence for a while.

Then: "Mitkey," called the Herr Professor. "Come on back und ve vill discuss this—"

He stepped through the doorway and saw them, there in the gray light of dawn, two small gray mice cuddled happily together. He couldn't tell which was which, because Mitkey's teeth had torn off the red and yellow garments which had suddenly been strange, confining and obnoxious things.

"Vot on earth?" asked Professor Oberburger. Then he remembered the current and guessed.

"Mitkey! Can you no longer talk? Iss der—"

Silence.

Then the Professor smiled. "Mitkey," he said, "my little star-mouse. I think you are more happier now."

He watched them a moment, fondly, then reached down and flipped the switch that broke the electrical barrier. Of course they didn't know they were free, but when the Professor picked them up and placed them carefully on the floor, one ran immediately for the hole in the wall. The other followed, but turned around and looked back—still a trace of puzzlement in the little black eyes, a puzzlement that faded.

"Gootbye, Mitkey. You vill be happier this vay. Und there vill always be cheese."

"Squeak," said the little gray mouse, and it popped into the hole.

"Gootbye—" it might, or might not, have meant.

Return of a Legend

Raymond Z. Gallun

Mars fever they called it. Could the wild boy cheat the Red Planet's skeleton deserts and the dogged trailers from Port Laribee?

Port Laribee with its score of Nisson huts, sealed against the lifeless atmosphere, the red dust and the cold, was a shabby piece of Earth dropped onto Mars.

There, Dave Kort was the first wilderness tramp to be remembered. In warm seasons he'd plod into Port Laribee, burdened by a pack that only the two-fifths of terrestrial gravity put within the range of human muscles. He was a great, craggy old man, incredibly grimed and browned, his frostbites bandaged with dry Martian leaves tied on with their own fiber.

His snag-toothed grin was bemused and secret through the scratched plastic of his air-hood. He'd trade carven stones, bits of ancient metal, or oddities of plant and animal life for chewing tobacco, chocolate, heavily lined clothes, mending supplies, and new parts for his battered portable air-compressor.

He'd refuse a bath with disdain. And at last his rusty, monosyllabic speech would wax eloquent—comparatively.

"So long, fellas," he'd say. "See yuh around."

The equinoctial winds, heralding autumn, would moan thinly like the ghosts of the Martians wiped out in war those ages back. Dust would blur the horizon of that huge, arid triangle of sea-bottom called Syrtis Major—still the least sterile land on the Red Planet. At night the dry cold would dip to ninety below zero, Fahrenheit.

The specialists of Port Laribee, who watched the spinning wind-gauges, thermometers and barometers, and devoted monastic years to learning about Mars, said that they'd never see Dave Kort again.

But for three successive summers after he had quit his job as helper among them, he showed up, tattered, filthy, thinned to a scarecrow, but grinning.

Young Joe Dayton, fresh from Earth and full of Mars-wonder, asked him a stock question that third summer. The answer was laconic. "Oh—I know the country. I get along."

But at the fourth winter's end, Dave Kort did not return. No one ever saw him again, nor found among the ruins and the quiet pastel hues of Mars the dried thing that had been Kort. Somewhere drifting dust had buried it. No one had quite understood him in life. If any affection had been aimed at him, it was for a story, not a man. The man died but the story thrived.

Dave Kort had lived off this wilderness, alone and with sketchy artificial aids, for three Martian years— almost six by Earth reckoning. It was quite a feat. For one thing, the open air of Mars has a pressure of only one-ninth of the terrestrial, and above ground it contains but a trace of oxygen.

How Kort had turned the trick was not completely inconceivable.

In making starch from carbon-dioxide and moisture under the action of sunlight, the green plant-life of Mars produces oxygen just as Earthly vegetation does. But instead of freeing it lavishly to the air, many of those Martian growths, hoarding the essentials of life on a dying world, compress their oxygen into cavities in stem and root and underground capsule, to support later a slow tissue-combustion like that of warm-blooded animals, thus protecting their vitals from cold and death.

Despoiling these stores of oxygen with a pointed metal pipette attached to a greedily sucking compressor was a known means of emergency survival on Mars. Thus you could laboriously replenish the oxygen flasks for your air-hood. Simple—yes. But tedious, grinding, endless. Dayton could imagine.

Food and shelter were also necessary. But under thickets there is a five-foot depth of fallen vegetation, dry, felty, slow to decay in this climate, accumulating autumn after autumn for Martian centuries. In this carpet are those oxygen-holding capsules and roots, often broken, freeing their contents for the spongy surrounding material to hold. There too grow much green algae—simpler plants of the same function. There are the fruit and seed-pods of the surface growths, sheltered from cold. And there, the remaining animal life has retreated.

Fuzzy, tawny things that twitter; fat, mammal-like exacavators that never care to see the sky, and many-joined creatures that resemble Earthly ants only in their industry and communal skills. Above ground they build their small, transparent air-domes—bubblelike structures formed of hardened secretion from their jaws. There they shelter their special gardens and sun their young.

So, for a man able to borrow methods unlike his human heritage, there were ways to keep alive in the raw Martian wilds.

Once, Lorring, the physician, said to Joe Dayton, "Kort must have burrowed, too—like a bear. Is that human? Of course the tip of the Syrtis Major triangle here at Port Laribee is far north. But even if he could have gotten all the way to the tropics, the nights are still bitter. Even so, the big question is not how he lived like he did, but why?"

Yes, this was a point which Dayton had often wondered about, frowning with thick, dark brows, while his wide mouth smiled quizzically above a generous jaw. What had impelled Kort to a solitude far deeper than that of an old-time hermit or desert-rat? Had he been a great child lumbering by instinct through the misfit fogs of his mind to a place where he felt at peace?

Dayton favored another explanation as the main one.

"Why, Doc?" he said to Lorring, as they played cards in the rec-hall. "The answer is in all of us, here. Or we would never have come to Mars. Where was there ever such a place of history, enigma, weird beauty, fascination to men? You can't be neutral. Hating Mars, you'd never stay. Half loving it, like most of us, you would—for a while. Loving it, you'd want a much closer look than is possible at Port Laribee, from which we sally forth like rubbernecks. Too bad that Mars is too rough for men, in the long run. Too bad that the Martians are extinct. Once there were even machines to maintain a better climate."

Other specialists were within hearing. They laughed, but they knew what Dayton meant. They'd seen the dun deserts, the great graven monoliths, dust-scoured, the heaps of rust. Being here had the charm of a quest for ancient treasure, marked by the mood of death.

Parsons, the metallurgist, said: "Funny, but I remember Kort's posture—bent, just like the figures in the bas-reliefs. Though Martian skeletal structure was far different. That sounds as if part of Mars sneaked into Kort's body, doesn't it? Hell, there's no pseudo-science here! Plodding through dust, and at low gravity, you just naturally develop that posture as a habit. Now call me nuts."

"You're nuts, Parsons," Kettrich, the biologist, obliged.

Not many days later, Frank Terry and his son came to Port Laribee. Bringing a seven-year-old boy—a bright little guy named Will—to unlivable Mars, marked the elder Terry at once as a screwball.

Was the mother dead or divorced? Was Terry a remittance man, exiled by his family? He seemed to have enjoyed the good things. . . Such curiosity was bad taste. Forget it.

"We like the sound of the place," Frank Terry explained. "We thought we'd take some photographs, really get friendly with the place. . ."

His listeners foresaw the withering of Terry's familiar enthusiasm, and his departure within a week. Except maybe Dayton guessed differently. The intellectual Terry was not much like Dave Kort. Yet perhaps a kinship showed in a certain expression, as if their natures had the same basis.

During the next Martian year, Dayton and the observatory crew saw the sporting-goods-store sheen vanish utterly from these two. They carried less and less equipment with each succeeding sally into the wilderness. Dried lichen, stuffed inside their airtight garments, soon served them as additional insulation against cold.

From their lengthening jaunts they brought back the usual relics—golden ornaments, carvings, bits of apparatus that had not weathered away. And the usual photographs of blue-green thickets, war-melted cities, domes celled like honeycombs, suggesting a larval stage in the life-cycle of the ancients, and of country littered with shattered crystal—much Martian land had once been roofed with clear quartz, against the harshening climate.

Frank Terry became bearded and battered. Will ceased to be a talkative, sociable youngster. Still devoted to his father, he turned shy, sullen, and alert in a new way.

He had a pet like an eight-inch caterpillar, though it was not that at all. It was warm-blooded, golden-furred, intelligent. It had seven beady eyes. It crept over the boy's shoulders, and down inside his garments, chirping eerily. Except for his father, it was the only companion the boy wanted.

So Summer ended, and the dark blue sky was murked by angry haze. Vitrac, chief scientist, said, "You're not going out again, are you, Terry?"

The kid gave the real answer, "Let's go, Dad. I want to. Besides, Digger is homesick."

The next morning, when the equinoctial storm closed in, the Terrys had vanished.

Joe Dayton led the search party. He found nothing. Mars is small but still vast. Its total surface equals all the land on Earth. Since the first men had come, not one in a thousand of its square miles had been touched by human boots.

Wandering explorers found Frank Terry's mummy late that spring, in a deep part of Syrtis Major, with old ocean salt around it. When they brought it to Port Laribee it was not completely dried out. So Terry must have survived through the winter.

The boy must surely be dead, too. But stories drifted back to the Port—of holes found in the felted soil, and of a small, heavily-burdened figure that scampered away at the sight of a man.

The general opinion was that this was pure romancing, to intrigue the tourists who came out that year in their bright, excited crowds, charmed by the Red Planet yet sheltered from it, equipped from shops recommended by the most debonair of space wanderers—if such existed. Many were eager to stay, girls among them, bright-faced, sure, with the thrill in their eyes and voices. Ah, yes—but how long would they have lasted in this too rich and rough a strangeness?

Joe Dayton shrugged, sad that his opinion had to be so mean. There were soberer arrivals, too. Relatives of Port Laribee staff: members, mostly. Willowby's wife. Doc Lorring's small daughter, Tillie, sent out for a visit. Among the tourists there were a few additional kids.

There was also the lost Frank Terry's elder brother, Dolph Terry, big, but prim beneath an easy smile. Also there was a Terry girl, Doran by name. She did not seem much like either of her brothers—the mystical wanderer, Frank Terry, nor the slightly stuffed-shirted Dolph. She was much younger than either of them, sun-browned, a bit puzzled at being on another world, not terribly pretty, but quick with good-humored shrugs and friendly chuckles whenever she could put aside her worry about her nephew.

Dayton had some belief in the tales from the wilderness. For he'd known young Will Terry. Besides, beneath the ineptness of kids, he recognized an adaptability beyond that of adults. So his work was cut out for him.

"After all, William was Frank's son," Dolph told

Dayton. "Frank was—what he was. But my sister and I are here to see that the boy is located. Perhaps he can still have a normal childhood."

"We'll do what we can," Dayton replied, smiling crookedly to dampen the man's naive and assertive air.

For the last half of the long summer the search went on; many visitors took brief part, ranging well beyond the short tractor lines which encompassed the tourist's usual view of Mars.

Dolph Terry was dogged, but clumsy and irritable. His sister's rugged cheerfulness and interest in her surroundings pleased Dayton.

Still, at the end—due as much as anything to sheer luck—it was Joe Dayton who captured Will Terry single-handed. It was almost autumn again. Joe flushed the scampering figure from a thicket. The boy's limp was to Dayton's advantage. He made a flying tackle, and the savage, grimy thing that was an eight-year-old human, was fighting in his grasp.

His crooned words, finding their way through the thin texture of two air-hoods and the tenuous atmosphere between, did not soften the ferocity of those pale eyes. Such eyes can be like a blank mask anyway—not unintelligent, but expressive of a different thought-plane.

"Easy, Will—easy, fella," Dayton said. "You couldn't last much longer out here. Your compressor must be nearly worn out."

Reassurance failed. "Lemme go!" the boy snarled blurredly, his speech rusted by solitude. Helped by his father, he had learned the tricks of survival here. His dimmed past was so different from his present life that perhaps it seemed fearfully alien to him. As he bore the struggling boy to the tractor-vehicle, Dayton had the odd idea that a Martian, trapped by a man, might behave like this.

He recalled old yarns of boys raised by wolves or apes. Here was the same simple loss of human ways—not by soul-migration, but the plain molding of habit by a bizarre environment.

At the Port Laribee hospital, Will Terry was at first

least disturbed when left alone. But his whimpers at night reminded Dayton of the mewling of a Martian storm.

Dolph Terry cursed the waiting for an Earth-liner and the lack of a psychiatrist on Mars. Doran had no luck either at making friends with Will. Meanwhile the tempests began.

But Doran had an idea. Visitors were still awaiting passage home, among them children.

"Kids are kids, Joe," she told Dayton. "They may be able to reach Will. I talked it over with Doc Lorring."

She was right. Gradually, then more quickly, the trapped-lynx glare faded from Will's eyes as he accepted the scared but fascinated companionship of the other youngsters in the hospital. He still had Digger. At last he let the others pet the fuzzy creature. The strangeness dimmed on both sides. Kid-brashness returned. Perhaps in the whimsy and fantasy of children, that could accept even the humanizing of beast and beetle, Will and his new friends found a common denominator for his life on Mars. He became a hero. Doran and Joe overheard some of his bragging.

"Sure I can work an air-compressor. Dad showed me. He used to say that Mars was home. I'm going back."

One morning Will was gone from the hospital. It came out that a hospital orderly had been diverted from watchfulness for a minute by other children. Two air-hoods, Mars-costumes, and compressors were gone. Also another boy named Danny Bryant.

The complaint of Lorring's own tomboy eight-year-old completed the picture, "They didn't want me along!"

That day the savage wind moaned and the dust trains across the sky were tawny. Danny Bryant's folks were near hysteria. In all the foolishness of boys, there seemed nothing to equal this. Dolph Terry seemed to wonder blankly what sort of wily thing his brother had sired and trained. The visitors who had been charmed by Mars were sullen and tense. The remaining kids were scared and solemn.

Doran's eyes were big with guilt and worry. "My idea caused the trouble, Joe," she told Dayton. "I've got to do something. I've got to follow Will and bring those boys back. I can live out there if Will can."

Dayton eyed her thoughtfully. It did not seem like such a tragedy to him, except of course, for the Bryants. He could understand this love for the wild Martian desert.

"Marry me, Doran, and we'll go together," Joe Dayton said.

So that was how it was. Dolph might think his whole family mad. Vitrac, chief scientist, who performed the ceremony, might think so too.

Joe and Doran ranged far ahead of the other searchers. Sometimes, in the hiss of the tempest, they thought they heard the weeping of a child. So they blundered through dust-drifts and murk, following what always proved a false lead.

The first night fell, a shrieking maelstrom of deathly cold, black as a pocket. An inflatable tent would have been a hardship for chill-stiffened fingers to set up in such a wind. They had no such burden. They burrowed beneath a thicket instead, into the layer of dry vegetation. For this there were no better tools than their heavy gloves. They dug deep, kicking the felty stuff behind them to plug the entrance, shutting out even the wail of the storm.

"The strangest honeymoon, ever!" Doran laughed.

Musty air was trapped around them, high in oxygen-content. To enrich it further they slashed hollow root-capsules with their knives. A little warmth was being generated in those roots. Above was the additional insulation and airseal of drifting dust.

Joe could breathe here without an air-hood, and hold his wife close in savage protection and regret and apology for the soft, man-made luxuries that should be, especially now, and were not. Instead they were in darkness, under Martian soil and dead leaves. A grub's paradise. Ancient beings of the Red Planet might have lived like this when the need arose, but it was an existence far off the beaten track for humans.

"When we get back I'll make it all up to you, Doran," Joe kept insisting.

There was a fear in him—of conforming for too long to the demands of this weird environment and of somehow losing a human heritage.

"I'm reading your mind, Joe," Doran laughed. "Don't worry. We both love the smell of coffee and bacon too much. And music, and nice furniture, and walks in the park. We're not like Frank was, or young Will perhaps still is. No, this will make us want such things more—tie us tighter to Earth."

At dawn they blundered on. During their third night underground they were raided while they slept. Some chocolate bars and other food-concentrates disappeared. And a pencil of Joe's. Their two-way radio would no longer work. The chuckling, chirping inquisitive creatures of the Martian soil had crept into its case and broken it.

Thus the Daytons, out of contact with Port Laribee, did not hear how Danny Bryant staggered back, dazed, frost-bitten, and half smothered, to his parents' arms.

The storm ended after five days. The small sun blazed in the steely sky, which seemed as brittle as frozen air. There was a sharp lifting of mood. Go back to Port Laribee? The Daytons were tempted. But they had not yet found the boys. Besides, they were far afield. And with much of their supplies used up or stolen, the work of mere survival consumed time and energy and slowed travel. So it was almost as well to push on, wasn't it?

It seemed that they were always using pointed pipette and compressor to refill oxygen flasks from the hollow parts of vegetation. At dawn they collected hoarfrost crystals wrung from the arid atmosphere by the nocturnal cold, for drinking water. They ate underground fruit and the starchy pulps of certain roots. Wary of poison, they tasted untried things cautiously.

Mars hogs that tunnelled in an eternal blind search for food were fair game in the darkness beneath the thicket leaf-carpets. Dayton had a tiny ato-stove that served for their meagre cooking.

Weeks passed and a strange life-pattern was set as the Daytons moved south, deeper into broadening Syrtis Major. Maybe it was a bit warmer. Some paper-dry growths were still blue-green. More were brown from the winter dryness. Necessities were harder to find.

Sometimes, among the pastel-tinted thickets and low hills, there were patches of real Martian desert, red and lifeless.

Night followed exhausting day, and how welcome was the warmth of a burrow where one could nurse the frostbites acquired in the frigid dawn.

Several times footprints, large-booted but short-paced, led the Daytons on, only to be lost in rocky ground and lichen.

Twice Joe and Doran crossed the war-fused wrecks of huge cities. Fallen hothouse roofs littered the ruins. The piles of rust must have been irrigation pumps, spaceship ramps, climate-controlled apparatus.

In tower, storehouse, and avenue were the skeletons, with their odd, vertical ribs to house huge lungs.

Some devices still worked. Joe found a rod, probably of corrosion-resistant platinum. He pressed its stud and for an instant, before it became useless, it flashed fire that melted part of a fanciful wall-carving.

The struggle to survive harshened further. Once it was bitter water, oozing up from some deep irrigation pipe, that staved off death by thirst.

Several times oxygen was obtained only by lying prone over a teeming colony of the chitinous creatures whose instinct was to roof with a protecting airdome of gluten anything that promised to be food. These Mars ants—ordinarily to be avoided—admitted air to the domes they built from their deepest buried tunnels and chambers.

Often Joe looked at his wife, knowing that they both had changed. They were tattered, and a little like the bas-relief figures. They were Dave Kort, and Frank and Will Terry over again. Doran's teeth were very white in a face browned by sunshine filtered only by the rare Martian air. She was very thin, but there was an oblique charm in her features. Or had his very conceptions of beauty altered subtly, conforming to a now familiar environment?

Thinking back to Port Laribee and Earth itself was often like recalling substanceless dreams, so different were such memories. And was the fading of revulsion for even the scurrying builders of the airdomes occasion for deeper fear because it represented the loss of another part of one's natural self?

Joe often worried. Others had been drawn to Mars too, eager to search out the mysteries of its past and people—all of this an intriguing fabric—but most Earthmen had the sense to realize in time that it was a graveyard world, unfit for humans. For to live the life of Mars you had to stop being human. Conditioning grimed into you like the red dust.

Nor was the trap just imaginary. The most frightening part was knowing that Doran was with child. Damn the pulse beats of life that had no regard for circumstances!

Joe could be glad only that she remained human enough to be pettish and optimistic by turns.

"We can't get back, can we, Joe?" she'd say. "But maybe it'll be all right. It's a long time, yet."

Should they try to hole up somewhere? That wasn't much good either. Even in spring there wouldn't be enough resources in one place to sustain life for long. They had to keep moving. So when again they saw those boot-tracks, they felt free to follow.

Milder days came. At noon the temperature reached fifty degrees, F. The country brightened in pastel beauty after the vernal storms. There were gorgeous flowerlike growths. The tracks would vanish and appear again, seeming to mark no single trail but a series of excursions from somewhere among the hills to the south.

Once Doran and Joe heard a thin halloo or scream of defiance.

One of their two air-compressors quit beyond repair, making it twice the job to fill their oxygen flasks. This could be fatal now.

Soon after they entered the hill gorges there was a rock fall, too close to be a thing of accident or coincidence. Later there was a swift-dying flicker that turned a spot of dust incandescent.

Later that afternoon, amid blue shadows from towering monoliths, Joe met an attack as sudden and savage as a bobcat's. The creature sprang down at him from a ledge, clawing, kicking, striking with a knife. Joe had a bad time until his greater strength won.

Doran helped hold her nephew down. Will Terry was battered, hardened, scarred—scarcely recognizable with his teeth bared.

But, oddly, Joe knew just what to say to soothe him.

"Will, you can see that we're like you. Maybe we don't want to be, but we are, now. We can't drag you back again to Port Laribee."

The kid relaxed a little. His pale eyes turned puzzled but wary.

"About the other boy, Will—Danny Bryant?" Doran asked.

Will's lip curled. "He was weak and dumb," he said, fumbling with unused words. "I took him back long ago."

"You did fine, Will," Joe said. "Now what have you found here in the hills? You've been camping in one place for a while. Show us."

Joe had to use harsh command against the sullenness still in the boy. He did so bluntly, driven by grim hope and need.

Thus, before sunset, Doran and he found something they needed.

"Dad wanted such a place," the kid said, half-proudly.

It was less than optimism promised—just a small, deep valley, pretty as a painting, but quietly forbidding, too. Joe had seen others almost like it. Martian growths clogged it, sprouting new blue-green leaves. The ruins were far less damaged than in the cities. There were countless little domes of the ant-creatures, indicating some underground water.

Nimbly Will led the way downward and across the

valley to a stout structure. It was not very unusual, just another relic in a region away from the fiercest path of war. Here might have been a last refuge, after the death of millions, the breakdown of machinery, and the rapid worsening of Martian climatic conditions. Crystal roofs lay shattered around the ornate central massiveness. But one wing with thicker glaze still stood—sealable.

Doran's eyes lighted as she and Joe and her nephew went into the deserted interior through the double doors of an airlock which some last, fleeing Martian had not closed.

Hardy wilderness plants had intruded into this hothouse but there still were troughs of soil, proving that this had been a garden sealed against cold, a place of fruit and flower.

"We might try to use this, Joe," Doran said, her voice thin in the heavy stillness.

He nodded. But his gratitude was tinged with scared and bitter overtones. He hurried to explore the central edifice, which must have been closed before the kid came, for the preservation of things inside was good. There were odd cylindrical cells, niches dark and dusty, cubicles piled with metal boxes. There was even what seemed a kind of machine-shop.

And there was a valve which, from the footprints in the dust, Will had tried to turn. Joe accomplished this now with a levering metal bar. Out in the dry hothouse pool a spout jetted rusty water.

The underground storage cisterns are intact," Joe was soon explaining. "I prayed there'd be some."

Joe Dayton was grateful, yet not happy.

Grimly he began again the bitter toil of survival, the others helping. Like bizarre harvesters they tore up great bundles of roots and stalks and piled them inside the hothouse. Briefly the blue sunset shadows were long, over that weird, beautiful valley. Then the dusk came, and the faint frost haze of the always frigid nights.

"We'd better hurry before we freeze," Joe growled irritably. "When we get a lot of this stuff inside we'll tramp on it to break the oxygen-capsules. By morning there should be breathable atmosphere under this roof. Later, vegetation planted inside will keep it fresh."

Joe Dayton's mood now had a taint of despair. Forced to try to settle in this place, he felt more than ever trapped. More than ever he felt as if the souls of those eon-dead beings depicted on carven walls that Phobos, the nearer moon, now illuminated, had been crowding into his human flesh and brain to push his own ego out. No, it was not witchcraft—it was simpler. Mars had shaped its ancient inhabitants. Now it was working on Earthly material with the same, subtle, ruthless fingers.

When the task in the hothouse was finished, Joe went with his wife and nephew to burrow again away from the cold, and to eat and to sleep, all in the manner which Mars compelled.

Joe wanted Doran and his child to keep their human ways. His child. That was his worst thought now.

His mind pictured Will—tattered, wild, strange in thought and feeling. He had lived his first years on Earth. So how would it be with a child *born* on Mars? Joe cursed into his furry beard—cursed the distance to Port Laribee which might as well not be there at all, so out of reach was it, so ineffectual, and so soon probably to be left deserted. Though bone weary, Joe did not sleep well that quiet night.

The next day, bathed and smiling, Doran still did not look quite Earthly to him. She was browned by Martian sun, but the real difference that had come into her strong beauty was a thing of multiple detail, like the mark of persons used to the sea contrasted with those born to the plains—but deeper.

Scrubbed fairly clean, Will remained an urchin of Mars. Also scrubbed, and shaved, Joe felt more comfortable. Yet he knew that basically this restored nothing.

A day later he was wandering around outside the hothouse, trying to plan needed agricultural projects, when a faint scrape of pebbles made him wheel warily.

"People! Rescue!" were his first eager thoughts.

But then he saw that the three figures, two large and one small, were creatures attuned to Mars in the same way as himself, and as helpless.

Yet when old friends were recognized, in spite of the deep changes, Joe Dayton felt a joyous lift.

"Doc Lorring!" he shouted. "Kettrich. And Tillie. Hey! Hey, Doran! Will! Come here!

Doctor Lorring's tomboy daughter, a bit younger than Will, showed a grinning dirty face through a battered air-hood and said, "Hi."

"We were trying to follow you most of the time, Dayton," Lorring stammered. "We hoped to find you and Doran, and maybe the Terry boy. But our tractor broke down, and we had to live off the land. While we still had the vehicle there didn't seem much reason why Tillie shouldn't come along. We'd begun to give up hope of finding any of you alive."

Minutes were spent questioning and explaining. They all went into the sealed hothouse. Kettrich, the biologist, had even saved a little coffee.

"For a celebration, if we ever located any of you missing ones," he said to Joe and Doran.

Kettrich sighed and went on, "Chief Vitrac, Lorson, and a dozen others are the only old timers left at the Port. The others have all gone, with Dolph Terry and the tourists. Humans are about done with Mars, though I suppose a few will trickle out here from time to time."

With contemplative relish Doran sipped coffee brewed with crudely filtered water on an ato-stove. She smiled like any woman who has her man, and has found a place and a purpose.

"Not for humans," she mused. "That's one way of putting it. Still, it doesn't necessarily mean us. Let's face facts," she continued. "A natural selection was going on all the time. Thousands of people left, disgusted. A very few stayed grimly, or got trapped. On Earth I never thought much about Mars, but now I've been here so long. We're different, perhaps proudly so. Oh, we still like the things that Earth-people like, maybe more than ever. But the Old Ones here also had their comforts. We have Earth flesh and bone;

we'll never be like them that way, and I'm glad. You can either say that Terrans are supremely adaptable, or that we are no longer quite human, and that there are Martians again. Because one *has* to be that to really live here, doesn't he? Mars won't be left wasted and sad. We're some of its first new people. Among the explorers there must be others. More and more will come. Gradually, through the centuries, we'll build Mars back toward what it was."

Dayton stared at his wife, then down at the ancient flagging, then at the others. Tillie tittered. She was as brown as Will Terry and almost as attached to the Red Planet. Around her mended glove a fuzzy creature twined, chirping. Will and Tillie were children of Mars.

Doran's assessment of a situation in plain talk took away its dread for Joe, giving his Mars-love a chance. He began to feel at home. "Is my wife talking sense?" he asked puzzledly.

Kettrich and Lorring had both been fascinated by this world, too—willing to devote years to it.

"Well, we can still radio Port Laribee," Lorring chuckled. "But in any case we're stuck here for a long time. Meanwhile, there's food growing wild around us. There's water. There are tools, machines, and supplies to puzzle out. And a valley to reclaim as a start. Beyond that, the job gets bigger and more interesting."

Before sunset that day, Joe and Doran Dayton walked alone in the valley. The Earth-star was already silvery in the dark blue west. The hills were dun-hued and peaceful. The domes of the Mars-ants gleamed. Fantastic spring flowers wavered in the wind. Small dust-whirls stirred among the ruins.

Joe Dayton looked forward, gladly now, to the birth of his child on the Red Planet.

"I hope that the Neo-Martians won't become so separate that they'll forget to be friends with Terrans," Doran mused.

Joe nodded as his arm crept around her waist. To him legendary history and present fact had merged. The wind's rustle was no longer the whisper of the dead past.

Quest of Thig

Basil Wells

Thig of Ortha was the vanguard of the conquering "Horde." He had blasted across trackless space to subdue a defenseless world —only to meet on Earth emotions that were more deadly than weapons.

Thig carefully smoothed the dark sand and seaweed of the lonely beach over the metal lid of the flexible ringed tunnel that linked the grubby ship from another planet with the upper air. He looked out across the heaving waters of the Sound toward Connecticut. He stared appraisingly around at the luxuriant green growth of foliage further inland and started toward the little stretch of trees and brush, walking carefully because of the lesser gravitation.

Thig was shorter than the average Earthman— although on Ortha he was well above the average in height—but his body was thick and powerfully muscled. His skull was well-shaped and large; his features were regular, perhaps a trifle oversize, and his hair and eyes were a curiously matching blend of reddish brown. Oddest of all, he wore no garments, other than the necessary belt and straps to support his rod-like weapon of white metal and his pouches for food and specimens.

The Orthan entered the narrow strip of trees and crossed to the little-used highway on the other side. Here he patiently sat down to wait for an Earthman or an Earthwoman to pass. His task now was to bring a native, intact if possible, back to the carefully buried space cruiser where his two fellows and himself would drain the creature's mentality of all its knowledge. In this way they could learn whether a planet was suited for colonization by later swarms of Orthans.

Already they had charted over a hundred celestial bodies but of them all only three had proven worthy of consideration. This latest planet, however, 72-P-3 on the chart, appeared to be an ideal world in every respect. Sunlight, plenty of water, and a dense atmospheric envelope made of 72-P-3 a paradise among planets.

The explorer from another world crouched into the concealment of a leafy shrub. A creature was approaching. Its squat body was covered with baggy strips of bluish cloth and it carried a jointed rod of metal and wood in its paw. It walked upright as did the men of Ortha.

Thig's cold eyes opened a trifle wider as he stared into the thing's stupid face. It was as though he was looking into a bit of polished metal at the reflection of himself!

The Earthman was opposite now and he must waste no more precious time. The mighty muscles of the Orthan sent him hurtling across the intervening space in two prodigious bounds, and his hands clamped across the mouth and neck of the stranger. . . .

Lewis Terry had been going fishing. For a week the typewriter mill that had ground out a thousand assorted yarns of the untamed West and the frigid desolation of the Northwoods had been silent. Lewis wondered if he was going stale. He had sat every day for eight hours in front of that shiny-buttoned bane of the typist, but there were no results. Feebly he had punched a key two days ago and a $ sign had appeared. He hadn't dared touch the machine since.

For Mr. Terry, that hard-hitting writer of two-gun action, had never been further west of Long Island than Elizabeth, and he had promised his wife, Ellen, that he would take the three children and herself on a trailer tour of the *West* that very summer. Since that promise, he could not write a word. Visions of whooping red-skinned Apaches and be-chapped outlaws raiding his little trailer home kept rolling up out of his subconscious. Yet he *had* to write at least three novelettes and a fistful of short stories in the next two weeks to finance the great adventure—or the trip was off.

So Lewis had left the weathered old cottage in the early dawn and headed for his tubby old boat at the landing in an attempt to work out a salable yarn. . . .

"Hey!" he shouted as a naked man sprang out of the bushes beside the road. "What's the trouble?"

Then he had no time for further speech; the massive arms of the stranger had wound around him and two hamlike hands shut off his speech and his wind. He fought futilely against trained muscles. The hand clamping his throat relaxed for a moment and hacked along the side of his head. Blackness flooded the brain of Lewis, and he knew no more.

"There it is," announced Thig, dropping the limp body of the captured Earthman to the metal deckplates. "It is a male of the species that must have built the cities we saw as we landed."

"He resembles Thig," announced Kam. "But for the strange covering he wears he might be Thig."

"Thig will be this creature!" announced Torp. "With a psychic relay we will transfer the Earthman's memories and meager store of knowledge to the brain of Thig! He can then go out and scout this world without arousing suspicion. While he is gone, I will take Kam and explore the two inner planets."

"You are the commander," said Thig. "But I wish this beast did not wear this clumsy sheathing upon his body. On Ortha we do not hamper the use of our limbs so."

"Do not question the word of your commander," growled Torp, swelling out his thick chest menacingly. "It is for the good of our people that you disguise yourself as an Earthman."

"For the good of the Horde," Thig intoned almost

piously as he lifted Terry's body and headed for the laboratory.

Service for the Horde was all that the men of Ortha knew. Carefully cultured and brought to life in the laboratories of their Horde, they knew neither father nor mother. Affection and love were entirely lacking in their early training and later life. They were trained antlike from childhood that only the growth and power of the Horde were of any moment. Men and women alike toiled and died like unfeeling robots of flesh and bone for the Horde. The Horde was their religion, their love-life, their everything!

So it was that the bodies of the Earthman and the Orthan were strapped on two parallel tables of chill metal and the twin helmets, linked to one another by the intricacies of the psychic relay, put upon their heads.

For ten hours or more the droning hum of the relay sucked Terry's brain dry of knowledge. The shock upon the nervous system of the Earthman proved too violent and his heart faltered after a time and stopped completely. Twice, with subtle drugs, they restored pseudo-life to his body and kept the electrical impulses throbbing from his tortured brain, but after the third suspension of life Thig removed his helmet.

"There is nothing more to learn," he informed his impassive comrades. "Now let us get on with the plastic surgery that is required. My new body must return to its barbaric household before undue attention is aroused. And when I return I will take along some of the gleaming baubles we found on the red planet—these people value them highly."

An hour later, his scars and altered cartilage already healed and painless, Thig again scraped sand over the entrance to the spaceship and set out along the moonlit beach toward the nearest path running inland to his home.

Memory was laying the country bare about him, Terry's own childhood memories of this particular section of Long Island. Here was the place where Jake and Ted had helped him dig for the buried treasure that old 'Notch-ear' Beggs had told them so exactly about. Remembrance of that episode gave Thig an idea about the little lump of jewels in his pocket. He had found them in a chest along the beach!

He was coming up on the porch now and at the sound of his foot on the sagging boards the screen door burst open and three little Earth-creatures were hugging at his legs. An odd sensation, that his acquired memories labeled as pleasure, sent a warm glow upward from around his heart.

Then he saw the slender red-haired shape of a woman, the mate of the dead man, he knew; and confusion struck his well-trained brain. Men had no mates on Ortha—sex had been overthrown with all the other primitive impulses of barbarism—so he was incapable of understanding the emotions that swept through his acquired memory.

Unsteadily he took her in his arms and felt her warm lips pressed, trembling, against his own. That same hot wave of pulsing blood choked achingly up into his throat.

"Lew, dear," Ellen was asking, "where have you been all day? I called up at the landing but you were not there. I wanted to let you know that Saddlebag Publications sent a check for $50 for "Reversed Revolvers" and three other editors asked for shorts soon."

"Shoulda got a hundred bucks for that yarn," grunted Thig, and gasped.

For the moment he had been Lewis Terry and not Thig! So thoroughly had he acquired the knowledge of Terry that he found himself unconsciously adopting the thinking and mannerism of the other. All the better this way, he realized—more natural.

"Sorry I was late," he said, digging into his pocket for the glittering baubles, "but I was poking around on the beach where we used to hunt treasure and I found an old chest. Inside it I found nothing but a handful of these."

He flashed the jewels in front of Ellen's startled eyes and she clung, unbelieving, to his arm.

"Why, Lew," she gasped, "they're worth a fortune! We can buy that new trailer now and have a rebuilt

motor in the car. We can go west right away. . . .
Hollywood, the Grand Canyon, cowboys!"

"Uh huh," agreed the pseudo-Lewis, memories of
the ferocious savages and gunmen of his stories ren-
dering him acutely unhappy. Sincerely he hoped that
the west had reformed.

"I saved some kraut and weiners," Ellen said. "Get
washed up while I'm warming them up. Kids ate all
the bread so I had to borrow some from the Eskoes.
Want coffee, too?"

"Mmmmmm," came from the depths of the chipped
white wash-basin.

"Home again," whispered Ellen as she stood beside
Thig twelve weeks later and gazed tearfully at the
weathered little gray house. She knelt beside the front
stoop and reached for the key hidden beneath it.

"The west was wonderful—tremendous, vast and
beautiful," she went on as they climbed the steps, "but
nowhere was there any place as beautiful as our own
little strip of sky and water."

Thig sank into a dusty old swing that hung on
creaking chains from the exposed rafters of the porch
roof. He looked down at the dusty gray car and the
bulbous silvery bulk of the trailer that had been their
living quarters for almost three months. Strange
thoughts were afloat in the chaos of his cool Orthan
brain.

Tonight or tomorrow night at the latest he must
contact his two fellows and report that Earth was a
planetary paradise. No other world, including Ortha,
was so well-favored and rich. An expeditionary force
to wipe the grotesque civilizations of Earth out of
existence would, of course, be necessary before the
first units of new Hordes could be landed. And there
Thig balked. Why must they destroy these people,
imperfect though their civilization might be, to make
room for the Hordes?

Thig tried to tell himself that it was the transmitted
thoughts of the dead Earthman that made him feel
so, but he was not too sure. For three months he had
lived with people who loved, hated, wept, and sac-

rificed for reasons that he had never known existed. He had learned the heady glory of thinking for himself and making his own decisions. He had experienced the primitive joy of matching his wits and tongue against the wits of other unpredictable human beings. There was no abrupt division of men and women into definite classes of endeavor. A laborer thought the same thoughts that a governor might think. Uncertainty added zest to every day's life.

The Orthan had come to question the sole devotion of the individual to the Horde to the exclusion of all other interests. What, he wondered, would one new world—or a hundred—populated by the Hordes add to the progress of humanity? For a hundred thousand years the Orthan civilization had remained static, its energies directed into certain well-defined channels. They were mindless bees maintaining their vast mechanical hives.

There was that moment on the brink of the Grand Canyon when Ellen had caught his arm breathlessly at all the beauty spread away there beneath them. There were mornings in the desert when the sun painted in lurid red the peaks above the harsh black-and-whites of the sagebrush and cactus slopes. There was the little boy, his body burning with fever, who nestled trustingly against his tense man's body and slept—the son of Ellen and the man he had destroyed.

Thig groaned. He was a weakling to let sentimentality so get the better of his judgment. He would go now to the spaceship and urge them to blast off for Ortha. He sprang off the porch and strode away down the road toard the beach.

The children ran to him, wanted to go along. He sent them away harshly, but they smiled and waved their brown little hands. Ellen came to the door and called after him.

"Hurry home, dear," she said. "I'll have a bite ready in about an hour."

He dared not say anything, for his voice would have broken and she would have known something was wrong. She was a very wise sort of person when something was troubling him. He saved his stubby paw of a hand to show that he had heard, and blindly hurried toward the Sound.

Oddly enough, as he hurried away along the narrow path through the autumn woods, his mind busied itself with a new epic of the west that lived no longer. He mentally titled it "Rustlers' Riot" and blocked in the outlines of his plot. One section of his brain was that of the careless author of gunslinging yarns, a section that seemed to be sapping the life from his own brain. He knew that the story would never be written, but he toyed with the idea.

So far had Thig, the emotionless robot-being from Ortha, drifted from the unquestioning worship of the Horde!

"You have done well," announced Torp when Thig had completed his report on the resources and temperatures of various sections of Terra. "We now have located three worlds fit for colonization and so we will return to Ortha at once.

"I will recommend the conquest of this planet, 72-P-3 at once and the complete destruction of all biped life upon it. The mental aberrations of the barbaric natives might lead to endless complications if they were permitted to exist outside our ordered way of life. I imagine that three circuits of the planet about its primary should prove sufficient for the purposes of complete liquidation."

"But why," asked Thig slowly, "could we not disarm all the natives and exile them on one of the less desirable continents—Antarctica, for example, or Siberia? They are primitive humans even as our race was once a race of primitives. Is it not our duty to help them to attain our own degree of knowledge and comfort?"

"Only the good of the Horde matters!" shouted Torp angrily. "Shall a race of feeble-witted beasts, such as these Earthmen, stand in the way of a superior race? We want their world, and so we will take it. The Law of the Horde states that all the universe is ours for the taking."

"Let us get back to Ortha at once then," gritted

out Thig savagely. "Never again do I wish to set foot upon the soil of this mad planet. There are forces at work upon Earth that we of Ortha have long forgotten."

"Check the blood of Thig for disease, Kam," ordered Torp shortly. "His words are highly irrational. Some form of fever perhaps native to this world. While you examine him I will blast off for Ortha."

Thig followed Kam into the tiny laboratory and found a seat beside the squat scientist's desk. His eyes roamed over the familiar instruments and gauges, each in its own precise position in the cases along the walls. His gaze lingered longest on the stubby black ugliness of a decomposition blaster in its rack close to the deck. A blast of the invisible radiations from that weapon's hot throat and flesh or vegetable fiber rotted into flaky ashes.

The ship trembled beneath their feet; it tore free from the feeble clutch of the sand about it, and they were rocketing skyward. Thig's broad fingers bit deep into the unyielding metal of his chair. Suddenly he knew that he must go back to Earth, back to Ellen and the children of the man he had helped destroy. He loved Ellen, and nothing must stand between them! The Hordes of Ortha must find some other world, an empty world—this planet was not for them.

"Turn back!" he cried wildly. "I must go back to Earth. There is a woman there, helpless and alone, who needs me! The Horde does not need this planet."

Kam eyed him coldly and lifted a shining hypodermic syringe from its case. He approached Thig warily, aware that disease often made a maniac of the finest members of the Horde.

"No human being is more important than the Horde," he stated baldly. "This woman of whom you speak is merely one unit of the millions we must eliminate for the good of the Horde."

Then it was that Thig went berserk. His fists slashed into the thick jaw of the scientist and his fingers ripped at the hard cords overlying the Orthan's vital throat tubes. His fingers and thumb gouged deep into Kam's startled throat and choked off any cry for assistance before it could be uttered.

Kam's hand swept down to the holster swung from his intricate harness and dragged his blaster from it. Thig's other hand clamped over his and for long moments they swayed there, locked together in silent deadly struggle. The fate of a world hung in the balance as Kam's other hand fought against that lone arm of Thig.

The scales swung in favor of Kam. Slowly the flaring snout of his weapon tilted upward until it reached the level of Thig's waist. Thig suddenly released his grip and dragged his enemy toward him. A sudden reversal of pressure on Kam's gun hand sent the weapon swivelling about full upon its owner's thick torso. Thig's fingers pressed down upon Kam's button finger, down upon the stud set into the grip of the decomposition blaster, and Kam's muscles turned to water. He shrieked.

Before Thig's eyes half of his comrade's body sloughed away into foul corruption that swiftly gave way to hardened blobs of dessicated matter. Horror for what he had done—that he had slain one of his own Horde—made his limbs move woodenly. All of his thoughts were dulled for the moment. Painfully slow, he turned his body around toward the control blister, turned around on leaden feet, to look full into the narrowed icy eyes of his commander.

He saw the heavy barrel of the blaster slashing down against his skull but he could not swing a fraction of an inch out of the way. His body seemed paralyzed. This was the end, he thought as he waited stupidly for the blow to fall, the end for Ellen and the kids and all the struggling races of Earth. He would never write another cowboy yarn—they would all be dead anyhow soon.

Then a thunderclap exploded against his head and he dropped endlessly toward the deck. Blows rained against his skull. He wondered if Torp would ever cease to hammer at him and turn the deadly ray of the weapon upon him. Blood throbbed and pounded with every blow. . . .

The blood pounded in his ears. Like repeated blows of a hammer they shook his booming head. No longer was Torp above him. He was in the corner of the laboratory, a crumpled blood-smeared heap of bruised flesh and bone. He was unfettered and the blood was caked upon his skull and in his matted hair. Torp must have thought he had killed him with those savage blows upon the head.

Even Torp gave way to the primitive rage of his ancestors at times; but to that very bit of unconscious atavism he now owed his life. A cool-headed robot of an Orthan would have efficiently used the blaster to destroy any possibility of remaining life in his unconscious body.

Thig rolled slowly over so that his eye found the door into the control room. Torp would be coming back again to dispose of their bodies through the refuse lock. Already the body of Kam was gone. He wondered why he had been left until last. Perhaps Torp wished to take cultures of his blood and tissues to determine whether a disease was responsible for his sudden madness.

The cases of fragile instruments were just above his head. Association of memories brought him the flash of the heavy blaster in its rack beneath them. His hand went up and felt the welcome hardness of the weapon. He tugged it free.

In a moment he was on his knees crawling across the plates of the deck toward the door. Halfway across the floor he collapsed on his face, the metal of the gun making a harsh clang. He heard Torp scuffle out of silence, and a choked cry in the man's throat squalled out into a senseless whinny.

Thig raised himself up on a quivering elbow and slid the black length of the blaster in front of him. His eyes sought the doorway and stared full into the glaring vacant orbs of his commander. Torp leaned there watching him, his breath gurgling brokenly through his deep-bitten lips. The clawing marks of nails, fingernails, furrowed his face and chest. He was a madman!

The deadly attack of Thig, his own violent avenging

of Kam's death, and now the apparent return to life
of the man he had killed had all served to jolt his
rigidly trained brain from its accustomed groove. The
shock had been too much for the established thought-
processes of the Orthan.

So Thig shot him where he stood, mercifully, before
that vacant mad stare set him to gibbering and
shrieking. Then he stepped over the skelton-thing that
had been Torp, using the new strength that victory
had given him to drive him along.

He had saved a world's civilization from extinction!
The thought sobered him; yet, somehow, he was
pleased that he had done so. After all, it had been
the Earthwoman and the children he had been thinking
of while he battled Kam, a selfish desire to protect
them all.

He went to the desk where Torp had been writing
in the ship's log and read the last few nervously
scrawled lines:

*Planet 72-P-3 unfit for colonization. Some perni-
cious disease that strikes at the brain centers and
causes violent insanity is existent there. Thig, just returned from a survey of the planet, went mad and
destroyed Kam. In turn I was forced to slay him. But
it is not ended. Already I feel the insidious virus
of. . . .*

And there his writing ended abruptly.

Thig nodded. That would do it. He set the automatic
pilot for the planet Ortha. Unless a rogue asteroid or
a comet crossed the ship's path she would return safely
to Ortha with that mute warning of danger on 72-P-3.
The body of Torp would help to confirm his final
message.

Then Thig crossed the cabin to the auxiliary life
boat there, one of a half-dozen spaceships in miniature
nested within the great ship's hull, and cut free from
the mother vessel.

He flipped the drive lever, felt the thrumming of
the rockets driving him from the parent ship. The
sensation of free flight against his new body was
strangely exhilarating and heady. It was the newest of
the emotions he had experienced on Earth since that

day, so many months before, when he had felt the warmness of Ellen's lips tight against his.

He swung about to the port, watched the flaming drive-rockets of the great exploratory ship hurl it toward far-away Ortha, and there was no regret in his mind that he was not returning to the planet of his first existence.

He thought of the dull greys and blacks of his planet, of the monotonous routine of existence that had once been his—and his heart thrilled to the memories of the starry night and perfect exciting day he had spent on his three-month trip over Earth.

He made a brief salute to the existence he had known, turned with a tiny sigh, and his fingers made brief adjustments in the controls. The rocket-thrum deepened, and the thin whistle of tenuous air clutching the ship echoed through the hull-plates.

He thought of many things in those few moments. He watched the roundness of Earth flatten out, then take on the cup-like illusion that all planets had for an incoming ship. He reduced the drive of his rockets to a mere whisper, striving to control the impatience that crowded his mind.

He shivered suddenly, remembering his utter callousness the first time he had sent a spaceship whipping down toward the hills and valleys below. And there was a sickness within him when he fully realized that, despite his acquired memory and traits, he was an alien from outer space.

He fingered the tiny scars that had completely obliterated the slight differences in his appearance from an Earthman's, and his fingers trembled a bit as he bent and stared through the vision port. He said a brief prayer in his heart to a God whose presence he now felt very deeply. There were tears in the depths of his eyes then, and memories were hot, bitter pains.

Earth was not far below him. As he let gravity suck him earthward, he heaved a gasp of relief. He was no longer Thig, a creature of a Horde's creation, but Lewis Terry, writer of lurid gun-smoking tales of the West. He must remember that always. He had destroyed the real Terry and now, for the rest of his life, he must make it up to the dead man's family.

The knowledge that Ellen's love was not really meant for him would be a knife twisting in his heart, but for her sake he must endure it. Her dreams and happiness must never be shattered.

The bulge of Earth was flattening out now, and he could see the outlines of Long Island in the growing twilight.

A new plot was growing in the brain of Lewis Terry, a yarn about a cowboy suddenly transported to another world. He smiled ironically. He had seen those other worlds. Perhaps some day he would write about them. . . .

He was Lewis Terry! He must remember that!

The Rocketeers Have Shaggy Ears

Keith Bennett

Some day there will be legend like this. Some day, from steamy Venus or arid Mars, the shaking, awe-struck words will come whispering back to us, building the picture of a glory so great that our throats will choke with pride—pride in the Men of Terra!

I

The Commander's voice went droning on, but Hague's fatigued brain registered it as mere sound with no words or meaning. He'd been dazed since the crash. Like a cracked phonograph, his brain kept playing back the ripping roar of jet chambers blowing out with a sickening lurch that had thrown every man in the control room to the floor. The lights had flickered out, and a sickening elevator glide began as Patrol Rocket One smashed down through the Venusian rainforest roof, and crashed in a clearing blasted by its own hurtling passage.

Hague blinked hard and tried to focus his brain on what hard-faced Commander Devlin was saying, something about the Base and Odysseus, the mother ship.

"We've five hundred miles before we'll be in their

vicinity, and every yard of it we walk. Hunting parties will shoot food animals. All water is to be boiled and treated with ultra-violet by my section. The photographers will march with the science section, which will continue classifying and writing reports. No actual specimens will be taken. We can't afford the weight."

To Hague, the other five men seated around the little charting table appeared cool, confidently ready to march through five hundred, or a thousand miles of dark, unexplored, steaming Hell that is Venusian rainforest. Their faces tight-set, icily calm, they nodded in turn as the Commander looked at each one of them; but Hague wondered if his own face wasn't betraying the fear lurking within him. Suddenly Commander Devlin grinned, and pulled a brandy bottle from his pocket, uncorking it as he spoke: "Well, Rocketeers, a short life and a merry one. I never did give a damn for riding in these tin cans." The tension broke, they were all smiling, and saying they'd walk into the base camp with some kind of a Venusian female under each arm for the edification of Officers' Mess.

Leaden doubt of his own untried abilities and nerve lay icy in Hague's innards, and he left after one drink. The others streamed from the brightly lighted hatch a moment later. The Commander made a short speech to the entire party. Then Navigator Clark, a smiling, wiry little man, marched out of the clearing with his advance guard. Their voices muffled suddenly as they vanished down a forest corridor that lay gloomy between giant tree holes.

Commander Devlin slapped Hague cheerfully on the shoulder as he moved past; and the second section, spruce and trim in blue-black uniforms, with silver piping, followed him. Crewmen Didrickson and Davis followed with rifles and sagging bandoliers of explosive bullets crossing their chests, and then Arndt, the lean craggy geologist, his arm in a sling; and marching beside him was rotund, begoggled Gault, the botanist. The little whippet tank clattered by next with Technician Whittaker grinning down at Hague from the turret.

"It pains me somethin' awful to see you walkin'

when I'm ridin'," Whittaker piped over the whippet's clanking growl.

Hague grinned back, then pinched his nose between two fingers in the ageless dumb show of disgust, pointed at the tank, and shook his head sadly. The two carts the whippet towed swayed by, and the rest of the column followed. First Bachmann, the doctor, and Sewell, his beefy crotchety assistant. The two photographers staggered past under high-piled equipment packs, and Hague wondered how long they would keep all of it. Lenkranz, Johnston, Harker, Szachek, Hirooka, Ellis—each carried a pack full of equipment. The rest filed by until finally Swenson, the big Swede technician, passed and the clearing was empty.

Hague turned to look over his own party. In his mind's eyes bobbed the neatly typed "Equipment, march order, light field artillery" lists he'd memorized along with what seemed a thousand other neatly typed lists at Gunnery School.

The list faded, and Hague watched his five-man gun-section lounge against their rifles, leaning slightly forward to ease the heavy webbing that supported their marching packs and the sectioned pneumatic gun.

"All right," Hague said brusquely. He dredged his brain desperately then for an encouraging speech, something that would show the crew he liked them, something the Commander might say, but he couldn't think of anything that sounded witty or rang with stirring words. He finally muttered a disgusted curse at his own blankheadedness, and said harshly, "All right, let's go."

The six men filed silently out of the clearing battered in the forest by Patrol Rocket One, and into damp gloom between gargantuan trunks that rose smoothly out of sight into darkness. Behind them a little rat-like animal scurried into the deserted slot of blasted trees, its beady black eyes studying curiously the silver ship that lay smashed and half-buried in the forest floor.

Base Commander Chapman shuffled hopelessly through the thick sheaf of onion-skin papers, and sank back sighing. Ammunition reports, supply reports, medical reports, strength reports, reconnaissance reports, radio logs, radar logs, sonar logs, bulging dossiers of reports, files full of them, were there; and elsewhere in the ship efficient clerks were rapping out fresh, crisp battalions of new reports, neatly typed in triplicate on onion-skin paper.

He stared across his crowded desk at the quiet executive officer.

"Yes, Blake, it's a good picture of local conditions, but it isn't exploration. Until the Patrol Rocket gets in, we can send only this local stuff, and it just isn't enough."

Blake shrugged.

"It's all we've got. We can send parties out on foot from the base here, even if we do lose men, but the dope they'd get would still be on a localized area."

The Commander left his desk, and stared through a viewport at the plateau, and beyond that at the jungled belt fringing an endless expanse of rainforest lying sullenly quiet under the roof of racing grey clouds.

"The point is we've got to have more extensive material than this when we fire our robot-courier back to earth. This wonderful mountain of papers—what do they do, what do they tell? They describe beautifully the physical condition of this Base and its complement. They describe very well a ten mile area around the Base—but beyond that area they tell nothing. It's wonderful as far as it goes, but it only goes ten miles, and that isn't enough."

Blake eyed the snowy pile of papers abstractedly. Then he jumped up nervously as another bundle shot into a receiving tray from the pheumatic message tube. He began pacing the floor.

"Well, what can we do? Suppose we send the stuff we have here, get it microfilmed and get it off—what then?"

The Commander swore bitterly, and turned to face his executive.

"What then?" he demanded savagely. "Are we going into that again? Why, the minute every other branch of the services realize that we haven't got any kind of thorough preliminary report on this section of Venus, they'll start pounding the war drums. The battleship admirals and the bayonet generals will get to work and stir up enough public opinion to have the United States Rocket Service absorbed by other branches—the old, old game of military politics."

Blake nodded jerkily. "Yes, I know. We'd get the leftovers after the battleships had been built, or new infantry regiments activated, or something else. Anyway we wouldn't get enough money to carry on rocket research for space explorations."

"Exactly," the Commander cut in harshly. "These rockets would be grounded on earth. The generals or admirals would swear that the international situation demanded that they be kept there as weapons of defense and that would be the end of our work."

"We've got to send back a good, thorough report, something to prove that the Rocket Service can do the job, and that it is worth the doing. And, until the patrol rocket gets back, we can't do it."

"Okay, Commander," Blake called as he went through the steel passage opening onto the mother ship's upper corridor, "I'll be holding the Courier Rocket until we get word."

Seven hours later it lightened a little, and day had come. Hague and the Sergeant had pulled the early morning guard shift, and began rolling the other four from their tiny individual tents.

Bormann staggered erect, yawned lustily, and swore that this was worse than spring maneuvers in Carolina.

"Shake it," Brian snarled savagely. "That whistle will blow in a minute."

When it did sound, they buckled each other into pack harness and swung off smartly, but groaning and muttering as the mud dragged at their heavy boots.

At midday, four hours later, there was no halt, and they marched steadily forward through steaming veils of oppressive heat, eating compressed rations as they walked. They splashed through a tiny creek that was solidly slimed, and hurried ahead when crawling things

wriggled in the green mass. Perspiration ran in streams
from each face filing past on the trail, soaked through
pack harness and packs; and wiry Hurd began to
complain that his pack straps had cut through his
shoulders as far as his navel. They stopped for a five
minute break at 1400, when Hurd stopped fussing
with his back straps and signalled for silence, though
the other five had been too wrapped in their own
discomfort to be talking.

"Listen! Do you hear it, Lieutenant? Like a horn?"
Hurd's wizened rat face knotted in concentration.
"Way off, like."

Hague listened blankly a moment, attempted an expression he fondly hoped was at once intelligent and
reassuring, then said, "I don't hear anything. You may
have taken too much fever dope, and it's causing a
ringing in your ears."

"Naw," with heavy disgust. "Listen! There it goes
again!"

"I heard it." That was Sergeant Brian's voice, hard
and incisive, and Hague wished he sounded like that,
or that he would have heard the sound before his second in command. All of the six were hunched forward, listening raptly, when the Lieutenant stood up.

"Yes, Hurd. Now I hear it."

The whistle blew then, and they moved forward.
Hague noticed the Sergeant had taken a post at the
rear of the little file, and watched their back trail warily
as the marched.

"What do you think it was, sir?" Bucci inquired
in the piping voice that sounded strange coming from
his deep chest.

"The Lord knows," Hague answered, and wondered how many times he'd be using that phrase in the
days to come. "Might have been some animal. They
hadn't found any traces of intelligent life when we left
the Base Camp."

But in the days that followed there was a new air
of expectancy in the marchers, as if their suspicions
had solidified into a waiting for attack. They'd been
moving forward for several days.

Hague saw the pack before any of his men did, and

thanked his guiding star that for once he had been a little more alert than his gun-section members.

The canvas carrier had been set neatly against one of the buttressing roots of a giant tree bole, and, from the collecting bottles strapped in efficient rows outside, Hague deduced that it belonged to Bernstein, the entomologist. The gunnery officer halted and peered back into the gloom off the trail, called Bernstein's name, and when there was no reply moved cautiously into the hushed shadows with his carbine ready. He sensed that Sergeant Brian was catfooting behind him.

Then he saw the ghostly white bundle suspended six feet above the forest floor, and moved closer, calling Bernstein's name softly. The dim bundle vibrated gently, and Hague saw that it hung from a giant white lattice radiating wheel-like from the green gloom above. He raised his hand to touch the cocoon thing, noted it was shaped like a man well-wrapped in some woolly material, and on a sudden hunch pulled his belt knife and cut the fibers from what would be the head.

It was Bernstein suspended there, his snug, silken shroud bobbing gently in the dimness. His dark face was pallid in the gloom, sunken and flaccid of feature, as though the juices had been sucked from his corpse, leaving it a limp mummy.

The lattice's sticky white strands vibrated—something moved across it overhead, and Hague flashed his lightpak up into the darkness. Crouched twenty feet above him, two giant legs delicately testing the strands of its lattice-like web, Hague saw the spider, its bulbous furred body fully four feet across, the monster's myriad eyes glittering fire-like in the glow of Hague's lightpak, as it gathered the great legs slightly in the manner of a tarantula ready to leap.

Brian's sharp yell broke Hague from his frozen trance. He threw himself down as Brian's rifle crashed, and the giant arachnid was bathed in a blue-white flash of explosive light, its body tumbling down across the web onto Hague where he lay in the mud. The officer's hoarse yells rang insanely while he pulled himself clear of the dead spider-beast, but he forced himself to quiet at the sound of the Sergeant's cool voice.

"All clear, Lieutenant. It's dead."

"Okay, Brian. I'll be all right now." Hague's voice shook, and he cursed the weakness of his fear, forcing himself to walk calmly without a glance over his shoulder until they were back on the trail. He led the other four gunners back to the spider and Bernstein's body, and as a grim object lesson, warned them to leave the trail only in pairs. They returned their weary footslogging pace down the muddy creek marked by Clark's crew. When miles had sweated by at the same steady pace, Hague could still feel in the men's stiff silence their horror of the thing Brian had killed.

Hours, and then days, rolled past, drudging nightmares through which they plowed in mud and steamy heat, with punctually once every sixteen hours a breathtaking, pounding torrent of rain. Giant drops turned the air into an aqueous mixture that was almost unbreathable, and smashed against their faces until the skin was numb. When the rain stopped abruptly the heat came back and water vapor rose steaming from the mud they walked through; but always they walked, shoving one aching foot ahead of the other through sucking black glue. Sometimes Bormann's harmonica would wheedle reedy airs, and they would sing and talk for a time, but mostly they swung forward in silence, faces drawn with fatigue and pale in the forest half light. Hague looked down at his hands, swollen, bloody with insect bites, and painfully stiff; and wondered if he'd be able to bend them round his ration pan at the evening halt.

Hague was somnambulating at the rear of his little column, listening to an ardent account from Bormann of what his girl might expect when he saw her again. Bucci, slowing occasionally to ease the pneumatic gun's barrel assembly across his shoulder, chimed in with an ecstatic description of his little Wilma. The two had been married just before the Expedition blasted Venusward out of an Arizona desert. Crosse was at the front end, and his voice came back nasally.

"Hey, Lieutenant, there's somebody sitting beside the trail."

"Okay. Halt." The Lieutenant swore tiredly and trotted up to Crosse's side. "Where?"

"There. Against the big root."

Hague moved forward, carbine at ready, and knew without looking that Sergeant Brian was at his shoulder, cool and self-sufficient as always.

"Who's there?" the officer croaked.

"It's me, Bachmann."

Hague motioned his party forward, and they gathered in a small circle about the Doctor, seated calmly beside the trail, with his back against a root flange.

"What's the matter, Doc? Did you want to see us?"

"No. Sewell seems to think you're all healthy. Too bad the main party isn't as well off. Quite a bit of trouble with fever. And, Bernstein gone, of course."

Hague nodded, and remembered he'd reported before.

"How's the Commander?" he inquired.

The Doctor's cherubic face darkened. "Not good. He's not a young man, and this heat and walking are wrecking his heart. And he won't ride the tank."

"Well, let's go, Doc." It was Brian's voice, cutting like a knife into Hague's consciousness. The Doctor looked tired and drawn.

"Go ahead, lads. I'm just going to sit here for a while." He looked up and smiled weakly at the astonished faces, but his eyes were bleakly determined.

"This is as far as I go. Snake bite. We've no anti-venom that seems to work. All they can do is to amputate, and we can't afford another sick man." He pulled a nylon wrapper from one leg that sprawled at an awkward angle beneath him. The bared flesh was black, swollen, and had a gangrenous smell. Young Crosse turned away, and Hague heard his retching.

"What did the Commander say?"

"He agreed this was best. I am going to die anyway."

"Will—will you be all right here? Don't you want us to wait with you?"

The Doctor's smile was weaker, and he mopped at the rivulets of perspiration streaking his mud-spattered face.

"No. I have an X-lethal dosage and a hypodermic. I'll be fine here. Sewell knows what to do." His round face contorted, "Now, for God's sake, get on, and let me take that tablet. The pain is driving me crazy."

Hague gave a curt order, and they got under way. A little further on the trail, he turned to wave at Doctor Bachmann, but the little man was already invisible in forest shadows.

The tenth day after the crash of Patrol Rocket One, unofficially known as the Ration Can, glimpses of skylight opened over the trail Clark's crew were marking; and Hague and his men found themselves suddenly in an opening where low, thick vines and luxuriant, thick-leaved shrubs struggled viciously for life. Balistierri, the zoologist, slight, p of a dark man always and almost a shadow now, stood wearily beside the trail waiting as they drew up. Their shade-blinded eyes picked out details in the open ground dimly. Hague groaned inwardly when he saw that this was a mere slit in the forest, and the great trees loomed again a hundred yards ahead. Balistierri seized Hague by the shoulder and pointed into the thick mat of green, smiling.

"Watch, all of you."

He blew a shrill blast on his whistle and waited, while Hague's gunners wondered and watched. There was a wild, silvery call, a threshing of wings, and two huge birds rose into the gold-tinted air. They flapped up, locked their wings, and glided, soared, and wheeled over the earth-stained knot of men—two great white birds, with crests of fire-gold, plumage snowy save where it was dusted with rosy overtones. Their call was bell-like as they floated across the clearing in a golden haze of sunlight filtered through clouds.

"They're—they're like angels." It was Bormann, the tough young sentimentalist.

"You've named them, soldier," Balistierri grinned. "I've been trying for a name; and that's the best I've heard. Bormann's angels they'll be. In Latin, of course."

Unfolding vistas of eternal zoological glory left Bormann speechless and red-faced. Sergeant Brian broke in.

"I guess they would have made those horn sounds. Right, Lieutenant?" His voice, dry and a little patronizing, suggested that this was a poor waste of valuable marching time.

"I wouldn't know, Sergeant," Hague answered, trying to keep dislike out of his voice, but the momentary thrill was broken and, with Balistierri beside him, Gunnery Officer Hague struck out on the trail that had been blasted and hacked through the clearing's wanton extravagance of greedy plant life.

As they crossed the clearing, Bucci tripped and sprawled full length in the mud. When he tried to get up, the vine over which he'd stumbled clutched with a woody tendril that wound snakelike tightly about his ankle; and, white faced, the rest of the men chopped him free of the serpentine thing with belt knives, bandaged the thorn wounds in his leg, and went on.

The clearing had one more secret to divulge, however. A movement in the forest edge caught Brian's eye and he motioned to Hague, who followed him questioningly as the Sergeant led him off trail. Brian pointed silently and Hague saw Didrickson, Sergeant in charge of Supplies, seated in the lemon-colored sunlight at the forest edge, an open food pack between his knees, from which he snatched things and swallowed them voraciously, feeding like a wild dog.

"Didrickson! Sergeant Didrickson!" the Lieutenant yelled. "What are you doing?"

The supply man stared back, and Hague knew from the man's face what had happened. He crouched warily, eyes wild with panic and jaw hanging foolishly slack. This was Didrickson, the steady, efficient man who'd sat at the chart table the night they began this march. He had been the only man Devlin thought competent and nerveless enough to handle the food. This was the same Didrickson, and madder now than a March hare, Hague concluded grimly. The enlisted man snatched up the food pack, staring at them in wild fear, and began to run back down the trail, back the way they'd come.

"Come back, Didrickson. We've got to have that food, you fool!"

The madman laughed crazily at the sound of the officer's voice, glaced back for a moment, then spun and ran.

Sergeant Brian, as always, was ready. His rifle cracked, and the explosive missile blew the running man nearly in half. Sergeant Brian silently retrieved the food pack and brought it back to Hague.

"Do you want it here, Lieutenant, or shall I take it up to the main party?"

"We'll keep it here, Sergeant. Sewell can take it back tonight after our medical check." Hague's voice shook, and he wished savagely that he could have had the nerve to pass that swift death sentence. Didrickson's crime was dangerous to every member of the party, and the Sergeant had been right to shoot. But when the time came—when perhaps the Sergeant wasn't with him—would he, Hague, react swiftly and coolly as an officer should? He wondered despairingly.

"All right, lads, let's pull," he said, and the tight-lipped gun crew filed again into the hushed, somber forest corridors.

II

Communications Technician Harker took a deep pull at his mug of steaming coffee, blinked his eyes hard at the swimming dials before him, and lit a cigarette. Odysseus warning center was never quiet, even now in the graveyard watch when all other lights were turned low through the great ship's hull. Here in the neat grey room, murmuring, softly clicking signal equipment was banked against every wall in a gleaming array of dials and meters, heavy power leads, black panels, and intricate sheafs of colored wire. The sonar kept up a sleepy drone, and radar scoped glowed fitfully with interference patterns, and the warning buzzer beeped softly as the radar echoed back to its receivers the rumor of strange planetary forces that radar hadn't been built to filter through. What made the interference, base technicians couldn't tell, but it practically paralyzed radio communication on all bands, and blanketed out even radar warnings.

The cigarette burned his fingertips, and Harker jerked awake and tried to concentrate on the letter he was writing home. It would be microfilmed, and go on the next courier rocket. A movement at the Warnings Room door brought Harker's head up, and he saw Commander Chapman, lean and grey, standing there.

"Good evening, sir. Come on in. I've got coffee on." The Communications Technician took a pot from the glow heater at his elbow, and set out another cup.

The Commander smiled tiredly, pulled out a stubby metal stool, and sat across the low table from Harker, sipping the scalding coffee cautiously. He looked up after a moment.

"What's the good word, Harker? Picked up anything?"

Harker ran his fingers through his mop of black hair and grimaced.

"Not a squeak, sir. No radio, no radar. Of course, the interference may be blanketing those. Creates a lot of false signals, too, on the radar screens. But we can't even pick 'em up with long-range sonar. That should get through. We're pretty sure they crashed, all right."

"How about our signals, Harker? Do you think we're getting through to them?"

Harker leaned back expansively, happy to expound his specialty.

"Well, we've been sending radio signals every hour on the hour, and radio voice messages every hour on the half-hour. We're sending a continuous sonar beam for their direction-finder. That's about all we can do. As for their picking it up, assuming the rocket has crashed and been totally knocked out, they still have a radio in the whippet tank. It's a transreceiver. And they have a portable sonar set, one of those little twenty-pound armored detection units. They'll use it as a direction finder."

Chapman swirled the coffee around in the bottom of his cup and stared thoughtfully into it.

"If they can get sonar, why can't we send them messages down the sonar beam? You know, flick it on and off in Morse code?"

"It won't work with a small detector like they have, sir. With our big set here, we could send them a message, but that outfit they have might burn out. It has a limited sealed motor supply that must break down an initial current resistance on the grids before the rectifiers can convert it to audible sound. With the set operating continuously, power drainage is small, but begin changing your signal beam and the power has to break down the grid resistance several hundred times for every short signal sent. It would burn out their set in a matter of hours.

"It works like a slide trombone, sort of. Run your slide way out, and you get a slowly vibrating column of air, and that is heard as a low note, only on sonar it would be a short note. Run your slide way up, and the vibrations are progessively faster and higher in pitch. The sonar set, at peak, is vibrating so rapidly that it's almost static, and the power flow is actually continuous. But, starting and stopping the set continuously, the vibrators never have a chance to reach a normal peak, and the power flow is broken at each vibrating in the receiver—and a few hours later your sonar receptor is a hunk of junk."

"All right, Harker. Your discussion is vague, but I get the general idea that my suggestion wasn't too hot. Well, have whoever is on duty call me if any signals come through." The Commander set down his cup, said good night, and moved off down the hushed corridor. Harker returned to his letter and a chewed stub of pencil, while he scowled in a fevered agony of composition. It was a letter to his girl, and it had to be good.

Night had begun to fall over the forest roof, and stole thickening down the muddy cathedral aisles of great trees, and Hague listened hopefully for the halt signal from the whippet tank, which should come soon. He was worried about Bucci, who was laughing and talking volubly; the officer decided he must have a touch of fever. The dark, muscular gunner kept talking about his young wife in what was almost a babble. Once he staggered and nearly fell, until Hurd took the pneumatic gun-barrel assembly and carried it on his own shoulders. They were all listening expectantly for the tank's klaxon, when a brassy scream ripped the evening to echoing shreds and a flurry of shots broke out ahead.

The scream came again, metallic and shrill as a locomotive gone amok; yells, explosive-bullet reports, and the sound of hammering blows drifted back.

"Take over, Brian," Hague snapped. "Crosse, Hurd—let's go!"

The three men ran at a stagger through the dragging mud around a turn in the trail, and dropped the pneumatic gun swiftly into place—Hurd at firing position, Crosse on the charger, and Hague prone in the slime snapping an ammunition belt into the loader.

Two emergency flares someone had thrown lit the trail ahead in a garish photographic fantasy of bright, white light and ink-black shadow, a scene out of Inferno. A cart lay on its side, men were running clear, the whippet tank lay squirming on its side, and above it towered the screaming thing. A lizard, or dinosaur, rearing up thirty feet, scaly grey, a man clutched in its two hand-like claws, while its armored tail smashed and smashed at the tank with pile-driver blows. Explosive bullets cracked around the thing's chest in blue-white flares of light, but it continued to rip at the man twisting pygmy-like in its claws—white teeth glinting like sabers as its blindly malevolent screams went on.

"On target," Hurd's voice came strained and low.

"Charge on," from Crosse.

"Let her go!" Hague yelled, and fed APX cartridges as the gun coughed a burst of armor-piercing, explosive shells into the rearing beast. Hague saw the tank turret swing up as Whittaker tried to get his gun in action, but a slashing slap of the monster's tail spun it back brokenly. The cluster of pneumatic shells hit then and burst within that body, and the great grey-skinned trunk was hurled off the trail, the head slapping against a tree trunk on the other side as the reptile was halved.

"Good shooting, Crosse," Hague grunted. "Get back with Brian. Keep the gun ready. That thing might have a mate." He ran toward the main party, and into the glare of the two flares.

"Where's Devlin?"

Clark, the navigation officer, was standing with a small huddle of men near the smashed supply cart.

"Here, Hague," he called. His eyes were sunken, his face older in the days since Hague had last seen him. "Devlin's dead, smashed between the cart and a tree trunk. We've lost two men, Commander Devlin and Ellis, the soils man. He's the one it was eating." He grimaced.

"That leaves twenty-three of us?" Hague inquired, and tried to sound casual.

"That's right. You'll continue to cover the rear. Those horn sounds you reported had Devlin worried about an attack from your direction. I'll be with the tank."

Sergeant Brian was stoically heating ration stew over the cook unit when Hague returned, while the crew sat in a close circle, alternately eying nervously the forest at their backs, and the savory steam that rose from Brian's mixture. There wasn't much for each of them, but it was hot and highly nutritious, and after a cigarette and coffee they would feel comfort for a while.

Crosse, seated on the grey metal charger tube he'd carried all day, fingered the helmet in his lap, and looked inquiringly at the Lieutenant.

"Well, sir, anybody hurt? Was the tank smashed?"

Hague squatted in the circle, sniffed the stew with loud enthusiasm, and looked about the circle.

"Commander Devlin's dead, and Ellis. One supply cart smashed, but the tank'll be all right. The lizard charged the tank. Balistierri thinks it was the lizard's mating season, and he figured the tank was another male and he tried to fight it. Then he stayed—to—lunch and we got him. Lieutenant Clark is in command now."

The orange glow of Brian's cook unit painted queer shadows on the strained faces around him, and Hague tried to brighten them up.

"Will you favor us with one of your inimitable harmonica arrangements, Maestro Bormann?"

"I can't right now. I'm bandaging Helen's wing." He held out something in the palm of his hand, and the heater's glow glittered on liquid black eyes. "She's like a little bird, but without her feathers. See?" He placed the warm lump in Hague's hand. "For wings, she's just got skin, like a bat, except she's built like a bird."

"You ought to show this to Balistierri, and maybe he'll name this for you, too."

Bormann's homely face creased into a grin. "I did, sir. At the noon halt when I found it. It's named after my girl. 'Bormann's Helen', only in Latin. Helen's got a broken wing."

As they ate, they heard the horn note again. Bucci's black eyes were feverishly bright, his skin hot and dry, and the vine scratches on his leg badly inflamed; and when the rest began to sing he was quiet. The reedy song of Bormann's harmonica piped down the quiet forest passages, and echoed back from the great trees; and somewhere, as Hague dozed off in his little tent, he heard the horn note again, sandwiched into mouth organ melody.

Two days of slogging through the slimy green mud, and at noon halt Sewell brought back word to be careful, that a man had failed to report at roll call that morning. The gun crew divided Bucci's equipment between them, and he limped in the middle of the file on crutches, fashioned from ration cart wreckage. Crosse, who'd been glancing off continually, like a wizened, curious rat, flung up his arm in a silent signal to halt, and Hague moved in to investigate, the ever-present Brian moving carefully and with jungle beast's silent poise just behind him. Crumpled like a sack of damp laundry, in the murk of two root buttresses, lay Romano, one of the two photographers. His Hasselbladt camera lay beneath his body crushing a small plant he must have been photographing.

From the back of Romano's neck protruded a gleaming nine-inch arrow shaft, a lovely thing of gleaming bronze-like metal, delicately thin of shaft and with fragile hammered bronze vanes. Brian moved up behind Hague, bent over the body and cut the arrow free.

They examined the thing, and when Brian spoke Hague was surprised that this time even the rock-steady Sergeant spoke in a hushed voice, the kind boys use when they walk by a graveyard at night and don't wish to attract unwelcome attention.

"Looks like it came from a blowgun, Lieutenant. See the plug at the back. It must be poisoned; it's not big enough to kill him otherwise."

Hague grunted assent, and the two moved back trailward.

"Brian, take over. Crosse, come on. We'll report this to Clark. Remember, from now on wear your body armor and go in pairs when you leave the trail. Get Bucci's plates onto him."

Bormann and Hurd set down their loads, and were buckling the weakly protesting Bucci into his chest and back plates, as Hague left them.

Commander Chapman stared at the circle of faces. His section commanders lounged about his tiny square office. "Well, then, what are their chances?"

Bjornson, executive for the technical section, stared at Chapman levelly.

"I can vouch for Devlin. He's not precisely a rule-book officer, but that's why I recommended him for this expedition. He's at his best in an unusual situation, one where he has to depend on his own wits. He'll bring them through."

Artilleryman Branch spoke in turn. "I don't know about Hague. He's young, untried. Seemed a little unsure. He might grow panicky and be useless. I sent him because there was no one else, unless I went myself."

The Commander cleared his throat brusquely. "I know you wanted to go, Branch, but we can't send out our executive officers. Not yet, anyway. What about Clark? Could he take over Devlin's job?"

"Clark can handle it," Captain Rindell of the Science Section, was saying. "He likes to follow the rule book, but he's sturdy stuff. He'll bring them through if something happens to Devlin."

"Hmmmm—that leaves Hague as the one questionable link in their chain of command. Young man, untried. Of course, he's only the junior officer. There's no use stewing over this; but I'll tell you frankly, that if those men can't get their records through to us before we send the next courier rocket to earth, I think the U.S. Rocket Service is finished. This attempt will be chalked up as a failure. The project will be abandoned entirely, and we'll be ordered back to earth to serve as a fighter arm there."

Bjornson peered from the space-port window and looked out over the cinder-packed parade a hundred feet below. "What makes you so sure the Rocket Service is in immediate danger of being scrapped?"

"The last courier rocket contained a confidential memo from Secretary Dougherty. There is considerable war talk, and the other Service Arms are plunging for larger armaments. They want their appropriations of money and stock pile materials expanded at our expense. We've got to show that we are doing a good job, show the Government a concrete return in the form of adequate reports on the surface of Venus, and its soils and raw materials."

"What about the 'copters?" Rindell inquired. "They brought in some good stuff for the reports."

"Yes, but with a crew of only four men, they can't do enough."

Branch cut in dryly. "About all I can see is to look hopeful. The Rocket would have exhausted its fuel long ago. It's been over ten weeks since they left Base."

"Assuming they're marching overland, God forbid, they'll have only sonar and radio, right?" Bjornson was saying. "Why not keep our klaxon going? It's a pretty faint hope, but we'll have to try everything. My section is keeping the listeners manned continually, we've got a sonar beam out, radio messages every thirty minutes, and with the klaxon we're doing all we can. I doubt if anything living could approach within a twenty-five mile range without hearing that klaxon, or without us hearing them with the listeners."

"All right." Commander Chapman stared hopelessly at a fresh batch of reports burdening his desk. "Send out ground parties within the ten-mile limit, but remember we can't afford to lose men. When the 'copters' are back in, send them both West." West meant merely in a direction west from Meridian O, as the mother rocket's landing place had been designated. "They can't do much searching over that rainforest, but it's a try. They might pick up a radio message."

Chapman returned grumpily to his reports, and the others filed out.

III

At night, on guard, Hague saw a thousand horrors peopling the Stygian forest murk; but when he flashed his lightpak into darkness there was nothing. He wondered how long he could stand the waiting, when he would crack as Supply Sergeant Didrickson had, and his comrades would blast him down with explosive bullets. He should be like Brian, hard and sure, and always doing the right thing, he decided. He'd come out of OCS Gunnery School, trained briefly in the newly-formed U.S. Rocket Service. Then the expedition to Venus—it was a fifty-fifty chance they said, and out of all the volunteers he'd been picked. And when the first expedition was ready to blast off from the Base Camp on Venus, he'd been picked again. Why, he cursed despairingly? Sure, he wanted to come, but how could his commanders have had faith in him, when he didn't know himself if he could continue to hold out.

Sounds on the trail sent his carbine automatically to ready, and he called a strained, "Halt."

"Okay, Hague. It's Clark and Arndt."

The wiry little navigation officer, and lean, scraggy Geologist Arndt, the latter's arm still in a sling, came into the glow of Hague's lightpak.

"Any more horns or arrows?" Clark's voice sounded tight, and repressed; Hague reflected that perhaps the strain was getting him too.

"No, but Bucci is getting worse. Can't you carry him on the cart?"

"Hague, I've told you twenty times. That cart is full and breaking down now. Get it through your head that it's no longer individual men we can think of now, but the entire party. If they can't march, they must be left, or all of us may die!" His voice was savage, and when he tried to light a cigarette his hand shook. "All right. It's murder, and I don't like it any better than you do."

"How are we doing? What's the over-all picture?" Both of the officers tried to smile a little at the memory of that pompous little phrase, favorite of a windbag they'd served under.

"Not good. Twenty-two of us now."

"Hirooka thinks we may be within radio range of Base soon," he continued more hopefully. "With this interference, we can't tell, though."

They talked a little longer, Arndt gave the gunnery officer a food-and-medical supply packet, and Hague's visitors became two bobbing lows of light that vanished down the trail.

A soul-crushing weight of days passed while they strained forward through mud and green gloom, like men walking on a forest sea-bottom. Then it was a cool dawn, and a tugging at his boot awoke the Lieutenant. Hurd, his face a strained mask, was peering into the officer's small shelter tent and jerking at his leg.

"Get awake, Lieutenant. I think they're here."

Hague struggled hard to blink off the exhausted sleep he'd been in.

"Listen, Lieutenant, one of them horns has been blowing. It's right here. Between us and the main party."

"Okay." Hague rolled swiftly from the tent as Hurd awoke the men. Hague moved swiftly to each.

"Brian, you handle the gun. Bucci, loader. Crosse, charger. Bormann, cover our right; Hurd the left. I'll watch the trail ahead."

Brian and Crosse worked swiftly and quietly with the lethal efficiency that had made them crack gunners at Fort Fisher, North Carolina. Bucci lay motionless at the ammunition box, but his eyes were bright, and he didn't seem to mind his feverish, swollen leg. The Sergeant and Crosse slewed the pneumatic gun to cover their back trail, and fell into position beside the gleaming grey tube. Hague, Bormann and Hurd moved quickly at striking tents and rolling packs, their rifles ready at hand.

Hague had forgotten his fears and the self-doubt, the feeling that he had no business ordering men like Sergeant Brian, and Hurd and Bormann. They were swallowed in intense expectancy as he lay watching the dawn fog that obscured like thick smoke the trail that led to Clarke's party and the whippet tank.

He peered back over his shoulder for a moment. Brian, Bucci, and Crosse, mud-stained backs toward him, were checking the gun and murmuring soft comments. Bormann looked at the officer, grinned tightly, and pointed at Helen perched on his shoulder. His lips carefully framed the words, "Be a pushover, Helen brings luck."

The little bird peered up into Bormann's old-young face, and Hague, trying to grin back, hoped he looked confident. Hurd lay on the other side of the trail, his back to Bormann, peering over his rifle barrel, bearded jaws rhythmically working a cud of tobacco he'd salvaged somewhere, and Hague suddenly thought he must have been saving it for the finish.

Hague looked back into the green light beginning to penetrate the trail fog, changing it into a glowing mass—then thought he saw a movement. Up the trail, the whippet tank's motor caught with a roar, and he heard Whittaker traversing the battered tank's turret. The turret gun boomed flatly, and a shell burst somewhere in the forest darkness to Hague's right.

Then there was a gobbling yell and gray man-like figures poured out onto the trail. Hague set his sights on them, the black sight-blade silhouetting sharply in the glowing fog. He set them on a running figure and squeezed his trigger, then again, and again, as new targets came. Sharp reports ran crackling among the great trees. Sharp screams came, and a whistling sound overhead that he knew were blowgun arrows. The pneumatic gun sputtered behind him, and Bormann's and Hurd's rifles thudded in the growing roar.

Blue flashes and explosive bullets made fantastic flares back in the forest shadows; and suddenly a knot of man-shapes were running toward him through the fog. Hague picked out one in the glowing mist, fired, another, fired. Gobbling yells were around him, and he shot toward them through the fog at point-blank range. A thing rose up beside him, and Hague yelled with murderous fury, and drove his belt-knife up into grey leather skin. Something burned his shoulder as he rolled aside and fired at the dark form standing over him with a poised, barbed spear. The blue-white flash was blinding, and he cursed and leaped up.

There was nothing more. Scattered shots, and the forest lay quiet again. After that shot at point-blank range, Hague's vision had blacked out.

"Any one else need first-aid?" he called, and tried to keep his voice firm. When there was silence, he said, "Hurd, lead me to the tank."

He heard the rat-faced man choke, "My God, he's blind."

"Just flash blindness, Hurd. Only temporary." Hague kept his face stiff, and hoped frantically that he was right, that it was just temporary blindness, temporary optic shock.

Sergeant Brian's icy voice cut in. "Gun's all right, Lieutenant. Nobody hurt. We fired twenty-eight rounds of H.E. No A.P.X. Get going with him, Hurd."

He felt Hurd's tug at his elbow, and they made their way up the trail.

"What do they look like, Hurd?"

"These men-things? They're grey, about my size, skin looks like leather, and their heads are flattish. Eyes on the side of their heads, like a lizard. Not a stitch of clothes. Just a belt with a knife and arrow holder. And they got webbed claws for feet. They're ugly-looking things, sir. Here's the tank."

Clark's voice came, hard and clear. "That you, Hague?" Silence for a moment. "What's wrong? You're not blinded?"

Sewell had dropped his irascibility, and his voice was steady and kindly.

"Just flash blindness, isn't it, sir? This salve will fix you up. You've got a cut on your shoulder. I'll take care of that too."

"How are your men, Hague?" Clark sounded as though he were standing beside Hague.

"Not a scratch. We're ready to march."

"Five hurt here, three with the advance party, and two at the tank. We got 'em good, though. They hit the trail between our units and got fire from both sides. Must be twenty of them dead."

Hague grimaced at the sting of something Sewell had squeezed into his eyes. "Who was hurt?"

"Arndt, the geologist; his buddy, Galut, the botanist; lab technician Harker, Crewman Harker, and Szachek, the meteorologist man. How's your pneumatic ammunition?"

"We fired twenty-eight rounds of H.E."

Cartographer Hirooka's voice burst in excitedly.

"That gun crew of yours! Your gun crew got twenty-one of these—these lizard men. A bunch came up our back trail, and the pneumatic cut them to pieces."

"Good going, Hague. We'll leave you extended back there. I'm pulling in the advance party, and there'll be just two groups. We'll be at point, and you continue at afterguard." Clark was silent for a moment, then his voice came bitterly, "We're down to seventeen men, you know."

He cursed, and Hague heard the wiry little navigator

slosh away through the mud and begin shouting orders. He and Hurd started back with Whittaker and Sergeant Sample yelling wild instructions from the tank as to what the rear guard might do with the next batch of lizard-men who came sneaking up.

Hague's vision was clearing, and he saw Balistierri and the photographer Whitcomb through a milky haze, measuring, photographing, and even dissecting several of the lizard-men. The back trail, swept by pneumatic gunfire was a wreck of wood splinters and smashed trees, smashed bodies, and cratered earth.

They broke down the gun, harnessed the equipment, and swung off at the sound of Clarke's whistle. Bucci had to be supported between two of the others, and they took turnabout at the job, sloshing through the water and mud, with Bucci's one swollen leg dragging uselessly between them. It was punishing work as the heat veils shimmered and thickened, but no one seemed to consider leaving him behind, Hague noticed; and he determined to say nothing about Clark's orders that the sick must be abandoned.

Days and nights flashed by in a dreary monotony of mud, heat, insects and thinning rations. Then one morning the giant trees began to thin, and they passed from rainforest into jungle.

The change was too late for Bucci. They carved a neat marker beside the trail, and set the dead youth's helmet atop it. Lieutenant Hague carried ahead a smudged letter in his shirt, with instructions to forward it to Wilma, the gunner's young wife.

Hague and his four gunners followed the rattling whippet tank's trail higher, the jungle fell behind, and their protesting legs carried them over the rim of a high, cloudswept plateau, that swept on to the limit of vision on both sides and ahead.

The city's black walls squatted secretively: four-square, black, glassy walls with a blocky tower set sturdily at each of the four corners, enclosing what appeared to be a square mile of low buildings. Grey fog whipped coldly across the flat bleakness and rustled through dark grass.

Balistierri, plodding beside Hague at the rear, stared

at it warily, muttering, "And Childe Roland to the dark tower came."

Sampler's tank ground along the base of the twelve-foot wall, turned at a sharp right angle, and the party filed through a square cut opening that once had been a gate. The black city looked tenantless. There was dark-hued grass growing in the misted streets and squares, and across the lintels of cube-shaped, neatly aligned dwellings, fashioned of thick, black blocks. Hague could hear nothing but whipping wind, the tank's clatter, and the quiet clink of equipment as men shuffled ahead through the knee-high grass, peering watchfully into dark doorways.

Clark's whistle shrilled, the tank motor died, and they waited.

"Hague, come ahead."

The gunnery officer nodded at Sergeant Brian, and walked swiftly to Clark, who was leaning against the tank's mud-caked side.

"Sampler says we've got to make repairs on the tank. We'll shelter here. Set your gun on a roof top commanding the street—or, better yet, set it on the wall. I'll want two of your gunners to go hunting food animals."

"What do you think this place is, Bob?"

"Beats me," and the navigator's wind-burned face twisted in a perplexed expression. "Lenkranz knows more about metals, but he thinks this stone is volcanic, like obsidian. Those lizard-men couldn't have built it."

"We passed some kind of bas-relief or mural inside the gate."

"Whitcomb is going to photograph them. Blake, Lenkranz, Johnson, and Hirooka are going to explore the place. Your two gunners, and Crewman Swenson and Balistierri will form the two hunting parties."

For five days, Hague and Crosse walked over the sullen plateau beneath scudding, leaden clouds, hunting little lizards that resembled dinosaurs and ran in coveys like grey chickens. The meat was good, and Sewell dropped his role of medical technician to achieve glowing accolades as an expert cook. Balistierri was in a zoologist's paradise, and he hunted over the windy plain with Swenson, the big white-haired Swede, for ten and twelve hours at a stretch. Balistierri would sit in the cook's unit glow at night, his thin face ecstatic as he described the weird life forms he and Swenson had tracked down during the day; or alternately he'd bemoan the necessity of eating what were to him priceless zoological specimens.

Whittaker and Sampler hammered in the recalcitrant tank's bowels and shouted ribald remarks to any one nearby, until they emerged the third day, grease-stained and perspiring, to announce that "She's ready to roll her g—d—cleats off."

Whittaker had been nursing the tank's radio trans-receiver beside the forward hatch this grey afternoon, when his wild yell brought Hague erect. The officer carefully handed Bormann's skin bird back to the gunner, swung down from the city wall's edge, and ran to Whittaker's side. Clark was already there when Hague reached the tank.

"Listen! I've got 'em!" Whittaker yelped and extended the crackling earphones to Clark.

A tinny voice penetrated the interference.

"Base . . . Peter One . . . Do you hear . . . to George Easy Peter One . . . hear me . . . out."

Whittaker snapped on his throat microphone.

"George Easy Peter One To Base. George Easy Peter One To Base. We hear you. We hear you. Rocket crashed. Rocket crashed. Returning overland. Returning overland. Present strength sixteen men. Can you drop us supplies? Can you drop us supplies?"

The earphones sputtered, but no more voices came through. Clark's excited face fell into tired lines.

"We've lost them. Keep trying, Whittaker. Hague, we'll march-order tomorrow at dawn. You'll take the rear again."

Grey, windy dawnlight brought them out to the sound of Clark's call. Strapping on equipment and plates, they assembled around the tank. They were rested, and full fed.

"Walk, you poor devils," Whittaker was yelling from his tank turret. "And, if you get tired, run awhile," he snorted, grinning heartlessly, as he leaned back in pretended luxury against the gunner's seat, a thinly padded metal strip.

Balistierri and the blond Swenson shouldered their rifles and shuffled out. They would move well in advance as scouts.

"I wouldn't ride in that armored alarm-clock if it had a built-in harem," Hurd was screaming at Whittaker, and hurled a well-placed mudball at the tankman's head as the tank motor caught and the metal vehicle lumbered ahead toward the gate, with Whittaker sneering but with most of his head safely below the turret rim. Beside it marched Clark, his ragged uniform carefully scraped clean of mud, and with him Lenkranz, the metals man. Both carried rifles and wore half-empty bandoliers of blast cartridges.

The supply cart jerked behind the tank, and behind it filed Whitcomb with his cameras; Johnston cartographer Hirooka perusing absorbedly the clip board that held his strip map; Blake, the lean and spectacled bacteriologist, brought up the rear. Hague waited until they had disappeared through the gate cut sharply in the city's black wall, then he turned to his gun crew.

Sergeant Brian, saturnine as always, swung past carrying the pneumatic barrel assembly, Crosse with the charger a pace behind. Next, Bormann, whispering to Helen, who rode his shoulder piping throaty calls. Last came Hurd, swaggering past with jaws grinding steadily at that mysterious cud. Hague cast a glance over his shoulder at the deserted street of black cubes, wondered at the dank loneness of the place, and followed Hurd.

The hours wore on as they swung across dark grass, through damp tendrils of cloud, and faced into whipping, cold wind, eyes narrowed against its sting. Helen, squawking unhappily, crawled inside Bormann's shirt and rode with just her brown bird-head protruding.

"Look at the big hole, Lieutenant," Hurd called above the wind.

Hurd had dropped behind, and Hague called a halt to investigate Hurd's find, but as he hiked rapidly back,

the wiry little man yelled and pitched out of sight.
Brian came running, and he and Hague peered over
the edge of the funnel-shaped pit, from which Hurd
was trying to crawl. Each time he'd get a third of the
way up the eighteen-foot slope, gravelly soil would
slide and he'd again be carried to the bottom.

"Throw me a line."

Brian pulled a hank of nylon line from his belt,
shook out the snarls, and tossed an end into Hurd's
clawing hands. Hague and the Sergeant anchored
themselves to the upper end and were preparing to
haul, when Hague saw something move in the gravel
beneath Hurd's feet, as the funnel bottom, and saw
a giant pincers emerging from loose, black gravel.

"Hurd look out!" he screamed.

The little man, white-faced, threw himself aside
as a giant beetle head erupted through the funnel bottom. The great pincer jaws fastened around Hurd's
waist as he struggled frantically up the pit's side. He
began screaming when the beetle monster dragged him
relentlessly down, his distorted face flung up at them
appealingly. Hague snatched at his rifle and brought
it up. When the gun cracked, the pincers tightened
on Hurd's middle, and the little man was snipped in
half. The blue-white flash and report of the explosive
bullet blended with Hurd's choked yells, the beetle
rolled over on its back, and the two bodies lay entan-
gled at the pit bottom. Brian and Hague looked at
each other in silent, blanched horror, then turned from
the pit's edge and loped back to the others.

Bormann and Crosse peered fearfully across the
wind-whipped grass and inquired in shouts what Hurd
was doing.

"He's dead, gone," Hague yelled savagely over the
wind's whine. "Keep moving. We can't do anything.
Keep going."

IV

At 1630 hours Commander Technician Harker
slipped on the earset, threw over a transmitting switch,
and monotoned the routine verbal message.

"Base to George Easy Peter One . . . Base to George

Easy Peter One . . . Do you hear me George Easy Peter One . . . Do you hear me George Easy Peter One . . . reply please . . . reply please." Nothing came from his earphones but bursts of crackling interference, until he tried the copters next, and "George Easy Peter Two" and "George Easy Peter Three" reported in. They were operating near the base.

He tried "One" again, just in case.

"Base to George Easy Peter One . . . Base to George Easy Peter One . . . Do you hear me . . . Do you hear me . . . out."

A scratching whisper resolved over the interference. Harker's face wore a stunned look, but he quickly flung over a second switch and the scratching voice blared over the mother ship's entire address system. Men dropped their work throughout the great hull, and clustered around the speakers.

"George One . . . Base . . . hear you . . . rocket crashed . . . overland . . . present strength . . . supplies . . . drop supplies."

Interference surged back and drowned the whispering voice, while through Odysseus' hull a ragged cheer grew and gathered volume. Harker shut off the address system and strained over his crackling earphones, but nothing more came in response to his radio calls.

He glanced up and found the Warning Room jammed with technicians, science section members, officers, men in laboratory smocks, or greasy overalls, or spotless Rocket Service uniforms, watching intently his own strained face as he tried to get through. Commander Chapman looked haggard, and Harker remembered that some one had once said that Chapman's young sister was the wife of the medical technician who'd gone out with Patrol Rocket One

Harker finally pulled off the earphones reluctantly and set them on the table before him. "That's all. You heard everything they said over the P.A. system. Nothing more is coming through."

Night came, another day, night again, and they came finally to the plateau's end, and stood staring from a windy escarpment across an endless roof of rainforest far below, grey-green under the continuous roof of lead-colored clouds. Hague, standing back a little, watched them. A thin line of ragged men along the rim, peering mournfully out across that endless expanse for a gleam that might be the distant hull of Odysseus, the mother ship. A damp wind fluttered their rags and plastered them against gaunt bodies.

Clark and Sampler were conferring in shouts.

"Will the tank make it down this grade?" Clark wanted to know.

For once, Sergeant Sampler's mobile, merry face was grim.

"I don't know, but we'll sure try. Be ready to cut that cart loose if the tank starts to slip."

Drag ropes were fastened to the cart, a man stationed at the tank hitch, and Sampler sent his tank lurching forward over the edge, and it slanted down at a sharp angle. Hague, holding a drag rope, set his heels and allowed the tank's weight to pull him forward over the rim; and the tank, cart, and muddy figures hanging to drag ropes began descending the steep gradient. Bormann, just ahead of the Lieutenant, strained back at the rope and turned a tight face over his shoulder.

"She's slipping faster!"

The tank was picking up speed, and Hague heard the clash of gears as Sampler tried to fight the downward pull of gravity. Gears ground, and Sampler forced the whippet straight again, but the downward slide was increasing. Hague was flattened under Bormann, heels digging, and behind him he could hear Sergeant Brian cursing, struggling to keep flat against the downward pull.

The tank careened sideways again, slipped, and Whittaker's white face popped from her turret.

"She's going," he screamed.

A drag rope parted. Clarke sprang like a madman between tank and cart, and cut the hitch. The tank, with no longer sufficient restraining weight, tipped with slow majesty outward, then rolled out and down, bouncing, smashing as if in a slow motion film, shedding parts at each crushing contact. It looked like a toy below them, still rolling and gathering speed, when Hague saw Whittaker's body fly free, a tiny rag doll at that distance, and the tank was lost to view when it bounced off a ledge and went floating down through space.

Clark signalled them forward, and they inched the supply cart downward on the drag ropes, legs trembling with strain, and their nerves twitching at the memory of Whittaker's chalky face peering from the falling turret. It was eight hours before they reached the bottom, reeling with exhaustion, set a guard, and tumbled into their shelter tents. Outside, Hague could hear Clark pacing restlessly, trying to assure himself that he'd been right to cut the tank free, that there'd been no chance to save Whittaker and Sampler when the tank began to slide.

Hague lay in his little tent listening to the footsteps splash past in muddy Venusian soil, and was thankful that he hadn't had to make the decision. He'd been saving three cigarettes in an oilskin packet, and he drew one carefully from the wrapping now, lit it, and inhaled deeply. Could he have done what Clark did—break that hitch? He still didn't know when he took a last lung-filling pull at the tiny stub of cigarette and crushed it out carefully.

As dawn filtered through the cloud layer, they were rolling shelter tents and buckling on equipment. Clarke's face was a worn mask when he talked with Hague, and his fingers shook over his pack buckles.

"There are thirteen of us. Six men will pull the supply cart, and six guard, in four-hour shifts. You and I will alternate command at guard."

He was silent for a moment, then watched Hague's face intently as he spoke again.

"It'll be a first-grade miracle if any of us get through. Hague, you—you know I had to cut that tank free." His voice rose nervously. "You know that! You're an officer."

"Yeah, I guess you did." Hague couldn't say it any better, and he turned away and fussed busily with the bars holding the portable Sonar detection unit to the supply cart.

They moved off with Hague leaning into harness pulling the supply cart bumpily ahead. Clarke stumbled jerkily at the head, with Blake, a lean, silent ghost beside him, rifle in hand. The cart came next with Hague, Bormann, Sergeant Brian, Crosse, Lenkranz and Sewell leaning in single file against its weight. At the rear marched photographer Whitcomb, Hirooka with his maps, and Balistierri, each carrying a rifle. The big Swede Swenson was last in line, peering warily back into the rainforest shadows. The thirteen men wound Indian file from sight of the flatheaded reptilian thing, clutching a sheaf of bronze arrows, that watched them.

Hague had lost count of days again when he looked up into the shadowy forest roof, his feet finding their way unconsciously through the thin mud, his ears registering automatically the murmurs of talk behind him, the supply cart's tortured creaking, and the continuous Sonar drone. The air felt different, warmer than its usual steam-bath heat, close and charged with expectancy, and the forest seemed to crouch in waiting with the repressed silence of a hunting cat.

Crosse yelled thinly from the rear of the file, and they all halted to listen, the hauling crew dropping their harness thankfully. Hague turned back and saw Crosse's thin arm waving a rifle overhead, then pointing down the trail. The Lieutenant listened carefully until he caught the sound, a thin call, the sound of a horn mellowed by distance.

The men unthinkingly moved in close and threw wary looks into the forest ways around them.

"Move further ahead, Hague. Must be more lizard men." Clark swore, with tired despair. "All right, let's get moving and make it fast."

The cart creaked ahead again, moving faster this time, and the snicking of rifle bolts came to Hague. He moved swiftly ahead on the trail and glanced up again, saw breaks in the forest roof, and realized that the huge trees were pitching wildly far above.

"Look up," he yelled, "wind coming!"

The wind came suddenly, striking with stone-wall solidity. Hague sprinted to the cart, and the struggling body of men worked it off the trail, and into a buttress angle of two great tree roots, lashing it there with nylon ropes. The wind velocity increased, smashing torn branches overhead, and ripping at the men who lay with their heads well down in the mud. Tiny animals were blown hurtling past, and once a great spider came flailing in cartwheel fashion, then smashed brokenly against a tree.

The wind drone rose in volume, the air darkened, and Hague lost sight of the other men from behind his huddled shelter against a wall-like root. The great trees twisted with groaning protest, and thunderous crashes came downward through the forest, with sometimes the faint squeak of a dying or frightened animal. The wind halted for a breathless, hushed moment of utter stillness, broken only by the dropping of limbs and the scurry of small life forms—then came the screaming fury from the opposite direction.

For a moment, the gunnery officer thought he'd be torn from the root to which his clawing fingers clung. Its brutal force smashed breath from Hague's lungs and held him pinned in his corner until he struggled choking for air as a drowning man does. It seemed that he couldn't draw breath, that the air was a solid mass from which he could no longer get life. Then the wind stopped as suddenly as it had come, leaving dazed quiet. As he stumbled back to the cart, Hague saw crushed beneath a thigh-sized limb a feebly moving reptilian head; and the dying eyes of the lizard-man were still able to stare at him in cold malevolence.

The supply cart was still intact, roped between buttressing roots to belt knives driven into the tough wood. Hague and Clark freed it, called a hasty roll, and the march was resumed at a fast pace through cooled, cleaner air. They could no longer hear horn sounds; but the grim knowledge that lizard-men were near them lent strength, and Hague led as rapidly as he dared, listening carefully to the Sonar's drone behind him, altering his course when the sound faded, and straightening out when it grew in volume.

A day slipped by and another, and the cart rolled ahead through thin greasy mud on the forest floor, with the Sonar's drone mingled with murmuring men's voices talking of food. It was the universal topic, and they carefully worked out prolonged menus each would engorge when they reached home. They forgot heat, insect bites, the sapping humidity, and talked of food—steaming roasts, flanked by crystal goblets of iced wine, oily roasted nuts, and lush, crisp green salads.

V

Hague, again marching ahead with Balistierri, broke into the comparatively bright clearing, and was blinded for a moment by the sudden, cloud-strained light after days of forest darkness. As their eyes accommodated to the lemon-colored glare, he and Balistierri sighted the animals squatting beneath low bushes that grew thickly in the clearing. They were monkey-like primates with golden tawny coats, a cockatoo crest of white flaring above dog faces. The monkeys stared a moment, the great white crests rising doubtfully, ivory canine teeth fully three inches long bared.

They'd been feeding on fruit that dotted the shrub-filled clearing; but now one screamed a warning, and they sprang into vines that made a matted wall on every side. The two rifles cracked together again, and three fantastically colored bodies lay quiet, while the rest of the troop fled screaming into tree tops and disappeared. At the blast of sound, a fluttering kaleidoscope of color swept up about the startled Rocketeers, and they stood blinded, while mad whorls of color whirled around them in a miniature storm.

"Giant butterflies," Balistierri was screaming in ecstasy. "Look at them! Big as a dove!"

Hague watched the bright insects coalesce into one agitated mass of vermillion, azure, metallic green, and sulphur yellow twenty feet overhead. The pulsating mass of hues resolved itself into single insects, with wings large as dinner plates, and they streamed out of sight over the forest roof.

"What were they?" he grinned at Balistierri. "Going to name them after Bormann?"

The slight zoologist still watched the spot where they'd vanished.

"Does it matter much what I call them? Do you really believe any one will ever be able to read this logbook I'm making?" He eyed the gunnery officer bleakly, then added, "Well, come on. We'd better skin these monks. They're food anyway."

Hague followed Balistierri, and they stood looking down at the golden furred primates. The zoologist knelt, fingered a bedraggled white crest, and remarked, "These blast cartridges don't leave much meat, do they? Hardly enough for the whole party." He pulled a tiny metal block, with a hook and dial, from his pocket, loped the hook through a tendon in the monkey's leg and lifted the dead animal.

"Hmmm. Forty-seven pounds. Not bad." He weighed each in turn, made measurements, and entered these in his pocket notebook.

The circle around Sewell, who presided over the cook unit, was merry that night. The men's eyes were bright in the heater glow as they stuffed their shrunken stomachs with monkey meat and the fruits the monkeys had been eating when Hague and Balistierri surprised them. Swenson and Crosse and Whitcomb, the photographer, overate and were violently sick; but the others sat picking their teeth contentedly in a close circle. Bormann pulled his harmonica from his shirt pocket, and the hard, silvery torrent of music set them to singing softly. Hague and Blake, the bacteriologist, stood guard among the trees.

At dawn, they were marching again, stepping more briskly over tiny creeks, through green-tinted mud, and the wet heat. At noon, they heard the horn again, and Clark ordered silence and a faster pace. They swung swiftly, eating iron rations as they marched. Hague leaned into his cart harness and watched perspiration staining through Bormann's shirted back just ahead of him. Behind, Sergeant Brian tugged manfully and growled under his breath at buzzing insects, slapping occasionally with a low howl of muted anguish. Helen, the skin bird, rode on Bormann's shoulder, staring aback into Hague's face with questioning chirps; and Hague was whistling softly between his teeth at her when Bormann stopped suddenly and Hague slammed into him. Helen took flight with a startled squawk, and Clark come loping back to demand quiet. Bormann stared at the two officers, his young-old face blank with surprise.

"I'm, I'm shot," he stuttered, and stared wonderingly at the thing thrusting from the side opening in his chest armor. It was one of the fragile bronze arrows, gleaming metallically in the forest gloom.

Hague cursed, and jerked free of the cart harness.

"Here, I'll get it free." He tugged at the shaft, and Bormann's face twisted. Hague stepped back. "Where's Sewell? This thing must be barbed."

"Back off the trail! Form a wide circle around the cart, but stay under cover! Fight 'em on their own ground!" Clark was yelling, and the men clustered about the cart faded into forest corridors.

Hague and Sewell, left alone, dragged Bormann's limp length beneath the metal cart. Hague leaped erect again, manhandled the pneumatic gun off the cart and onto the trail, spun the charger crank, and lay down in firing position. Behind him, Sewell grunted, "He's gone. Arrow poison must have paralyzed his diaphragm and chest muscles."

"Okay. Get up here and handle the ammunition." Hague's face was savage as the medical technician crawled into position beside him and opened an ammunition carrier.

"Watch the trail behind me," Hague continued, slamming up the top cover plate and jerking a belt through the pneumatic breech. "When I yell charge, spin the charger crank; and when I yell off a number, set the meter arrow at that number." He snapped the cover plate shut and locked it.

"The other way! They're coming the other way!" Sewell lumbered to his knees, and the two heaved the gun around. A blowgun arrow rattled off the cart body above them, and gobbling yells filtered among the trees with an answering crack of explosive cartridges. A screaming knot of grey figures came sprinting down on the cart. Hague squeezed the pneumatic's trigger, the gun coughed, and blue-fire-limned lizard men crumpled in the trail mud.

"Okay, give 'em a few the other way."

The two men horsed the gun around and sent a buzzing flock of explosive loads down the forest corridor opening ahead of the cart. They began firing carefully down other corridors opening off the trail, aiming delicately less their missiles explode too close and the concussion kill their own men; but they worked a blasting circle of destruction that smashed the great trees back in the forest and made openings in the forest roof. Blue fire flashed in the shadows and froze weird tableaus of screaming lizard-men and hurtling mud, branches, and great splinters of wood.

An exulting yell burst behind them. Hague saw Sewell stare over his shoulder, face contorted, then the big medical technician sprang to his feet. Hague rolled hard, pulling his belt knife, and saw Sewell and a grey man-shape locked in combat above him, saw leathery grey claws drive a bronze knife into the medic's unarmored throat; and then the gunnery officer was on his feet, knife slashing, and the lizard-man fell across the prone Sewell. An almost audible silence fell over the forest, and Hague saw Rocketeers filtering back onto the cart trail, rifles cautiously extended at ready.

"Where's Clark?" he asked Lenkranz. The grey-haired metals man gazed back dully.

"I haven't seen him since we left the trail. I was with Swenson."

The others moved in, and Hague listed the casualties. Sewell, Bormann, and Lieutenant Clark. Gunnery Officer Clarence Hague was now in command. That the Junior Lieutenant now commanded Ground Expeditionary Patrol Number One trickled into his still numb brain; and he wondered for a moment what the Base Commander would think of their chances if he knew. Then he took stock of his little command.

There was young Crosse, his face twitching nervously. There was Blake, the tall, quiet bacteriologist; Lenkranz, the metals man; Hirooka, the Nisei; Balistierri; Whitcomb, the photographer, with a battered Hasselbladt still dangling by its neck cord against his armored chest. Swenson was still there, the big Swede crewman; and imperturable Sergeant Brian, who was now calmly cleaning the pneumatic gun's loading mechanism. And Helen, Bormann's skin bird, fluttering over the ration cart, beneath which Bormann and Sewell lay in the mud.

"Crosse, Lenkranz, burial detail. Get going." It was Hague's first order as Commander. He thought the two looked most woebegone of the party, and figured digging might loosen their nerves.

Crosse stared at him, and then sat suddenly against a tree bole.

"I'm not going to dig. I'm not going to march. This is crazy. We're going to get killed. I'll wait for it right here. Why do we keep walking and walking when we're going to die anyway?" His rising voice cracked, and he burst into hysterical laughter. Sergeant Brian rose quietly from his gun-cleaning, jerked Crosse to his feet, and slapped him into quiet. Then he turned to Hague.

"Shall I take charge of the burial detail, sir?"

Hague nodded; and suddenly his long dislike of the iron-hard Sergeant melted into warm liking and admiration. Brian was the man who'd get them all through.

The Sergeant knotted his dark brows truculently at Hague. "And I don't believe Crosse meant what he said. He's a very brave man. We all get a little jumpy. But he's a good man, a good Rocketeer."

Three markers beside the trail, and a pile of dumped equipment marked the battleground when the cart swung forward again. Hague had dropped all the recording instruments, saving only Whitcomb's exposed films, the rations, rifle ammunition, and logbooks that had been kept by different members of the science section. At his command, Sergeant Brian reluctantly smashed the pneumatic gun's firing mechanism, and left the gun squatting on its tripod beside charger and shell belts. With the lightened load, Hague figured three men could handle the cart, and he took his place with Brian and Crosse in the harness. The others no longer walked in the trail, but filtered between great root-flanges and tree boles on either side, guiding themselves by the Sonar's hum.

They left no more trail markers, and Hague cautioned them against making any unnecessary noise.

"No trail markers behind us. This mud is watery enough to hide footprints in a few minutes. We're making no noise, and we'll drop no more refuse. All they can hear will be the Sonar, and that won't carry far."

On the seventy-first day of the march, Hague squatted, fell almost to the ground, and grunted, "Take ten."

He stared at the stained, ragged scarecrows hunkered about him in forest mud.

"Why do we do it?" he asked no one in particular. "Why do we keep going, and going, and going? Why don't we just lie down and die? That would be the easiest thing I could think of right now." He knew that Rocket Service officers didn't talk that way, but he didn't feel like an officer, just a tired, feverish, bone-weary man.

"Have we got a great glowing tradition to inspire us?" he snarled. "No, we're just the lousy Rocketeers that every other service arm plans to absorb. We haven't a Grant or a John Paul Jones to provide an example in a tough spot. The U.S. Rocket Service has nothing but the memory of some ships that went out and never came back; and you can't make a legend out of men who just plain vanish."

There was silence, and it looked as if the muddy figures were too exhausted to reply. Then Sergeant Brian spoke.

"The Rocketeers have a legend, sir."

"What legend, Brian?" Hague snorted.

"Here is the legend, sir. 'George Easy Peter One'."

Hague laughed hollowly, but the Sergeant continued as if he hadn't heard.

"Ground Expeditionary Patrol One—the outfit a plant couldn't lick. Venus threw her grab bag at us, animals, swamps, poison plants, starvation, fever, and we kept right on coming. She just made us smarter, and tougher, and harder to beat. And we'll blast through these lizard-men and the jungle, and march into Base like the whole U.S. Armed Forces on review."

"Let's go," Hague called, and they staggered up again, nine gaunt bundles of sodden, muddy rags, capped in trim black steel helmets with cheek guards down. The others slipped off the trail, and Hague, Brian, and Crosse pulled on the cart harness and lurched forward. The cart wheel-hub jammed against a tree bole, and as they strained blindly ahead to free it, a horn note drifted from afar.

"Here they come again," Crosse groaned.

"They—won't be—up—with us—for days." Hague grunted, while he threw his weight in jerks against the tow line. The cart lurched free with a lunge, and all three shot forward and sprawled raging in the muddy trail.

They sat wiping mud from their faces, when Brian stopped suddenly, ripped off his helmet and threw it aside, then sat tensely forward in an attitude of strained listening. Hague had time to wonder dully if the man's brain had snapped, before he crawled to his feet.

"Shut up, and listen," Brian was snarling. "Hear it! Hear it! It's a klaxon! Way off, about every two seconds!"

Hague tugged off his heavy helmet, and strained every nerve to listen. Over the forest silence it came with pulse-like regularity, a tiny whisper of sound.

He and Brian stared bright-eyed at each other, not quiet daring to say what they were thinking. Crosse got up and leaned like an empty sack against the cartwheel with an inane questioning look.

"What is it?" They stared at him without speaking, still listening intently, "It's the Base. That's it, it's the Base!"

Something choked Hague's throat, then he was yelling and firing his rifle. The rest came scuttling out of the forest shadow, faces breaking into wild grins, and they joined Hague, the forest rocking with gunfire. They moved forward, and Hirooka took up a thin chant:

> Ooooooh, the Rocketeers
> have shaggy ears.
> They're dirty——

The rest of their lyrics wouldn't look well in print; but where the Rocketeers have gone, on every frontier of space, the ribald song is sung. The little file moved down the trail toward the klaxon sound. Behind them, something moved in the gloom, resolved itself into a reptile-headed, man-like thing that reared a small wood trumpet to fit its mouth; a soft horn note floated clear; and other shapes became visible, sprinting forward, flitting through the gloom . . .

When a red light flashed over Chapman's desk, he flung down a sheaf of papers and hurried down steel-walled corridors to the number one shaft. A tiny elevator swept him to Odysseus' upper side, where a shallow pit had been set in the ship's scarred skin, and a pneumatic gun installed. Chapman hurried past the gun and crew to stand beside a listening device. The four huge cones loomed dark against the clouds, the operator in their center was a blob of shadow in the dawn-light, where he huddled listening to a chanting murmur that came from his headset. Blake came running onto the gundeck; Bjornson and the staff officers were all there.

"Cut it into the Address system," Chapman told the Listener operator excitedly; and the faint sounds were amplified through the whole ship. From humming Address amplifiers, the ribald words broke in a hoarse melody.

> The rocketeers have shaggy ears,
> They're dirty——

The rest described in vivid detail the prowess of rocketeers in general.

"How far are they?" Chapman demanded.

The operator pointed at a dial, fingered a knob that altered his receiving cones split-seconds of angle. "They're about twenty-five miles, sir."

Chapman turned to the officers gathered in an exultant circle behind him.

"Branch, here's your chance for action. Take thirty men, our whippet tank, and go out to them. Bjornson, get the 'copters aloft for air cover."

Twenty minutes later, Chapman watched a column assemble beneath the Odysseus' gleaming side and march into the jungle, with the 'copters buzzing west a moment later, like vindictive dragon flies.

Breakfast was brought to the men clustered at Warnings equipment, and to Chapman at his post on the gundeck. The day ticked away, the parade ground vanished in thickening clots of night; and a second dawn found the watchers still at their posts, listening to queer sounds that trickled from the speakers. The singing had stopped; but once they heard a note that a horn might make, and several times gobbling yells that didn't sound human. George One was fighting, they knew now. The listeners picked up crackling of rifle fire, and when that died there was silence.

The watchers heard a short cheer that died suddenly, as the relief column and George One met; and they waited and watched. Branch, who headed the relief column, communicated with the mother ship by the simple expedient of yelling, the sound being picked up by the listeners.

"They're coming in, Chapman. I'm coming behind to guard their rear. They've been attacked by some kind of lizard-men. I'm not saying a thing—see for yourself when they arrive."

Hours rolled past, while they speculated in low tones, the hush that held the ship growing taut and strained.

"Surely Branch would have told us if anything was wrong, or if the records were lost," Chapman barked angrily. "Why did he have to be so damned melodramatic?"

"Look, there—through the trees. A helmet glinted!"

The laconic Bjornson had thrown dignity to the winds, and capered like a drunken goat, as Rindell described it later.

Chapman stared down at the jungle edging the parade ground and caught a movement.

A man with a rifle came through the fringe and stood eyeing the ship in silence, and then came walking forward across the long, cindered expanse. From this height, he looked to Chapman like a child's lead soldier, a ragged, muddy, midget scarecrow. Another stir in the trees, and one more man, skulking like an infantry flanker with rifle at ready. He, too, straightened and came walking quietly forward. A file of three men came next, leaning into the harness of a little metal cart that bumped drunkenly as they dragged it forward. An instant of waiting, and two more men stole from the jungle, more like attacking infantry than returning heroes. Chapman waited, and no more came. This was all.

"My God, no wonder Branch wouldn't tell us. There were thirty-two of them." Rindell's voice was choked.

"Yes, only seven." Chapman remembered his field glasses and focused them on the seven approaching men. "Lieutenant Hague is the only officer. And they're handing us the future of the U.S. Rocket Service on that little metal cart."

The quiet shattered and a yelling horde of men poured from Odysseus' hull and engulfed the tattered seven, sweeping around them, yelling, cheering, and carrying them toward the mother ship.

Chapman looked a little awed as he turned to the officers behind him. "Well, they did it. We forward these records, and we've proven that we can do the job." He broke into a grin. "What am I talking about? Of course we did the job. We'll always do the job. We're the Rocketeers, aren't we?"

The Diversifal

Ross Rocklynne

Side by side they would live, year after year, hating each other more fiercely each day. And in the end, if their mission succeeded, the creature would die and the man would find insanity.

"No," said the shadowy man who sat high above the floor on the chair of the time-machine, "you can't do that."

"Can't, eh?"

"No!"

"Sorry."

For a second, Bryan was shaken with indecision. *This is intolerable,* he thought. *I'll turn the doorknob. After all, he has no real jurisdiction over my actions. Nor has he, in spite of the stakes involved, any right to meddle in my life the way he has.*

His rebel thoughts endured for only that second. His grip loosened on the doorknob; his gloved hand fell away. He actually took a few steps backward, as if he would negate that action which led toward disaster. Then he turned quickly, urged his undernourished body back up the threadbare hall into his equally threadbare room. Off came his shapeless hat and overcoat, which was ripped at seams and

175

pockets, and he sat down, brain numb, the sensations of his stomach forgotten in the greater hunger.

Where is she? *Who is she?*

He did not have the courage to meet the cold eyes of the man who sat in shadowy outline amongst nebulous, self-suspended machinery, although that being watched him with merciless inflexibility of purpose. He had only the courage to speak, while his eyes fixed dully on the gingerbread metal bed with its sagging mattress.

"The Alpha Group?"

"The Alpha Group," the shadowy man spoke coldly, in agreement. "*Punctus* four. You would have met *her*."

"I thought so. I felt it."

"You felt nothing of the sort. You have an exaggerated notion of the perceptive qualities of your psyche," he retorted.

"I named the Alpha Group," said Bryan wearily.

"Because for the first three or four years of our association, the Alpha Group will predominate. And because you have come to associate certain of my facial expressions and tonal qualities with the group. There was no telepathic pick-up from the girl. She is not aware that you exist. Nor will she ever be aware, as long as you choose to work in close collaboration with me—and as a humanitarian yourself, you will not refuse to collaborate."

Bryan leaned back in the worn armchair, grinning twistedly, though his heart was lead in his breast. He held the long-lashed eyes of the god-like creature with a flickering sidewise glance. "Perhaps you will choose to stop collaborating with me."

The nostrils of the being flared. "No. Never. We will continue—we must continue to work together until the Alpha, Delta, and Gamma groups are exhausted—or until—"

"Or until I commit suicide as you suggested."

"Yes."

Bryan lost his tensity, and his fear that he could not bear it, might disobey a command from this creature. Suddenly, he was amused. Bryan was chained to this creature, but no less than this creature was chained to him—chained to him for ten long years, or until he might take his own life.

Creature? Yes. For certainly any animal that is not *Homo sapiens* is a creature. Even if he be *Homo superior*, of the year Eight-hundred thousand A.D., and has invented a time-machine, and has but one powerful, compelling thought in mind—to save the human race. Or that race of creatures which had stemmed from the human race. That was it. After fighting and imagining, aspiring and succeeding, for a good many millions of years, man was about to be snuffed out. So the shadowy being—*Homo superior*—had told Bryan on that day a week ago when he had appeared in this room. The human race, far in the future, would destroy itself unless—unless Bryan Barrett did not do something that he had done, did not become something that he had become.

The thoughts of the creature had impinged on his brain clearly after the first moments of fright. Bryan had listened, and believed.

"So I'm a diversifal," he had muttered. "Bryan Barrett, liberal, radical, diversifal."

"You *are* a diversifal. I can coin no other word to fit."

"And *she* is a diversifal."

"Yes."

"And our child would be a mutant."

"Yes."

"I thought," Bryan had said, his thoughts sinking heavily into a morass of intangibles, "I thought, if one wants to follow the theory to its logical conclusion, that there are an infinite number of probable worlds."

"Are there?" The depthless eyes of the being, looking down at Bryan from his shadowy height above the floor, had been contemptuous with disinterest. "I know of only two. They are the only two with which I am concerned. A thousand years into my future they warred—and humanity destroyed itself. This I know. This I must prevent. From your unborn mutant child my race stems."

"Your race?" Bryan had exclaimed.

"Yes."

"You are seeking to prevent your own world of probability?"

"Yes." The long-lashed eyes flickered. The being leaned forward a little, staring down at Bryan. "Why not, Bryan Barrett? Does it matter? It is my world of probability which discovered the manner of traveling to the other world. It is my world which waged the war. It is my world, your world, which is—will be—at fault. I am selfless. You know what it is to be selfless. You can understand. And, after all, you are the diversifal—the splitting factor."

Bryan was inwardly shaken. The selfless superman. Or, and this was more likely, the selfless scientist. The picture, in its entirety, had come quite clearly to Bryan Barrett. He was a diversifal, because in him impinged events any of which might lead to the creation of a certain time-branch; a time-branch which must not be created if humanity in a far-distant era were to survive. The concept of worlds of *if* was not new to Bryan, nor was the idea of the future of man outside his thoughts. He dealt with the future, with the liberation of man from his bondage to tyranny. He was fighting for future wherein man would know no poverty, no social backwardness—for a time when man could come into his own, blossom forth and make true use of the boundless resources that were possible. Small wonder, then, that he could accept the idea of a man from the far future without trouble, and could decide to give ten years of his life to the cause for which this man from the future was fighting.

But already the first week of that ten years had become a nightmare.

"You've kept me here," he now told the being, "three days, without any food except some stale cakes. Why?"

"Because the events of the Alpha Group are worked around your every probable action like a net. If you left this house before morning, you would meet her." His sharp-pointed face turned hard. "The psychological data I have on her is sketchy. I can control your actions. I cannot control hers, nor guess what they would be. And also, had you left here at any time during the last three days, you would have made an acquaintance whom you would not see again for eight, perhaps nine years."

"The Gamma Group!"

"The Gamma Group. That acquaintance would show up as a probable event in the Gamma Group which would lead to tickets to a musical comedy in a New York—" He stopped speaking, but Bryan Barrett, without knowing it, was watching him with cunning expression. The man from the future sneered. "Your obvious, unconscious desire to trick me would sicken even you, Bryan. Every word I speak is to your unconscious merely a clue to her identity. You must fight that."

Sweat started on Bryan's square, thinning face. He bowed forward, feeling as if he were about to burst. "I can leave here tomorrow morning?" His voice was muffled.

"Yes. And your way of life must change. You will go to Hannicut, editor of *The Daily News-Star,* and tell him you'd like to take that job he offered you last year."

Bryan came to his feet in a blaze of anger. "No! You know why I didn't take that job!"

"I know why. But it is still necessary for you to lose your integrity if we are to succeed. Go to Hannicut and tell him you're willing to falsify the news either by commission or omission. Also you will cancel your membership in the so-called radical organization, *Freedom For All.* And in any other liberal organization you may belong to."

He looked calmly down into Bryan's stricken, agonized face. "I know what those associations mean to you—and to freedom-loving men everywhere. I am truly sorry. I conceive the future to be more important that this present, however. This, Bryan Barrett, is your first step to wealth and power. A financial gulf must be created as an additional precaution between you and her. A gulf that a poverty-stricken person

can never cross. She is poor. She will always be
poor. . . ."

It was strange the way that nightmarish week turned
into a month, that month into a year. Hannicut, editor
of *The Daily News-Star,* performed a blunder from
the viewpoint of the man who owned that newspaper
and a hundred others throughout the world: he printed
a story which told the truth about a recent labor-big
business dispute. Hannicut's boss fired him, and in
elevating Bryan Barrett to the post warned him never
to give labor a break, else he'd go the way of Hannicut.

"Take the job," came the cold thoughts of the man
from the future, and his name Bryan Barrett now
knew—Entoré.

Bryan got the first damp issue back from the press
room the next day, and looked at it with sickened
eyes. He left the office with his hat pulled low over
his eyes. Newsboys were hawking the edition—big
scareheads which told of another strike in the coal
mines, and never mentioned one word about the strike
a certain big-business corporation was pulling against
the government. Which never said a thing about the
filibuster a certain senator had pulled in Congress to
defeat a pro-minority bill.

In the second week of Bryan's editorship, he started
to leave the office. Back in Bryan's hotel suite, Entoré,
man from the future, sent another wordless command.

"Do not leave the office now."

"No?" Bryan muttered the word from the graying
mustache he now wore.

"No. Two men are waiting downstairs—two rowdies
from the *Freedom For All* League. They are intending
to throw bricks."

Bryan's fists clenched. "There are no rowdies in
the *Freedom For All* League. No matter what the
newspapers claim."

"These men once knew you, when you fought
tyranny together. They are law-abiding men. But
something has snapped in them. In their eyes, you
are a traitor. They could never punish you by law.

They are willing to sacrifice their own lives if they can kill you."

"Thanks."

Bryan sank into a chair in the corner of his office. His head bowed, and he knew there was gray in his hair, gray that the last year had put there. Later Entoré spoke again. Bryan left.

He had no sooner reached the street and signaled a taxi than Entoré spoke again. "Do not take that taxi. Walk one block left. The Alpha Group. That taxi will have a minor street accident. Among those who gather in the crowd will be she."

Bryan stood with his hand upraised. The taxi was sloping in toward him. His heart thudded. He felt a voiceless, impassioned longing, as if a mind, a human mind, were reaching across distances and touching his without saying anything. Her mind. Then he turned and walked one block left and took another taxi. He sat in the taxi, cold and graying, a man who was rising in power and wealth as the editor of a great metropolitan daily. A man who by all the rules of human conduct was a quisling of the worst sort. Yet, could *they*, his former friends and fellow fighters, know what hell he was going through now because he was looking farther into the future than they could ever hope to look? They were fighting against the corruptness of present civilization. Someday their fight would bear fruit in a nation-wide and, later on, a world-wide Utopia. Bryan Barrett had been forced to look farther ahead than that. To and beyond the year 800,000 A.D. They would never understand.

"Turn your head to the right," came the command.

Automatically, Bryan turned his head. "Why?" he asked dully.

"The Gamma Group, seven years from now. Had you kept your eyes on the left side of the street, *punctus* nineteen of the Gamma group would have occurred. You would have seen a woman who resembled your mother so strongly that later on this week you would write a letter to her in your hometown, wondering if she had been in New York. She would have answered quickly, wondering why you wrote so seldom, and telling you she hadn't been in New York, but that, come to think of it, she would make the trip to see you. You would have met her in Penn Station, and in the excitement would have lost your billfold. A traveller would have found the billfold, taken the money, and dropped the billfold in a drawer at his home. Seven years later, his wife, cleaning house, would have found the billfold and returned it to you. You would have rewarded the woman. A few days later, you would meet her on the street; with her, a friend—"

"She!" Bryan interposed huskily.

"Yes," Entoré said. "The possibilites of meeting her through the Gamma Group of events are the shadowy ones. One by one I am destroying the possibility of events both in the Delta and the Gamma Groups. But both will be relatively strong long after the Alpha Group no longer exists."

Bryan went back to his hotel suite without eating. Entoré was there, staring at him with an impersonal, cold glance.

Bryan said, his hand still on the closed door, "I won't be able to stand much more of this."

Entoré leaned forward on the console of his machine. "I, too, am sacrificing," he pointed out.

"Are you?" Bryan's eyes and voice tore across at him with sarcasm. "You can disappear back to your own time for an hour, a week, a year, if you choose, and return back to this same second of time without my being aware that you had gone. You have relief from the vigil. I have none. Ten years?" His laugh was brittle. "I'll go crazy!"

Entoré said nothing.

Bryan ground out, "You'd want me confined in a sanatarium, Entoré. That would be similar to death, as far as destroying the Groups goes. No, thanks. I'll hang on."

He looked back at Entoré, as impersonally as Entoré was looking at him. Bryan thought, as he looked at the assemblage of machinery: *He's shadowy,*

*vague. He has no real substance in this world. I can
see through him and his machinery, a little. But he's
partly solid. I've touched the machine. I've had to
push hard to get my hand through. Maybe a bullet . . .*

He thrust the thought away, seeing in a flash what
horrors it could bring. Kill Entoré? Kill him? He
who had, with his own science of a far future, assembled groups of event-data which alone could guide
Bryan Barrett, diversifal, along the path he must take,
rather than the path he would normally take? And
yet, what if some day, in a burst of rage . . . ?

Bryan Barrett planned nothing of that sort. Another
year passed, and another. The circulation of *The Daily
News-Star* rose. Bryan could have pointed to Entoré,
when rich friends pointed to Bryan as one of the great
editors of the times. Entoré could look around
corners, see what was coming from the future. Entoré
could scoop them all. If a war was going to break out,
Bryan could have correspondents on the spot days
before the event. If there was to be a mine explosion,
Bryan could, if he wished, write the story ahead of
time, himself. His salary rose to a fabulous figure. And
he remembered, hollowly, Entoré's purpose. A financial gulf must be created between him and her. She
would always be poor. . . .

Bryan Barrett did not consciously plan to kill Entoré It was merely that events pointed in that
direction—events as sure and far-reaching as those
events of the Delta and Gamma Groups which now
and again Entoré forced him to by-pass. There was
the instance of the gun. Bryan was passing an alley-way
in the fourth year of his association with Entoré.
Had it not been for the reflection from the store window, Bryan would not have seen the assassin. He
ducked as the gun roared. With a continuation of the
motion, he hurled himself into the alley, for a long
second wrestled mightily with death. He jerked the
gun from the man's hands, threw him against the wall.
His eyes widened.

"Drake!"

"Okay, Bryan," the shabbily dressed man spat at

him. "I'll admit I was out to get you. I'll stay here until the police come. And when they try me, I'll tell things to the courtroom you never would allow to get into your paper. How you and your boss put the pressure to bear, and disbanded the *Freedom For All* League."

Bryan paled, dropped the gun into his pocket. "Drake," he said, "get moving. Nothing happened. I was acting under my boss' orders when I printed that anti-League propaganda. I wouldn't have done it myself. But you wouldn't understand. Go on."

Bryan quickly turned away, walked in the other direction. By the time the crowd formed, both participants in the scene were gone. But something had snapped in Bryan's mind. He walked faster, faster, as fast as his thoughts. An hour later, he burst into his suite, his hand in his pocket around the gun.

"Entoré!" he snapped, taking two stiff-legged steps toward the suspended creature. "All day, you've been in communication with me. Yet, as I was coming home from the office, somebody tried to kill me. Why didn't you warn me about that?"

Entoré's face remained cold. "Were you killed?"

"What does that matter? It was a lucky accident I wasn't. A matter of a reflection in a window, something even you couldn't have foreseen with your high and mighty science. Entoré, *you wanted me to die!*"

Entoré said nothing for awhile, his face a study. Finally, as if admitting something that had only hovered on the fringes of his mind, he said, "Bryan, I suppose we have both at last come to hate each other. But I have never once tried to lead you into any situation that would mean your death."

"Except this evening!"

But already the force of Bryan's rage had died. Entoré's logic was indisputable. He hadn't been killed. He felt the cold, hard mass of the gun in his pocket. He wondered if Entoré knew about that. He wondered how deeply Entoré could probe into his thoughts.

Entoré repeated, with an abstraction that was entirely strange in him, "No, Bryan. No. I have never thought of that, never thought of consciously plotting your death, although it would free me."

His eyes flickered; and Bryan, turning, went with the steps of an old man toward the bedroom. He took off the coat, hung it up. The gun was still in the pocket. Bryan tried to force the thought of the gun from his mind, to get the memory of it deep into his unconscious.

The gun stayed there in that coat for three years.

The Alpha Group was now destroyed. The Alpha Group, running thick with events which would have led him to her. And the Delta Group, too, was now so blocked off, and the probabilities of a meeting occurred in such long, involved chains that Entoré could destroy *puncti* merely by dictating to Bryan Barrett in such small matters as the color of a necktie, or a choice of dessert, or—well, how could the color of a necktie start a chain of events which would lead to her? This way: A tie bought hastily, worn once, disliked—given to the new hotel maid. The maid is making a quilt from old neckties, and several others are given to her. When she completes the quilt, she sells it to a small department store. The department store displays the quilt in the window. The maid informs Bryan, pridefully. On his way from lunch, Bryan feels obliged to stop by and look at the quilt. But he is in somewhat of a hurry, turns, looking at his watch, bumps head-on into *her*. . . . But Entoré prevented Bryan from buying the chartreuse necktie.

In the eighth year, the Delta Group of events ceased to exist. They were now in the shadowy realms of the Gamma Group. Those events which were far-flung echoes of the past.

"There's not much chance, now, eh?" Bryan queried.

"Not much chance."

Bryan sat down. He was forty years of age, and the years had treated him harshly. He was tired, in mind and body. Fine lines had been etched deep in his face; strands of gray ran thickly through his hair.

He was tall, and gaunt, and inclined to stoop at the shoulders, as from a physical burden. He moved through life with a slow, firm tread which was not so much an indication of his bodily strength as of his will, which he whipped to action as he would a stubborn animal.

Entoré had in no way changed.

"I would like," Bryan muttered, in the voice of a man asleep, "I would like to meet her."

"I know," said Entoré.

"Tomorrow night," said Bryan, "I am going incognito to a public meeting of the so-called *United Liberty Lovers* League. It is a sham organization, masquerading under a name which indicates its opposite nature. I intend to expose the League in my paper."

"No," said Entoré.

Bryan looked up, his face savage. "Yes! Eight years ago, I deserted every ideal that made me worthy of life. I was in some measure responsible for the disbanding of a league that was fighting corruption—the kind of corruption my newspaper has dealt in. I intend to make one strong bid for my self-respect."

"You will no longer have your position if you print such a story. The man who owns the paper sponsors the organization you intend to expose."

"That's all right," said Bryan, still savagely. He rose, pounding one fist with restrained emphasis into the palm of his left hand. "I've never gone against you, Entoré. Never. Not in the slightest detail. This time I must. If this is a step that will create a chain of events which is undesirable, there's still a way for you to lead me back to a safe path."

Entoré's depthless eyes flickered. His small mouth turned slowly hard. "If you wish," he said coldly. "But you must obey me in small particulars."

Byran nodded curtly.

Bryan Barrett never reached the meeting hall of the sham organization, *United Liberty Lovers* League, the next night.

"Do not go by way of Columbus Circle," Entoré's thoughts came.

Bryan leaned forward, spoke to the taxi driver, giving him another route, a route that led toward death. Bryan saw the moving van coming with ponderous sureness from a side-street, bearing down broadside on the taxi. The driver cramped the wheel hard, screamed. The monster loomed, and Bryan moved, his nerves pulling at his muscles like reins holding the head of a spirited horse. He halfway rolled from the middle of the seat, with one foot kicked the door lever and shoved the door open. He threw himself from the taxi, hit shoulder first in the street, scraped his face on hard pavement. He lay like one dead. When he came to, he arose from the crowd that circled him, pushed his way through like a swimmer breaking water. Somebody tried to stop him, but he went, staggering at first, and then quickly.

He got back in another taxi. Entoré did not speak to him once during that trip. He did not speak when Bryan came into the hotel suite. Bryan emptied his mind of coherence. He went into the bedroom, took off his coat. He put on another coat, and tried not to realize that the gun was in that pocket.

Then he came out into the living-room and took a stance looking up at Entoré.

"You tried to kill me," he said.

Entoré said coldly, looking at the blood on his face, "I am ignorant of all events after the taxi changed course. You deliberately closed your mind to me. However, I am glad you didn't go to the League meeting. It would have set in motion a number of *puncti* which would have been hard to destroy. There now remains a chance—one bare chance that you will ever meet her. Once that *punctus* is destroyed. You will be pleased to know—as I will be pleased—that our association can then be disbanded."

Bryan started to shake inwardly. Then the trembling was transmitted to his outward person.

"Entoré," he had to whisper, "I know something now I didn't know before. You're a superman, and you're a congenital liar. You can lie with a straight

face when you know big events hang on your lies.
More, you can convince yourself that your lies are
true—and maybe that's a valuable survival charac-
teristic. Because you lied to me when you first appeared to me eight years ago."

He gulped in air, tried to control his trembling.
He spoke again.

"Most of what you said was true. I believe most
of it. But you just caught yourself up on one big lie.
You knew how selfless I could be, because I believed
in an ideal. You appealed to my selflessness by putting
yourself in the same category. You told me it was your
world of probability you were trying to destroy. Put
that way, I could do nothing less than promise to
collaborate with you completely. However, if by the
destruction of one more *punctus,* the last chance of
my meeting her is destroyed, then, in that same instant,
your world will be destroyed, and *you* will be
destroyed, too. You will cease to exist. Yet you speak
of disbanding our association. If you spoke the truth,
it would be disbanded automatically—and you would
not have a chance to be pleased or displeased. Entoré," said Bryan, reaching into the pocket and taking
out the gun, "you have tried to kill me once too often.
You won't get another chance."

He fired. He fired point-blank. And in his innermost
heart he did not think he would succeed, did not want
to succeed.

The bullet struck Entoré in the chest.

Entoré's passionless eyes widened. The delicate
shadowy fingers clasped suddenly at the open hole
in his chest that suddenly gushed with pink, barely
discernible blood. He choked. Then he fell forward
across the console of his machine.

"I am dying!" The hideous, incredulous thought-
words ripped at Bryan's brain. He saw Entoré's
fingers scrambling at buttons on the control of his
suspended machinery. The machinery and Entoré
suddenly disappeared, like smoke dissipated before
a breeze. There was emptiness.

The gun dropped from Bryan's fingers, as if it were
a serpent which had struck him. He stood frozen for

a long moment, icy cold horror pouring along the winding arteries of his body, pervading his brain.

"Entoré!" he cried. "Entoré! Come back!"

But Entoré would not come back. In his last moments, Entoré had sent himself spinning back to his own time. Bryan sank, stupefied, into a chair.

Bryan left the hotel suite the next morning. He moved slowly, like a blind man who feels he is liable to stumble over the brink of a precipice at any moment. He walked along the street listening for Entoré's thought-voice.

Suddenly he stopped in mid-pace, turned, walked back, and then a block in the other direction. He started to board a bus, then changed his mind.

At breakfast, he ordered mechanically—then, in fright, changed the order completely.

When the day was done, he lay in bed, rigid with nervous exhaustion, knowing he had set himself an impossible task. Two years of this. And his battle against mechanical or impulsive actions was no substitute for Entoré's knowledge of *puncti*.

He thought of Entoré, as he lay rigid in darkness. Entoré had been a liar. And yet his lie did not matter. The same result, the preservation of humanity in the far distant future, would be achieved whether Entoré's world or the other world ceased to have being. The murder of Entoré had solved nothing, but had left Bryan in a tangle of complexities from which there was only one straightforward path: suicide.

A month passed. And Bryan suddenly saw that insanity was another way out. He was surely growing insane. He was trying to control the minutiae of his existence, and doing so was like an entity in his own head, ripping his mind to shreds. He looked at his hand—large, bony—and it shook visibly. He looked straight down at the glass-top of his desk, and saw a hollow-cheeked, sunken-eyed specter. He sank back into his chair, closed his eyes wearily. And as he sat thus, he made his decision.

With the decision came a vast, flooding peace, a cauterizing of the disease that was growing in his mind. He opened his eyes as if he were looking on a new world. A world where he, Bryan Barrett, did as he pleased without censorship from Entoré or from himself. He rose quickly.

On his desk, he heard the rustle of papers. He turned, filled with a drunken elation. The wind was flicking over pages of the rival newspaper on his desk much as a human hand could flick them over. Bryan put a paperweight on each corner, sank gloatingly into his chair. Events were flowing as they should flow, even in the small matter of wind blowing a newspaper.

Small?

Something exploded in his brain like a bell struck violently.

He came to his feet, bent over the newspaper, staring at the advertisement which leaped with smashing impact toward his eyes. An advertisement smugly explaining the virtues of a musical comedy that was in its sixth month.

Years ago, Entoré had said something about a musical comedy. Of an acquaintance who would later show up in the Gamma Group with tickets for a musical comedy. Only, Entoré had destroyed that possibility by making certain Bryan did not make the acquaintance in the first place.

He reached for the phone automatically. The wells of resistance had been pumped dry. That evening he sat in a rear theatre seat, far from the stage. And yet he saw her. Third act, second row, in the middle. Long before the show ended, he was standing at the stagedoor, waiting for her to come out. She came soon. She halted in the door. Then she saw him. Without hesitance, she walked toward him and without saying anything, fell into step beside him and they walked down the street.

Their conversation until they sat in the restaurant with the dinner plates cleared away was nothing that either of them would remember. Then it was Bryan who spoke.

"You'd never married?"

"No. And you?"

"Never. We've been kept apart."

"I know," she said quietly. "Entoré."

He looked across the table at her, unable to feel the shock of that suddenly imparted information. Her name was Ann. She was small and dainty of body, but the beauty that had been hers was fading into the serene depth of her eyes.

He said at last, "Entoré came to you first, did he?"

"He did. And I refused him."

"Why?"

"Because I was living in the present, and eight-hundred thousand years from now is eight-hundred thousand years."

He struggled with that logic, but there were implications in it which escaped him. "But," he persisted, "the race of man would die. It would end because of us."

She leaned forward a little tensely, a little pleadingly, and the dark eyes flooded their inner beauty over her face so that he caught his breath. She wanted to explain something to him, but she had no words to say it. She sank back, mutely. He sat silently, holding himself in an iron control, and then it was that the barrier leaped up between them. For hours they sat there, talking of other things that neither would remember.

Finally she rose, quickly, holding her purse with both hands. "I must leave now," she told him. He rose, too. Panic flickered on her face, and her hands —thin, fragile hands—wound around the purse. "I have a feeling—as strong as the feeling that your eyes were on me from the audience—that if I leave now, we'll never meet each other again. Do you want it that way? Do you *really* want it that way?"

"It's the way it must be," he said, and it was as if his Nemesis, Entoré, had forced the damning words from his lips.

A second after she had turned, walking so quickly that it seemed she was running away, turned and disappeared up the short flight of stairs toward the traffic-roaring street, he could still see that startled, destroying pain that wrenched her face. It was the incredulity that even the hope of the empty years of her life had been taken from her to leave a harrowing memory of near-happiness only.

Only a second he stood there, remembering that tortured expression. Then a thunderbolt exploded inside him. *This is the present, and eight hundred thousand years is eight hundred thousand years—as long as eternity, as meaningless!*

"Ann!" he shouted—screamed the name as he stood on the street. She was not in sight. And he knew he would never see her again. The black, nauseous wind of self-hatred poured madly through his brain, and carried the mocking memory of Entoré. The last *punctus* of the Gamma Group of events had been dissipated. He was truly his own master again. He had the choice of facing straight ahead into the unwelcome future or—of fastening his mind on some more pleasant memory of the past, fastening it there permanently, and assuming the expression of an idiot.

Duel on Syrtis

Poul Anderson

Bold and ruthless, he was famed throughout the System as a big-game hunter. From the firedrakes of Mercury to the ice-crawlers of Pluto, he'd slain them all. But his trophy-room lacked one item; and now Riordan swore he'd bag the forbidden game that roamed the red deserts . . . a Martian!

The night whispered the message. Over the many miles of loneliness it was borne, carried on the wind, rustled by the half-sentient lichens and the dwarfed trees, murmured from one to another of the little creatures that huddled under crags, in caves, by shadowy dunes. In no words, but in a dim pulsing of dread which echoed through Kreega's brain, the warning ran—

They are hunting again.

Kreega shuddered in a sudden blast of wind. The night was enormous around him, above him, from the iron bitterness of the hills to the wheeling, glittering constellations light-years over his head. He reached out with his trembling perceptions, tuning himself to the brush and the wind and the small burrowing things underfoot, letting the night speak to him.

Alone, alone. There was not another Martian for a hundred miles of emptiness. There were only the tiny animals and the shivering brush and the thin, sad blowing of the wind.

The voiceless scream of dying traveled through the brush, from plant to plant, echoed by the fear-pulses of the animals and the ringingly reflecting cliffs. They were curling, shriveling and blackening as the rocket poured the glowing death down on them, and the withering veins and nerves cried to the stars.

Kreega huddled against a tall gaunt crag. His eyes were like yellow moons in the darkness, cold with terror and hate and a slowly gathering resolution. Grimly, he estimated that the death was being sprayed in a circle some ten miles across. And he was trapped in it, and soon the hunter would come after him.

He looked up to the indifferent glitter of stars, and a shudder went along his body. Then he sat down and began to think.

It had started a few days before, in the private office of the trader Wisby. "I came to Mars," said Riordan, "to get me an owlie."

Wisby had learned the value of a poker face. He peered across the rim of his glass at the other man, estimating him.

Even in God-forsaken holes like Port Armstrong one had heard of Riordan. Heir to a million-dollar shipping firm which he himself had pyramided into a System-wide monster, he was equally well known as a big game hunter. From the firedrakes of Mercury to the ice crawlers of Pluto, he'd bagged them all. Except, of course, a Martian. That particular game was forbidden now.

He sprawled in his chair, big and strong and ruthless, still a young man. He dwarfed the unkempt room with his size and the hard-held dynamo strength in him, and his cold green gaze dominated the trader.

"It's illegal, you know," said Wisby. "It's a twenty-year sentence if you're caught at it."

"Bah! The Martian Commissioner is at Ares, halfway round the planet. If we go at it right, who's ever to know?" Riordan gulped at his drink. "I'm well aware that in another year or so they'll have tightened up enough to make it impossible. This is the last chance for any man to get an owlie. That's why I'm here."

Wisby hesitated, looking out the window. Port Armstrong was no more than a dusty huddle of domes, interconnected by tunnels, in a red waste of sand stretching to the near horizon. An Earthman in airsuit and transparent helmet was walking down the street and a couple of Martians were lounging against a wall. Otherwise nothing—a silent, deadly monotony brooding under the shrunken sun. Life on Mars was not especially pleasant for a human.

"You're not falling into this owlie-loving that's corrupted all Earth?" demanded Riordan contemptuously.

"Oh, no," said Wisby. "I keep them in their place around my post. But times are changing. It can't be helped."

"There was a time when they were slaves," said Riordan. "Now those old women on Earth want to give 'em the vote." He snorted.

"Well, times are changing," repeated Wisby mildly. "When the first humans landed on Mars a hundred years ago, Earth had just gone through the Hemispheric Wars. The worst wars man had ever known. They damned near wrecked the old ideas of liberty and equality. People were suspicious and tough—they'd had to be, to survive. They weren't able to—to empathize with the Martians, or whatever you call it. Not able to think of them as anything but intelligent animals. And Martians made such useful slaves—they need so little food or heat or oxygen, they can even live fifteen minutes or so without breathing at all. And the wild Martians made fine sport—intelligent game, that could get away as often as not, or even manage to kill the hunter."

"I know," said Riordan. "That's why I want to hunt one. It's no fun if the game doesn't have a chance."

"It's different now," went on Wisby. "Earth has been at peace for a long time. The liberals have gotten the upper hand. Naturally, one of their first reforms was to end Martian slavery."

Riordan swore. The forced repatriation of Martians working on his spaceships had cost him plenty. "I haven't time for your philosophizing," he said. "If you can arrange for me to get a Martian, I'll make it worth your while."

"How much worth it?" asked Wisby.

They haggled for a while before settling on a figure. Riordan had brought guns and a small rocketboat, but Wisby would have to supply radioactive material, a "hawk," and a rockhound. Then he had to be paid for the risk of legal action, thought that was small. The final price came high.

"Now, where do I get my Martian?" inquired Riordan. He gestured at the two in the street. "Catch one of them and release him in the desert?"

It was Wisby's turn to be contemptuous. "One of them? Hah! Town loungers! A city dweller from Earth would give you a better fight."

The Martians didn't look impressive. They stood only some four feet high on skinny, claw-footed legs, and the arms, ending in bony four-fingered hands, were stringy. The chests were broad and deep, but the waists were ridiculously narrow. They were viviparous, warm-blooded, and suckled their young, but gray feathers covered their hides. The round, hook-beaked heads, with huge amber eyes and tufted feathers ears, showed the origin of the name "owlie." They wore only pouched belts and carried sheath knives; even the liberals of Earth weren't ready to allow the natives modern tools and weapons. There were too many old grudges.

"The Martians always were good fighters," said Riordan. "They wiped out quite a few Earth settlements in the old days."

"The wild ones," agreed Wisby. "But not these. They're just stupid laborers, as dependent on our civilization as we are. You want a real old-timer, and I know where one's to be found."

He spread a map on the desk. "See, here in the Hraefnian Hills, about a hundred miles from here.

These Martians live a long time, maybe two centuries, and this fellow Kreega has been around since the first earthmen came. He led a lot of Martian raids in the early days, but since the general amnesty and peace he's lived all alone up there, in one of the old ruined towers. A real old-time warrior who hates Earthmen's guts. He comes here once in a while with furs and minerals to trade, so I know a little about him." Wisby's eyes gleamed savagely. "You'll be doing us all a favor by shooting the arrogant bastard. He struts around here as if the place belonged to him. And he'll give you a run for your money."

Riordan's massive dark head nodded in satisfaction.

The man had a bird and a rockhound. That was bad. Without them, Kreega could lose himself in the labyrinth of caves and canyons and scrubby thickets —but the hound could follow his scent and the bird could spot him from above.

To make matters worse, the man had landed near Kreega's tower. The weapons were all there—now he was cut off, unarmed and alone save for what feeble help the desert life could give. Unless he could double back to the place somehow—but meanwhile he had to survive.

He sat in a cave, looking down past a tortured wilderness of sand and bush and wind-carved rock, miles in the thin clear air to the glitter of metal where the rocket lay. The man was a tiny speck in the huge barren landscape, a lonely insect crawling under the deep-blue sky. Even by day, the stars glistened in the tenuous atmosphere. Weak pallid sunlight spilled over rocks tawny and ocherous and rust-red, over the low dusty thorn-bushes and the gnarled little trees and the sand that blew faintly between them. Equatorial Mars!

Lonely or not, the man had a gun that could spang death clear to the horizon, and he had his beasts, and there would be a radio in the rocketboat for calling his fellows. And the glowing death ringed them in, a charmed circle which Kreega could not cross without bringing a worse death on himself than the rifle would give—

Or was there a worse death than that—to be shot by a monster and have his stuffed hide carried back as a trophy for fools to gape at? The old iron pride of his race rose in Kreega, hard and bitter and unrelenting. He didn't ask much of life these days— solitude in his tower to think the long thoughts of a Martian and create the small exquisite artworks which he loved; the company of his kind at the Gathering Season, grave ancient ceremony and acrid merriment and the chance to beget and rear sons; an occasional trip to the Earthling settling for the metal goods and the wine which were the only valuable things they had brought to Mars; a vague dream of raising his folk to a place where they could stand as equals before all the universe. No more. And now they would take even this from him!

He rasped a curse on the human and resumed his patient work, chipping a spearhead for what puny help it could give him. The brush rustled dryly in alarm, tiny hidden animals squeaked their terror, the desert shouted to him of the monster that strode toward his cave. But he didn't have to flee right away.

Riordan sprayed the heavy-metal isotope in a ten-mile circle around the old tower. He did that by night, just in case patrol craft might be snooping around. But once he had landed, he was safe—he could always claim to be peacefully exploring, hunting leapers or some such thing.

The radioactivity had a half-life of about four days, which meant that it would be unsafe to approach for some three weeks—two at the minimum. That was time enough, when the Martian was boxed in so small an area.

There was no danger that he would try to cross it. The owlies had learned what radioactivity meant, back when they fought the humans. And their vision, extending well into the ultra-violet, made it directly visible to them through its fluorescence—to say nothing of the wholly unhuman extra senses they had. No,

Kreega would try to hide, and perhaps to fight, and eventually he'd be cornered.

Still, there was no use taking chances. Riordan set a timer on the boat's radio. If he didn't come back within two weeks to turn it off, it would emit a signal which Wisby would hear, and he'd be rescued.

He checked his other equipment. He had an airsuit designed for Martian conditions, with a small pump operated by a power-beam from the boat to compress the atmosphere sufficiently for him to breathe it. The same unit recovered enough water from his breath so that the weight of supplies for several days was, in Martian gravity, not too great for him to bear. He had a .45 rifle built to shoot in Martian air; that was heavy enough for his purposes. And, of course, compass and binoculars and sleeping bag. Pretty light equipment, but he preferred a minimum anyway.

For ultimate emergencies there was the little tank of suspensine. By turning a valve, he could release it into his air system. The gas didn't exactly induce suspended animation, but it paralyzed efferent nerves and slowed the overall metabolism to a point where a man could live for weeks on one lungful of air. It was useful in surgery, and had saved the life of more than one interplanetary explorer whose oxygen system went awry. But Riordan didn't expect to have to use it. He certainly hoped he wouldn't. It would be tedious to lie fully conscious for days waiting for the automatic signal to call Wisby.

He stepped out of the boat and locked it. No danger that the owlie would break in if he should double back; it would take tordenite to crack that hull.

He whistled to his animals. They were native beasts, long ago domesticated by the Martians and later by man. The rockhound was like a gaunt wolf, but huge-breasted and feathered, a tracker as good as any Terrestrial bloodhound. The "hawk" had less resemblance to its counterpart of Earth: it was a bird of prey, but in the tenuous atmosphere it needed a six-foot wingspread to lift its small body. Riordan was pleased with their training.

The hound bayed, a low quavering note which would

have been muffled almost to inaudibility by the thin air and the man's plastic helmet had the suit not included microphones and amplifiers. It circled, sniffing, while the hawk rose into the alien sky.

Riordan did not look closely at the tower. It was a crumbling stump atop a rusty hill, unhuman and grotesque. Once, perhaps ten thousand years ago, the Martians had had a civilization of sorts, cities and agriculture and a neolithic technology. But according to their own traditions they had achieved a union or symbiosis with the wild life of the planet and had abandoned such mechanical aids as unnecessary. Riordan snorted.

The hound bayed again. The noise seemed to hang eerily in the still, cold air, to shiver from cliff and crag and die reluctantly under the enormous silence. But it was a bugle call, a haughty challenge to a world grown old—stand aside, make way, here comes the conqueror!

The animal suddenly loped forward. He had a scent. Riordan swung into a long, easy low-gravity stride. His eyes gleamed like green ice. The hunt was begun!

Breath sobbed in Kreega's lungs, hard and quick and raw. His legs felt weak and heavy, and the thudding of his heart seemed to shake his whole body.

Still he ran, while the frightful clamor rose behind him and the padding of feet grew ever nearer. Leaping, twisting, bounding from crag to crag, sliding down shaly ravines and slipping through clumps of trees, Kreega fled.

The hound was behind him and the hawk soaring overhead. In a day and a night they had driven him to this, running like a crazed leaper with death baying at his heels—he had not imagined a human could move so fast or with such endurance.

The desert fought for him; the plants with their queer blind life that no Earthling would ever understand were on his side. Their thorny branches twisted away as he darted through and then came back to rake the flanks of the hound, slow him—but they could not stop his brutal rush. He ripped past their strengthless clutching fingers and yammered on the trail of the Martian.

The human was toiling a good mile behind, but showed no sign of tiring. Still Kreega ran. He had to reach the cliff edge before the hunter saw him through his rifle sights—had to, had to, and the hound was snarling a yard behind now.

Up the long slope he went. The hawk fluttered, striking at him, seeking to lay beak and talons in his head. He batted at the creature with his spear and dodged around a tree. The tree snaked out a branch from which the hound rebounded, yelling till the rocks rang.

The Martian burst onto the edge of the cliff. It fell sheer to the canyon floor, five hundred feet of iron-streaked rock tumbling into windy depths. Beyond, the lowering sun glared in his eyes. He paused only an instant, etched black against the sky, a perfect shot if the human should come into view, and then he sprang over the edge.

He had hoped the rockhound would go shooting past, but the animal braked itself barely in time. Kreega went down the cliff face, clawing into every tiny crevice, shuddering as the age-worn rock crumbled under his fingers. The hawk swept close, hacking at him and screaming for its master. He couldn't fight it, not with every finger and toe needed to hang against shattering death, but—

He slid along the face of the precipice into a gray-green clump of vines, and his nerves thrilled forth the appeal of the ancient symbiosis. The hawk swooped again and he lay unmoving, rigid as if dead, until it cried in shrill triumph and settled on his shoulder to pluck out his eyes.

Then the vines stirred. They weren't strong, but their thorns sank into the flesh and it wouldn't pull loose. Kreega toiled on down into the canyon while the vines pulled the hawk apart.

Riordan loomed hugely against the darkening sky. He fired, once, twice, the bullets humming wickedly

close, but as shadows swept up from the depths the
Martian was covered.

The man turned up his speech amplifier and his
voice rolled and boomed monstrously through the
gathering night, thunder such as dry Mars had not
heard for millennia: "Score one for you! But it isn't
enough! I'll find you!"

The sun slipped below the horizon and night came
down like a falling curtain. Through the darkness
Kreega heard the man laughing. The old rocks trembled with his laughter.

Riordan was tired with the long chase and the
niggling insufficiency of his oxygen supply. He wanted
a smoke and hot food, and neither was to be had. Oh,
well, he'd appreciate the luxuries of life all the more
when he got home—with the Martian's skin.

He grinned as he made camp. The little fellow was
a worthwhile quarry, that was for damn sure. He'd
held out for two days now, in a little ten-mile circle
of ground, and he'd even killed the hawk. But Riordan
was close enough to him now so that the hound could
follow his spoor, for Mars had no watercourses to
break a trail. So it didn't matter.

He lay watching the splendid night of stars. It would
get cold before long, unmercifully cold, but his sleeping
bag was a good-enough insulator to keep him warm
with the help of solar energy stored during the day
by its Gergen cells. Mars was dark at night, its moons
of little help—Phobos a hurtling speck, Deimos merely
a bright star. Dark and cold and empty. The
rockhound had burrowed into the loose sand nearby,
but it would raise the alarm if the Martian should come
sneaking near the camp. Not that that was likely—he'd
have to find shelter somewhere too, if he didn't want
to freeze.

*The bushes and the trees and the little furtive
animals whispered a word he could not hear, chattered
and gossiped on the wind about the Martian who kept
himself warm with work. But he didn't understand
that language which was no language.*

Drowsily, Riordan thought of past hunts. The big

game of Earth, lion and tiger and elephant and buffalo and sheep on the high sun-blazing peaks of the Rockies. Rain forests of Venus and the coughing roar of a many-legged swamp monster crashing through the trees to the place where he stood waiting. Primitive throb of drums in a hot wet night, chant of beaters dancing around a fire—scramble along the hell-plains of Mercury with a swollen sun licking against his puny insulating suit—the grandeur and desolation of Neptune's liquid-gas swamps and the huge blind thing that screamed and blundered after him—

But this was the loneliest and strangest and perhaps most dangerous hunt of all, and on that account the best. He had no malice toward the Martian; he respected the little being's courage as he respected the bravery of the other animals he had fought. Whatever trophy he brought home from this chase would be well earned.

The fact that his success would have to be treated discreetly didn't matter. He hunted less for the glory of it—though he had to admit he didn't mind the publicity—than for love. His ancestors had fought under one name or another—viking, Crusader, mercenary, rebel, patriot, whatever was fashionable at the moment. Struggle was in his blood, and in these degenerate days there was little to struggle against save what he hunted.

Well—tomorrow—he drifted off to sleep.

He woke in the short gray dawn, made a quick breakfast, and whistled his hound to heel. His nostrils dilated with excitement, a high keen drunkenness that sang wonderfully within him. Today—maybe today!

They had to take a roundabout way down into the canyon and the hound cast about for an hour before he picked up the scent. Then the deep-voiced cry rose again and they were off—more slowly now, for it was a cruel stony trail.

The sun climbed high as they worked along the ancient river-bed. Its pale chill light washed needle-sharp crags and fantastically painted cliffs, shale and sand and the wreck of geological ages. The low harsh brush crunched under the man's feet, writhing and crackling its impotent protest. Otherwise it was still, a deep and taut and somehow waiting stillness.

The hound shattered the quiet with an eager yelp and plunged forward. Hot scent! Riordan dashed after him, trampling through dense bush, panting and swearing and grinning with excitement.

Suddenly the brush opened underfoot. With a howl of dismay, the hound slid down the sloping wall of the pit it had covered. Riordan flung himself forward with tigerish swiftness, flat down on his belly with one hand barely catching the animal's tail. The shock almost pulled him into the hole too. He wrapped one arm around a bush that clawed at his helmet and pulled the hound back.

Shaking, he peered into the trap. It had been well made—about twenty feet deep, with walls as straight and narrow as the sand would allow, and skillfully covered with brush. Planted in the bottom were three wicked-looking flint spears. Had he been a shade less quick in his reactions, he would have lost the hound and perhaps himself.

He skinned his teeth in a wolf-grin and looked around. The owlie must have worked all night on it. Then he couldn't be far away—and he'd be very tired—

As if to answer his thoughts, a boulder crashed down from the nearer cliff wall. It was a monster, but a falling object on Mars has less than half the acceleration it does on Earth. Riordan scrambled aside as it boomed onto the place where he had been lying.

"Come on!" he yelled, and plunged toward the cliff.

For an instant a gray form loomed over the edge, hurled a spear at him. Riordan snapped a shot at it, and it vanished. The spear glanced off the tough fabric of his suit and he scrambled up a narrow ledge to the top of the precipice.

The Martian was nowhere in sight, but a faint red trail led into the rugged hill country. *Winged him, by God!* The hound was slower in negotiating the shale-covered trail; his own feet were bleeding when he came up. Riordan cursed him and they set out again.

They followed the trail for a mile or two and then it ended. Riordan looked around the wilderness of trees and needles which blocked view in any direction. Obviously the owlie had backtracked and climbed up one of those rocks, from which he could take a flying leap to some other point. But which one?

Sweat which he couldn't wipe off ran down the man's face and body. He itched intolerably, and his lungs were raw from gasping at his dole of air. But still he laughed in gusty delight. What a chase! What a chase!

Kreega lay in the shadow of a tall rock and shuddered with weariness. Beyond the shade, the sunlight danced in what to him was a blinding, intolerable dazzle, hot and cruel and life-hungry, hard and bright as the metal of the conquerors.

It had been a mistake to spend priceless hours when he might have been resting working on that trap. It hadn't worked, and he might have known that it wouldn't. And now he was hungry, and thirst was like a wild beast in his mouth and throat, and still they followed him.

They weren't far behind now. All this day they had been dogging him; he had never been more than half an hour ahead. No rest, no rest, a devil's hunt through a tormented wilderness of stone and sand, and now he could only wait for the battle with an iron burden of exhaustion laid on him.

The wound in his side burned. It wasn't deep, but it had cost him blood and pain and the few minutes of catnapping he might have snatched.

For a moment, the warrior Kreega was gone and a lonely, frightened infant sobbed in the desert silence. *Why can't they let me alone?*

A low, dusty-green bush rustled. A sandrunner piped in one of the ravines. They were getting close.

Wearily, Kreega scrambled up on top of the rock and crouched low. He had backtracked to it; they should by rights go past him toward his tower.

He could see it from here, a low yellow ruin worn by the winds of millennia. There had only been time to dart in, snatch a bow and a few arrows and an axe. Pitiful weapons—the arrows could not penetrate the Earthman's suit when there was only a Martian's thin grasp to draw the bow, and even with a steel head the axe was a small and feeble thing. But it was all he had, he and his few little allies of a desert which fought only to keep its solitude.

Repatriated slaves had told him of the Earthlings' power. Their roaring machines filled the silence of their own deserts, gouged the quiet face of their own moon, shook the planets with a senseless fury of meaningless energy. They were the conquerors, and it never occurred to them that an ancient peace and stillness could be worth preserving.

Well—he fitted an arrow to the string and crouched in the silent, glimmering sunlight, waiting.

The hound came first, yelping and howling. Kreega drew the bow as far as he could. But the human had to come near first—

There he came, running and bounding over the rocks, rifle in hand and restless eyes shining with taut green light, closing in for the death. Kreega sung softly around. The beast was beyond the rock now, the Earthman almost below it.

The bow twanged. With a savage thrill, Kreega saw the arrow go through the hound, saw the creature leap in the air and then roll over and over, howling and biting at the thing in its breast.

Like a gray thunderbolt, the Martian launched himself off the rock, down at the human. If his axe could shatter that helmet—

He struck the man and they went down together. Wildly, the Martian hewed. The axe glanced off the plastic—he hadn't had room for a swing. Riordan roared and lashed out with a fist. Retching, Kreega rolled backward.

Riordan snapped a shot at him. Kreega turned and fled. The man got to one knee, sighting carefully on the gray form that streaked up the nearest slope.

A little sandsnake darted up the man's leg and

wrapped about his wrist. Its small strength was just enough to pull the gun aside. The bullet screamed past Kreega's ears as he vanished into a cleft.

He felt the thin death-agony of the snake as the man pulled it loose and crushed it underfoot. Somewhat later, he heard a dull boom echoing between the hills. The man had gotten explosives from his boat and blown up the tower.

He had lost axe and bow. Now he was utterly weaponless, without even a place to retire for a last stand. And the hunter would not give up. Even without his animals, he would follow, more slowly but as relentlessly as before.

Kreega collapsed on a shelf of rock. Dry sobbing racked his thin body, and the sunset wind cried with him.

Presently he looked up, across a red and yellow immensity to the low sun. Long shadows were creeping over the land, peace and stillness for a brief moment before the iron cold of night closed down. Somewhere the soft trill of a sandrunner echoed between low wind-worn cliffs, and the brush began to speak, whispering back and forth in its ancient wordless tongue.

The desert, the planet and its wind and sand under the high cold stars, the clean open land of silence and loneliness and a destiny which was not man's, spoke to him. The enormous oneness of life on Mars, drawn together against the cruel environment, stirred in his blood. As the sun went down and the stars blossomed forth in awesome frosty glory, Kreega began to think again.

He did not hate his persecutor, but the grimness of Mars was in him. He fought the war of all which was old and primitive and lost in its own dreams against the alien and the desecrator. It was as ancient and pitiless as life, that war, and each battle won or lost meant something even if no one ever heard of it.

You do not fight alone, whispered the desert. *You fight for all Mars, and we are with you.*

Something moved in the darkness, a tiny warm form running across his hand, a little feathered mouse-like thing that burrowed under the sand and lived its s fugitive life and was glad in its own way of living. But it was a part of a world, and Mars has no pity in its voice.

Still, a tenderness was within Kreega's heart, and he whispered gently in the language that was not a language, *You will do this for us? You will do it, little brother?*

Riordan was too tired to sleep well. He had lain awake for a long time, thinking, and that is not good for a man alone in the Martian hills.

So now the rockhound was dead too. It didn't matter; the owlie wouldn't escape. But somehow the incident brought home to him the immensity and the age and the loneliness of the desert.

It whispered to him. The brush rustled and something wailed in darkness and the wind blew with a wild mournful sound over faintly starlit cliffs, and it was as if they all somehow had voice, as if the whole world muttered and threatened him in the night. Dimly, he wondered if man would ever subdue Mars, if the human race had not finally run across something bigger than itself.

But that was nonsense. Mars was old and worn-out and barren, dreaming itself into slow death. The tramp of human feet, shouts of men and roar of sky-storming rockets were waking it—but to a new destiny, to man's. When Ares lifted its hard spires above the hills of Syrtis, where then were the ancient gods of Mars?

It was cold, and the cold deepened as the night wore on. The stars were fire and ice, glittering diamonds in the deep crystal dark. Now and then he could hear a faint snapping borne through the earth as rock or tree split open. The wind laid itself to rest, sound froze to death, there was only the hard clear starlight falling through space to shatter on the ground.

Once something stirred. He woke from a restless sleep and saw a small thing skittering toward him. He groped for the rifle beside his sleeeping bag, then laughed harshly. It was only a sandmouse. But it proved that the Martian had no chance of sneaking up on him while he rested.

He didn't laugh again. The sound had echoed too hollowly in his helmet.

With the clear bitter dawn he was up. He wanted to get the hunt over with. He was dirty and unshaven inside the unit, sick of iron rations pushed through the airlock, stiff and sore with exertion. Lacking the hound, which he'd had to shoot, tracking would be slow, but he didn't want to go back to Port Armstrong for another. No, hell take that Martian, he'd have the devil's skin soon!

Breakfast and a little moving made him feel better. He looked with a practiced eye for the Martian's trail. There was sand and brush over everything; even the rocks had a thin coating of their own erosion. The owlie couldn't cover his tracks perfectly—if he tried, it would slow him too much. Riordan fell into a steady jog.

Noon found him on higher ground, rough hills with gaunt needles of rock reaching yards into the sky. He kept going, confident of his own ability to wear down the quarry. He'd run deer to earth back home, day after day until the animal's heart broke and it waited quivering for him to come.

The trail looked clear and fresh now. He tensed with the knowledge that the Martian couldn't be far away.

Too clear! Could this be bait for another trap? He hefted the rifle and proceeded more warily. But no, there wouldn't have been time—

He mounted a high ridge and looked over the grim, fantastic landscape. Near the horizon he saw a blackened strip, the border of his radioactive barrier. The Martian couldn't go further, and if he doubled back Riordan would have an excellent chance of spotting him.

He tuned up his speaker and let his voice roar into the stillness: "Come out, owlie! I'm going to get you; you might as well come out now and be done with it!"

The echoes took it up, flying back and forth between the naked crags, trembling and shivering under the brassy arch of sky. *Come out, come out, come out—*

The Martian seemed to appear from thin air, a gray ghost rising out of the jumbled stones and standing poised not twenty feet away. For an instant, the shock of it was too much; Riordan gaped in disbelief. Kreega waited, quivering ever so faintly as if he were a mirage.

Then the man shouted and lifted his rifle. Still the Martian stood there as if carved in gray stone, and with a shock of disappointment Riordan thought that he had, after all, decided to give himself to an inevitable death.

Well, it had been a good hunt. "So long," whispered Riordan, and squeezed the trigger.

Since the sandmouse had crawled into the barrel, the gun exploded.

Riordan heard the roar and saw the barrel peel open like a rotten banana. He wasn't hurt, but as he staggered back from the shock Kreega lunged at him.

The Martian was four feet tall, and skinny and weaponless, but he hit the Earthling like a small tornado. His legs wrapped around the man's waist and his hands got to work on the airhose.

Riordan went down under the impact. He snarled, tigerishly, and fastened his hands on the Martian's narrow throat. Kreega snapped futilely at him with his beak. They rolled over in a cloud of dust. The brush began to chatter excitedly.

Riordan tried to break Kreega's neck—the Martian twisted away, bored in again.

With a shock of horror, the man heard the hiss of escaping air as Kreega's beak and fingers finally worried the airhose loose. An automatic valve clamped shut, but there was no connection with the pump now—

Riordan cursed, and got his hands about the Martian's throat again. Then he simply lay there, squeezing, and not all Kreega's writhing and twistings could break that grip.

Riordan smiled sleepily and held his hands in place. After five minutes or so Kreega was still. Riordan kept right on throttling him for another five minutes, just to make sure. Then he let go and fumbled at his back, trying to reach the pump.

The air in his suit was hot and foul. He couldn't quite reach around to connect the hose to the pumps—

Poor design, he thought vaguely. *But then, these airsuits weren't meant for battle armor.*

He looked at the slight, silent form of the Martian. A faint breeze ruffled the gray feathers. What a fighter the little guy had been! He'd be the pride of the trophy room, back on Earth.

Let's see now— He unrolled his sleeping bag and spread it carefully out. He'd never make it to the rocket with what air he had so it was necessary to let the suspensine into his suit. But he'd have to get inside the bag, lest the nights freeze his blood solid.

He crawled in, fastening the flaps carefully, and opened the valve on the suspensine tank. Lucky he had it—but then, a good hunter thinks of everything. He'd get awfully bored, lying here till Wisby caught the signal in ten days or so and came to find him, but he'd last. It would be an experience to remember. In this dry air, the Martian's skin would keep perfectly well.

He felt the paralysis creep up on him, the waning of heartbeat and lung action. His senses and mind were still alive, and he grew aware that complete relaxation has its unpleasant aspects. Oh, well—he won. He'd killed the wiliest game with his own hands.

Presently Kreega sat up. He felt himself gingerly. There seemed to be a rib broken—well, that could be fixed. He was still alive. He'd been choked for a good ten minutes, but a Martian can last fifteen without air.

He opened the sleeping bag and got Riordan's keys. Then he limped slowly back to the rocket. A day or two of experimentation taught him how to fly it. He'd go to his kinsmen near Syrtis. Now that they had an Earthly machine, and Earthly weapons to copy—

But there was other business first. He didn't hate Riordan, but Mars is a hard world. He went back and dragged the Earthling into a cave and hid him beyond all possibility of human search parties finding him.

For a while he looked into the man's eyes. Horror stared dumbly back at him. He spoke slowly, in halting English: "For those you killed, and for being a stranger on a world that does not want you, and against the day when Mars is free, I leave you."

Before departing, he got several oxygen tanks from the boat and hooked them into the man's air supply. That was quite a bit of air for one in suspended animation. Enough to keep him alive for a thousand years.